"*The Forger's Forgery* . . . was a great read, cleverly constructed, very entertaining, exciting, and humoristic."

—**FRISO LAMMERTSE**, Author of *Van Meegeren's Vermeers*

"With his first novel, *Heels over Head*, Clay Small made his debut as a gifted writer. In *The Forger's Forgery*, Small weaves a suspenseful thriller set between Dallas and the art world of Amsterdam, a city close to his heart. It's fast-paced and full of conflict, twists, and surprises. I found it impossible to put down."

—**BRADFORD GARDNER**, Managing Director,
Boston Financial Management

"Clay has a gift for engaging the reader, taking them to places they want to go, entertaining them, and using his legal knowledge to create multiple mysteries that the reader looks forward to solving."

—**RAYMOND JACOBSON**, McDermott, Will & Emery

"Perhaps one reason why *The Forger's Forgery* is a complex mystery—and yet realistic—is that it is based on a true story of master forger Han van Meegeren, who forged the works of Dutch masters in the 1930s and 1940s in a notorious crime that was clever, unprecedented, and difficult to solve. In *The Forger's Forgery*, author Clay G. Small is masterful at his depiction of Dutch culture and people, the art world, and the forgers who influence its development, making their illicit money on creations that are masterful in their own right. As the mystery evolves, the art worlds of both Amsterdam and Texas come to life, as environments are influenced by forgery events that connect disparate lives and people, changing and challenging the art world."

—**D. DONOVAN**, Senior Reviewer, Midwest Book Review

"*The Forger's Forgery* taught this Amsterdam resident a thing or two about the city I live in. The intriguing history around Han van Meegeren is exciting. Clay Small combines cultural detail, rich geographic description, and countless plot twists to create an engaging and satisfying novel. Absolutely masterful!"

—**KATE GORDON**, Amsterdam

"Intricate plot, characters you'd like to get to know (well . . . not all of them), and just enough non-fiction to be both fun and educational. That's Clay G. Small's latest book in the Henry Lindon saga, *The Forger's Forgery*. Clay's depictions are so clear you can almost see the yellow-stained fingers holding a Gauloises cigarette. And when finished, you find yourself excited to see that Clay leaves a hint that the saga will continue."

—**CRAIG ENOCH**, Justice, Texas Supreme Court (Ret.)

"What a ride! In *The Forger's Forgery,* Clay Small skillfully weaves together fact and fiction while taking the reader on a journey into lesser-known aspects of the art world accompanied by the loveable, though fallible, Henry Lindon."

—**LEANNE OLIVER,** General Counsel,
PepsiCo Foods North America

THE
FORGER'S
FORGERY

a novel

CLAY G. SMALL

RIVER GROVE
BOOKS

Published by River Grove Books
Austin, TX
www.rivergrovebooks.com

Distributed by River Grove Books

Design and composition by Greenleaf Book Group
Cover design by Greenleaf Book Group
Cover images: ©Dennis Van de Water, Viorel Sima used under license from Shutterstock.com; ©andresr used under license from istockphoto.com

Publisher's Cataloging-in-Publication data is available.

Print ISBN: 978-1-63299-367-0

eBook ISBN: 978-1-63299-368-7

First Edition

This one is for Mighty Max.

I'm big on keep'n in mind the difference between havin'
somethin' to do and havin' to do somethin'.
—Marvin Lindon

THANKS

I deeply appreciate those who were willing to read early drafts, including Chad, Mark, John, Hubo, Ed, Leah, Ryan, Molly, and Allison. Thanks to Sally, Chelsea, Kristine, and the rest of the gang at Greenleaf. Thanks to Diane for her constant efforts to keep things moving down the right track. And, most importantly, thanks to my wife, Ellen, for her patience with my many hours of solitude.

PART I

AMSTERDAM

1

The overnight flight across the Atlantic was turbulent and sleepless. As his taxi entered Amsterdam's center city, he was grateful for the serenity of a Sunday morning in January. At least for the moment, he was removed from his domestic turmoil simmering on the other side of the ocean.

Henry reread the letter from the University of Amsterdam about his stay as a visiting professor. His living accommodations were to be at apartment 2 at Roetersstraat 8-1, and his contact was Senior Professor Bernadette Gordon. He rechecked his information to make sure she lived in apartment 3. When the taxi pulled up in front of Roetersstraat 8-1, Henry was pleased to see that the dark brick, nineteenth-century building was directly across the street from the university's glass-and-steel urban campus.

With the driver's help, Henry wrestled his two oversized bags onto the sidewalk. Adjacent to Roetersstraat 8-1 he noticed multiple block-long bike racks supporting hundreds of student bicycles. He dragged his bags to the building's door and pushed the intercom button for Professor Gordon's apartment. A cheerful woman's voice answered, "*Goedemorgen.*"

"Hi, it's Henry Lindon, the visiting professor from Southerland University in Dallas."

"Oh, yes, we have been expecting you. I will buzz you in."

Henry wondered who the "we" were. With the door's buzz, Henry stepped into a tiny foyer, about a yard square, littered with flyers for various takeout and delivery restaurants. Getting his bags into the foyer was made even more difficult by the bicycle pump wedged into one corner. With trepidation, he looked up the nearly vertical, ladder-like staircase. The narrow steps could barely accommodate a half of one of his feet.

He began the Herculean task of hauling one of his huge bags up the tight staircase. Twenty steps later he reached the first landing, relieved to see the number 2 on the door. Breathing heavily, he heard the apartment door above him open and then a cheerful jangling noise.

As someone descended the curving stairs toward him, a voice called out in a Dutch accent, "Hello! Welcome to Amsterdam." Because of the turn in the stairs leading to the floor above him, Henry couldn't immediately see the entire person who was descending. First to appear were black running shoes and then slender legs in spandex, followed by a black sweater with rolled-up sleeves and dozens of silver bracelets bouncing on a woman's left arm. Finally, he came face-to-face with a striking, willowy woman with straight, jet-black hair cut in a sweeping hipster style, whose face-framing bangs rested on rectangular silver-framed glasses. She was blessed with the dewy, pale complexion and high cheek color of a Dutch girl raised on fresh country cheese.

Giving Henry a surprisingly firm handshake, she said, "I am Professor Bernadette Gordon. It is nice to meet you in person. You find me getting ready for my morning run."

"Pleased to meet you. That's some set of stairs."

"Oh, you will get used to it. They will keep you fit," Bernadette said pulling a red circle key ring out of her sweater pocket. "Let me show you your apartment." As she inserted the key into the door, she glanced down the stairs and said, "I see you have another bag. Did someone come with you?"

"No, I just wasn't sure what to pack. My wife, Marylou, will join me later. She's visiting our daughter and granddaughter in California before coming to Amsterdam." *Maybe she's coming, maybe not.*

"That is nice," she said taking hold of Henry's first bag. "I will wait in the apartment for you."

Henry looked down the staircase; the trip down would be treacherous. "One slip and I'll be an aching pile of bones at the bottom," he said to himself.

Descending sideways while firmly gripping the banister, he eventually grabbed his second overstuffed bag and started manhandling it up stair by stair with his left hand, while pulling himself up the banister with his right. "With this bag banging on the stairs, I'll wake the entire building," he whispered.

"Excuse me, what did you say?" he heard from above. Looking up, he saw a young girl about eleven standing on the landing in front of his apartment. *Mini-me*, Henry thought. She had the same jet-black hair and creamy complexion as her mother.

"Hello there, just talking to myself." He was greeted by a smile, then silence, and a neutral hand wave.

As he finally approached the landing, he realized it was too narrow for his bag, the girl, and himself. His lower back was starting to cramp. Trying to catch his breath, he called out, "Professor Gordon, can I speak with you?"

Bernadette's head appeared out of the open door. She looked at Henry, then at the girl. "Oh, where are my manners? Professor Lindon, I am pleased to introduce my daughter, Lola."

Henry was looking for help, not an introduction. But, self-conscious about the size of his bag, he didn't want to make matters worse by appearing impolite. As he reset his grip on the bag so he could extend his right hand to the girl, he lost his balance, tilted backward, and began to flail his arms. He made a stabbing grab for the rail and yanked himself forward into a face plant on the stairs. He saved himself from falling, but his bag hurtled down the stairs. It slid, tumbled, and then it bounced. Miraculously, halfway down the stairs, the racket stopped when it wedged itself under the bannister.

No one moved. Wide-eyed, mother and daughter stared at Henry. Then, Lola put her hand over her mouth to stifle a giggle. Bernadette made a feeble attempt to shush Lola, but quickly joined her daughter in peals of laughter with hands on her knees.

Henry still lay flat on the stairs trying to collect his dignity. *So much for a good first impression!* Rising to his knees, he looked up at the laughing mother and daughter and said, "Nice to meet you, Lola," igniting further merriment.

"Well, Professor Lindon," said a smiling Bernadette, "I think that is what you Americans call a grand entrance! Let us try to move you and your bags safely inside."

After retrieving his bag, Henry entered the small apartment composed of two modestly decorated rooms. Bernadette pushed open the French doors separating the main room and the bedroom, revealing a room dominated by its ceiling. The thick and complex flourish of nineteenth-century decorative plaster gave the apartment an air of old-world charm. The room's bay window had a window seat—a perch from which to view the active street life below.

Bernadette asked, "Is this nice for you?"

"It's perfect," Henry answered, walking back into the main room. "I'm looking forward to getting to know the city."

"Professor Lindon, this neighborhood is called Plantage. It is more leafy and quiet than the rest of the city center. Down the street is the oldest zoo in Europe, and in the other direction is one of the last windmills in the city. I think you will find it very nice here."

"I'm sure I will, and please, call me Henry."

"Oh, very well, and you should call me Bernadette. Lola and I would be most happy if you would join us tonight for a simple dinner to welcome you to the university. We eat early, six o'clock."

"Yes," Henry responded a little too quickly. "That is very kind of you."

As mother and daughter walked back up the stairs to their own apartment, Bernadette called back. "Today will be an uncommonly warm day, so enjoy your afternoon. All of Amsterdam will be outside enjoying the weather . . . and . . . be careful on the stairs." A wave of her hand set her bracelets chiming.

■ ■ ■

After unpacking his bags, Henry put on his running clothes and went for a jog down Roetersstraat in an effort to energize himself. Turning left on Niewe Prinsengracht, he ran along the canal, past permanently moored houseboats in various stages of decay or renovation. On the stern of one boat, a skull-and-crossbones pirate flag and the Amsterdam city flag of three x's on a background of red and black waved in the breeze. Beneath the flags, a man lay spread-eagle under a blanket. Henry hoped he was sleeping off Saturday night.

He took another left at the Amstel, where the houseboats on the river morphed into house barges. One well-preserved barge had been fitted with beautiful Frank Lloyd Wright–style stained-glass windows reflecting cheerfully in the afternoon sunshine. Across the street from the barges were rows of carefully preserved seventeenth-century townhouses. He continued up the river to the majestic Amstel Hotel, headquarters for Nazi military brass during the occupation.

The streets were alive with walkers, dogs, joggers, bicycles, baby carriages, and café sitters, all taking advantage of the sunny afternoon. The metal tables and chairs of the café had been rearranged so that all the patrons faced the sun. Plying the river were a dozen glass-top canal boats showing global tourists the wonders of Amsterdam.

As Henry jogged over a canal bridge, he heard opera. He stopped and down the canal spotted a gray boat that looked like a miniature destroyer—without its superstructure. The boat's dozen passengers blended their voices melodically into what sounded like an Italian opera. As the boat glided under the bridge, Henry and the singers exchanged cheerful waves.

Leaning over the bridge railing, Henry took a deep breath. Things were finally going his way. Amsterdam and Dallas could not be more different. He was in a place where his problems could fade away. *But would his issues boomerang back if Marylou decided to join him in Amsterdam?* He made a silent pledge to focus his thoughts on the moment.

Back at the street corner of his apartment, Henry stopped at the neighborhood wine store. The inventory twinkled in the afternoon light. He dithered back and forth between an overpriced Chassagne-Montrachet and a reasonably priced chardonnay.

As he walked back into the apartment building with his purchase in hand, Henry's thoughts were on dinner with the beautiful academic. He wondered if she invited all visiting professors to dinner. Or had she seen something special in him?

He showered and tried on three different shirts, choosing a black one with a slimming effect. Uncharacteristically, he spent five minutes ensuring his slightly unruly wavy hair was properly brushed. He thought about calling Marylou but decided to wait a day to let emotions settle. Finally, he made a cup of green tea, sat on the window seat, and watched the bustling flow of students across the street at the University of Amsterdam. He conjectured as to who might soon be in his class.

Below him, he saw the building's door open. Walking down the stairs with an empty canvas bag in one hand and a cell phone at her ear was Lola. He wondered where her mother was. "Is Lola out on a busy city street by herself?" he asked himself.

He watched her go down Roetersstraat, talking cheerfully on her phone and then turning left out of sight. His curiosity piqued, he stayed seated, watching for her return. Twenty minutes later, with the phone still glued to her ear, Lola reappeared with a long loaf of Italian bread protruding from her bag. She pulled a key ring out of her jeans pocket and went up the stairs.

■ ■ ■

At six o'clock, Henry knocked on Bernadette's door; it opened with the tinkling sound of bracelets. She was wearing black jeans, bright white Converse sneakers, and a loosely fitted white blouse. Henry admired the self-confidence of a woman who didn't dress for her dinner guest.

Bernadette's apartment was about twice the size of Henry's from what he could tell. The walls were hung with scores of oil-paint-stained wooden palettes of various sizes, shapes, colors, and ages. The palettes announced the apartment as a place dedicated to art.

Two things caught Henry's eye: Lola in an apron stirring something on the stove, and, in a corner of the room, two six-foot-high neatly stacked columns of the same book. The apartment shone with Dutch domesticity—all precise and tidy.

Politely accepting the bottle of Chassagne-Montrachet, Bernadette said, "Please excuse our mess. I am preparing for a series of book events in the coming weeks." She walked over to the piles and pulled one of the books off the top. It was titled *Perfect Strangers*.

"This is for you, Henry. Please sit," she said, gesturing to one of two couches in the room. "I treat myself to a cold Jenever as an aperitif before dinner—would that be nice for you?"

"Absolutely," Henry responded. Turning to the kitchen, he called out, "Good evening, Lola. Are you tonight's chef?"

Still stirring slowly, she responded, "Good evening, Professor Lindon. We are pleased to have you join us. I hope you will find my cooking acceptable. It is only spaghetti."

Bernadette returned with two tulip glasses of Jenever frosted by the freezer. Handing a glass to Henry, she lifted hers and said, "Welcome to the University of Amsterdam. Here we say *proost*."

Henry raised his glass, saying, "Proost." He took an immediate liking to the frigid aniseed-flavored liquor.

"Please, tell me about your book," Henry said, turning over the book in his hands and examining Bernadette's flattering profile photo on the back cover. "Is *Perfect Strangers* your first book?"

"No, but it is my first novel. My other books are about techniques of Dutch artists—boring academic books no one reads. This one is historical fiction based on the infamous Dutch forger named Han van Meegeren. Do you know about him and his forged Vermeers?"

"I certainly know Vermeer. His painting *Girl with a Pearl Earring* is a favorite of mine. But I'm not . . . "

Before Henry could finish, Lola interrupted with an athletic hurdle over the back of the sofa, plopping down next to her mother. With a wave of the pale blue SPA water bottle in her hand, she said, "Mother, please, no van Meegeren tonight. I am so tired of that evil little man. Please, since Professor Lindon is here, can we talk about the United States?" Turning to face Henry, she beamed an uninhibited, toothy smile. "If Mother's book sells well in the United States, we will visit there. I want to go to Las Vegas! I want to meet Jerry Springer. Do you know him?"

Embarrassed that anyone in Holland would have any idea about Jerry Springer, Henry answered, "No, I do not. Why are you interested in Jerry Springer?"

"His show is on every afternoon at four o'clock. My friend Emma told me that *The Jerry Springer Show* is about what really goes on in the United States."

Bernadette laughed at her inquisitive child. "We will see about that. I promise not to talk about 'that evil little man' anymore tonight, other than to say that Tuesday afternoon at three o'clock I will be lecturing at the university about van Meegeren. It will be part of my class on Dutch art history. Would you be interested in attending the lecture?"

"I'd be honored," Henry said with an appreciative nod.

Bernadette stood and, lightly touching Henry's shoulder on her way to the narrow dining room, said, "Wonderful, I think you will enjoy it."

Over a spaghetti dinner complemented by rocket salad and warm Italian bread spread with pungent garlic butter, the conversation focused on the coming weeks' activities at the University of Amsterdam and Lola's school. After dinner, the trio retired back to the living room couches with cups of coffee.

"Lola, you are a wonderful cook. Where did you learn your way around a kitchen?"

"From my mother's cookbooks. She prefers to stay out of both the kitchen and the grocery store," Lola replied guilelessly.

Henry was curious to watch the mother's reaction to her precocious daughter.

"That is certainly the truth!" Bernadette cheerfully responded. "In Holland when children begin what we call *middelbare school*, they are given a fair amount of freedom. They have their own phones, bigger bikes, manage their money, and are responsible for their schedules. We believe that with freedom comes responsibility. For Lola it is going out shopping and cooking. It works well for us."

"That's wonderful," said Henry. "I wish it was the same in America. Today we have 'helicopter parents' constantly hovering over their children. If they could, they'd wrap their kids in a cocoon of bubble wrap. I'm not an expert, but I think helicoptering reflects an endemic sense of anxiety in America."

"Oh, that is sad. We Dutch may be boring and steady but certainly not anxious. With the pace of change, perhaps we should be. But as you will find, all most of us want is *gezellig*."

Henry found Bernadette's back-of-the-throat pronunciation of the "gugh" charming. He asked, "What is *gezellig*?"

"That was nice pronunciation of a difficult Dutch word, Henry. The word does not translate well into English. It is best to think of it as a cozy time with friends, like tonight. After you have been here for a while, you will understand. One more thing before I forget. This building is obviously old, and unfortunately the heat goes out from time to time. Please knock on my door, no matter what the hour, if your heat fails."

"I'll do that," Henry said as he got to his feet. "But now I need some sleep. If I don't see you tomorrow, I'll be at the lecture Tuesday afternoon. Good night and thank you both for a beautiful evening."

Less than an hour later, Henry was sound asleep with his copy of *Perfect Strangers* open across his chest. He dreamt he was skating down a frozen Amsterdam canal, stride for stride, with Jerry Springer.

Tuesday afternoon, Henry sat in the back of a cavernous lecture hall at the University of Amsterdam watching the students file in, open their backpacks, and turn on their computers. Cheerful conversations bounced around the room. Two minutes before class was scheduled to begin, Henry heard the jingle of bracelets announcing Bernadette's entry into the hall. She bustled down the aisle with a large brown leather saddlebag hanging at her hip from a long strap across her shoulder. She carried a metal coffee container and wore forest-green slacks with a matching vest and green Converse sneakers.

With practiced movements, she removed a power stick from her bag, plugged it into the lectern, and set down her lecture notes. She scanned the lecture hall and made eye contact with Henry, giving him a coquettish wave with the fingers wrapped around her coffee container.

"Damn, she's hot," Henry murmured.

"Excuse me?" said the young woman to his right.

"Sorry . . . it's . . . just so hot in here, don't you think?" said a flustered Henry. He was relieved that Bernadette had started her slide presentation.

On the screen flashed a photograph of her book cover:

Perfect Strangers

Bernadette Gordon

"Today we examine a subject close to my heart—Han van Meegeren. On the screen is the cover of my novel, *Perfect Strangers*, based on the life of van Meegeren. More on that book later.

"Art forgery has been with us for hundreds of years. As you can imagine, the unmasking of a forgery in a museum collection is a museum director's darkest nightmare. There is no question that the world's art collections are replete with forgeries yet to be exposed. As the price of fine art has skyrocketed, forgery has flourished.

"In Han van Meegeren, Holland produced the most colorful forger of all time. His forgeries were proudly displayed in the world's greatest museums and private collections. But he cannot be considered the greatest art forger of all time. The greatest are those whose names we do not know—they have not been caught!"

Stepping out from behind the lectern, Bernadette straightened her shoulders and stretched her neck. Smiling broadly, she continued, "But before we can talk about the forger van Meegeren, we must at least mention the genius who led to van Meegeren's infamous forgeries—the transcendent Vermeer." The screen filled with the image of Vermeer's famous *The Art of Painting*. Henry sat up straighter. He felt emboldened by the fact he knew the painting was generally considered a self-portrait of the artist at work in his studio. He wondered if his undergraduate days as an art history major might finally pay off.

Taking a moment for her students to appreciate the masterpiece, Bernadette continued, "We all know about the great 'Sphinx of Delft,' an artist whose world-famous paintings capture timeless calm and restraint. He inspires a cult-like following from both art aficionados and the man on the street."

Bernadette clicked slowly and silently through some of Vermeer's most renowned paintings, including *Girl with a Pearl Earring, View of Delft, The Milkmaid, A Girl Asleep,* and *Little Street.* Students in the lecture hall pointed out their personal favorites to their friends.

"Is our fascination with Vermeer because we know so little about him? We know he lived in mid-seventeenth-century Delft, left only thirty-five accredited paintings, fathered fifteen children, and, in a staunchly Calvinist country, converted to Catholicism. He used unique yellows and ultramarine blue in his paintings. In that era, ultramarine was made from the lapis lazuli stone, which was more expensive than gold. He painted domestic scenes of women that remain vibrant centuries later. The great artist died young, penniless, and virtually unknown.

"But here are a few things about Vermeer that are often overlooked." Visibly warming to her subject matter, Bernadette slowly pressed her arms in and out as if playing an accordion. "Early in his career, he painted religious canvases that have little in common with the domestic scenes we cherish today."

On the screen flashed Vermeer's *Saint Praxedis* followed by *Christ in the House of Martha and Mary.*

"These canvases and their religious themes are markedly different from Vermeer's domestic scenes renowned worldwide. There is no known transition from his early works to his beloved later genre. It is not uncommon for artists to have multiple creative periods and styles. Picasso, van Gogh, and Monet are just three examples.

"However, it was the stark differences between Vermeer's early paintings and his later masterpieces that van Meegeren ingeniously grasped to fuel his great fraud centuries later. Before we move on to van Meegeren, are there any questions about Vermeer?"

A sprinkling of hands went up, and Bernadette pointed to a student with a blond corona of hair, sitting in the middle of the hall. "Professor, those last two paintings you showed, the religious ones. Do you like them?"

"What art I do or do not favor is not relevant," responded Bernadette with a shrug of both shoulders and a mischievous smile. "But, as long as you asked . . . NO!

"One more question, and then we will take a quick break," Bernadette said, pointing to a tall, slouching student in the sixth row.

"Are art historians sure those two paintings—the ones you don't like— are Vermeers?" the young man asked. "They don't look anything like, you know, *The Milkmaid* or the *Girl with a Pearl Earring*, or any of the others."

"Thanks for that," replied Bernadette. "You provided the perfect segue into the story of the criminal, and unlikely Dutch hero, Han van Meegeren. As we will see, he took full advantage of the discrepancies between Vermeer's early efforts and later styles. But now it is time for a coffee."

3

Henry trailed the students out of the lecture hall to the coffee kiosk line. The students in front of him ordered coffee and a stroopwafel. Henry copied the order and returned to the lecture hall. He was enjoying the stroopwafel's sweet, cinnamon syrup sandwiched between cracker-thin waffles, when he heard Bernadette admonish a student in the front row, "Please, enjoy a coffee but no eating in the lecture hall. It is not polite."

Henry discreetly slid his stroopwafel into his coat pocket and checked around him to see if anyone witnessed his *faux pas*. The student immediately to his left gave him a wink and said, "You are not the first."

Henry nodded, mouthing, "Thanks."

He looked up at the screen that held a photograph of a white-haired, dapper man sitting in a courtroom. It was the same photo of van Meegeren as on the front cover of *Perfect Strangers*.

Pointing at the image with her laser pointer, Bernadette began, "Here is where van Meegeren ended his career—in the dock, accused of trafficking in Dutch art treasures with the Nazi occupiers. More specifically, selling a Vermeer to the malevolent psychopath Reichsmarschall Hermann Göring. Göring was the Nazi who directed the Luftwaffe's destruction of Rotterdam on May 14, 1940. At the time of this photograph, van Meegeren was a self-acknowledged philanderer, drug addict, syphilitic, alcoholic, and, of course, a forger. But, first some background on his path to the courthouse.

"Van Meegeren was a *bon vivant* with the look of a leprechaun," she said with a toss of her wrist that jangled her bracelets. "He began his career in The Hague specializing in society portraits and making a living sufficient to fuel his increasingly rampant alcoholism and infidelity. Copies of one of his works, a pencil drawing of Princess Juliana's pet deer, became the most widely owned piece of art in the Netherlands."

An image of the delicate drawing of the princess's fawn lit up on the screen. "In the late 1920s, one in five households in the Netherlands owned a copy of this drawing.

"Van Meegeren was indisputably an accomplished artist. His turn to the dark side appears to have been sparked by his 1920 solo show at the Blessing Gallery. The art world had embraced modernism, and van Meegeren's religious-themed canvases were viewed as out of step with the times. Critics dismissed them as being technically excellent but lacking any kind of inner creative life.

"By all accounts, van Meegeren was devastated by the critics' rejection. He had great expectations for his role in society as a renowned artist. Predictably, failed expectation became the mother of resentment."

Warming to her topic, Bernadette restarted her accordion arm gesture. Henry found the flow of her arms infatuating. She was totally unaffected and unguarded. He realized that spontaneity was a large part of her appeal.

"Van Meegeren left Holland for France, where forgery became his full-time job. Was it for the money or as a means of revenge against his critics? Forgery gave him the vehicle to both demonstrate his artistic prowess and make fools of the art critics who mistakenly certified his paintings as those of great masters. Whatever the true motivation, forgery proved incredibly lucrative, making van Meegeren the wealthiest artist of his time.

"He eventually made an ingenious breakthrough that paved the way for his most successful forgeries—Bakelite." Bernadette flashed up a photo of colorful pool balls made of the early plastic.

"In the mid-nineteenth century, art restorers discovered that alcohol dissolved new oil paint but had no effect on paint that had hardened over decades if not centuries. The alcohol test was key in testing a painting's authenticity. When van Meegeren mixed Bakelite into his oil paints and then slowly baked the canvas in an oven, the age of the paint became unsusceptible to any age-testing with alcohol. Van Meegeren's artistic talent, combined with this technical breakthrough, set the stage for his spectacular success as a forger.

"His first big splash as a Vermeer forger came with *Lady and Gentleman at the Spinet*." Bernadette played forward a PowerPoint slide of the painting. Highlighting the painting's elements with her pointer, she said, "Here we see so many facets familiar in Vermeer's work. The checkered floor, the mysterious letter dangling from the woman's hand, the ancient oil painting on the back wall, the use of the golden yellow on the woman's dress—all signal Vermeer.

"Van Meegeren then had a crowning bit of luck. One of the foremost Dutch art critics of the time was Abraham Bredius. A pompous, difficult man of wealth, he devoted his life to Dutch art. Bredius publicly authenticated van Meegeren's *Lady and Gentleman at the Spinet* as a Vermeer. With that accreditation, van Meegeren's career as a Vermeer forger was launched."

An unrelenting hand shot up on the left side of the lecture hall. Henry smiled knowingly. As a professor, he was familiar with this particular student species. Perhaps ignored as children, but more likely coddled, calling attention to themselves was their universe. This species, intent on asking their question, was oblivious to a professor's nonverbal signals to hold the question for later. From the tone of Bernadette's voice acknowledging the student, Henry concluded it was not the first time this student had interrupted one of her lectures.

"Professor, is it not ridiculous that centuries after his death, people would believe that paintings by such a famous artist would just magically appear out of thin air? Should we all start searching grandmother's attic?"

"Good question, Ms. van de Paverd," Bernadette said while stepping out from behind the podium. "A couple of factors helped make it all believable. First, for centuries, Vermeer was all but forgotten. His popularity did not really ignite until the 1920s, and then especially in the United States. So, no one was searching for his paintings. Second, three authentic Vermeers had been discovered in the twentieth century. The unearthing of another Vermeer was plausible."

The vibration on Henry's phone announced a text. As discreetly as possible, he checked to see who was texting. It was his wife, Marylou— "Please call now." He looked up to see an enthusiastic Bernadette lithely move to the other side of the podium to emphasize a point. He was pulled in two different directions. He knew he should call Marylou but was reluctant to miss any part of Bernadette's lecture. He wondered whether it was really the lecture he'd miss or simply the opportunity to watch Bernadette.

Saying "pardon me" to each of the students between him and the aisle, Henry squeezed out of the row and up the aisle to the exit. Once he found a private area in the hall, he called Marylou.

"Hello, Henry, I hope I'm not disturbing anything important."

"No, not really. Just attending a lecture."

"What's it on?"

"A forger named Han van Meegeren; he famously forged Vermeers. It's fascinating stuff. What's up?"

"I'm back in Dallas after a terrific trip to San Francisco. Our granddaughter is precious and their new townhouse is tiny but very cute. I'm heading your way in five days and wanted to check on the weather and what type of clothes I should pack."

A sting of irritation hit Henry. Had he been pulled out of Bernadette's lecture to talk about the weather? He closed his eyes and his hand went to his cowlick.

"It's great news that you're coming. Well, it's winter here on the North Atlantic, so it's damp and cold. Obviously, you'll need a coat and some sweaters."

"That's what I thought. I can tell by your tone that you're anxious to get back to the lecture."

"Sorry, is there anything else?"

"In fact there is. I'm bringing a big surprise with me to Amsterdam. Bye, Henry."

Before he could ask about the surprise, Marylou terminated the call. Aware he had mishandled the situation, he contemplated calling back. It was the right thing to do. But conscious that he would miss much of Bernadette's lecture, he decided the call could wait. Besides, a call back might lead to a conversation he wanted to avoid.

■■■

Taking the first seat on the aisle, Henry listened to Bernadette respond to a student's question. From what he could decipher, the question had been about brush technique. Bernadette glanced at the slender silver watch intertwined with her arm full of silver bracelets. "In the interest of time, we need to move on to how van Meegeren, a self-acknowledged forger accused of treason, was resurrected to hero status in post-war Holland."

Bernadette clicked to *The Supper at Emmaus*—a placid, flat, washed-out painting of Christ and three disciples at supper. "Take a moment to look at this painting. It has no relationship to the Vermeer paintings we all know. Not only does it lack any artistic relationship to Vermeer's paintings, but look at its imperfections. For instance, look at the disciple on the right. His shirtsleeve, rather than connecting to his shoulder, goes to nowhere. There is nothing appealing about this painting. Yet, with the help of yet another authentication by the art connoisseur Bredius, van Meegeren was able to pass off this unappealing painting as a Vermeer."

19

Bernadette paused to emphasize her next point. "The key to van Meegeren's deception was the fantasy he manufactured—that new examples of Vermeer's early religious paintings had been discovered. The logic was simple: they did not look like his later works of domestic tranquility because they were a missing part of Vermeer's early religious oeuvre. In 1936, this banal *The Supper at Emmaus* became the toast of the art world. The Boijmans Museum in Rotterdam heroically paid a fortune for the painting to keep a Vermeer safe from foreign ownership. It became the pride of its collection.

"Now to Hermann Göring." Bernadette clicked on a photograph of the corpulent, self-assured Göring in full white military uniform with gold trim and a spray of medals. He proudly held the diamond-studded, ivory-and-gold military baton awarded to him by Adolf Hitler.

"Göring was a man of enormous appetites and an even larger ego. He, along with Hitler, was obsessed with collecting—in reality *stealing*—the world's art treasures. But Göring pined for what Hitler already had: a Vermeer. Hitler confiscated *The Astronomer* from Edouard de Rothschild's enormous Paris art collection, and Göring yearned for his own work by the great master."

On the lecture screen appeared another drab, uninteresting painting, *Christ with the Woman Taken in Adultery*.

"Göring's opportunity came in 1943 when he heard from a Nazi banker in Amsterdam that this remarkably unappealing painting, supposedly by Vermeer, had become available." Bernadette stopped speaking, turned to look at the painting on the screen, and shot her arms into the air in a gesture of disbelief.

"Van Meegeren," she continued, "told an intermediary that the painting came from the collection of an elderly widow in dire need of money to immigrate to America. Off the painting went to Berlin for Göring's viewing, and by all accounts, it was love at first sight. After considerable negotiation with intermediaries, Göring traded 137 paintings from his collection for the single Vermeer. It was his pride and joy."

Inserting a bit of levity into her lecture, Bernadette flashed on the screen a photo of two bottles—Pride furniture polish and Joy detergent. Noticing a sidelong glance from a student, Henry realized he was laughing too enthusiastically.

"Now flash-forward to Holland in 1945," Bernadette said, her voice edged with sadness. "The Nazis pillaged Holland of food supplies and fuel. Citizens stripped the cities and countryside of any wood to burn for heat and even began eating tulip bulbs.

"But not van Meegeren. His enormous forgery profits bought him this beautiful townhouse at Keizersgracht 321." A photo of the four-story orange-brick townhouse flashed on the screen. "He also purchased fifty-seven other properties in and around Amsterdam. Included in these properties was a studio where he held notorious gin- and cocaine-fueled orgies. While the rest of Amsterdam suffered unspeakable indignities, van Meegeren partied on.

"His party ended on May 8, 1945—V-E Day." A black-and-white photo showed a packed street with joyful people waving Dutch and American flags. "There were exuberant celebrations across Holland. Predictably, there was also a thirst for revenge against those who had collaborated with the Nazis. Public beatings and humiliations in the streets were commonplace. Those who profited from the occupation were favorite targets. On May 29, 1945, van Meegeren was arrested and charged with selling a Dutch national treasure, a Vermeer, to the Nazi Göring. The alleged treasure was the forged Vermeer *Christ with the Woman Taken in Adultery*.

"After two weeks of endless interrogation, van Meegeren stunned his captors by saying, 'I did it, I painted it.' He was ultimately forced to acknowledge that many of the paintings in prestigious collections across the globe were his forgeries, including the pride of Rotterdam's Boijmans Museum, *The Supper at Emmaus*."

Bernadette moved from behind the podium and stood close to the students in the front row. The entire lecture hall went silent. The screen lit up with a photo of van Meegeren standing in front of a large canvas with a paintbrush in one hand and his palette under his other arm.

"To prove he had in fact painted Göring's 'Vermeer,' and therefore had not committed treason by selling a national treasure, van Meegeren offered to paint another Vermeer. The court provided van Meegeren with the necessary tools to do so. The process became a media circus.

"With the court-supervised completion of *Jesus Teaching in the Temple*, the public's opinion of van Meegeren reversed. Overnight, the despised Nazi collaborator morphed into the lovable court jester who had defrauded the loathed Göring. He was the little Dutchman who had outwitted the monster who had flattened Rotterdam. Myths built up around van Meegeren. *The Saturday Evening Post* ran an article entitled 'The Man Who Swindled Goering,' and a comic book for Dutch school students appeared titled *The van Meegeren Matter*. Remarkably, a poll in *The Netherlands* newspaper listed him as the second most popular man in the country.

"In retrospect, the outpouring of public adoration came from two polar-opposite directions—what the Americans call a 'perfect storm.'" Bernadette glanced at Henry and gave him a subtle smile.

"On one hand, van Meegeren filled the nation's need for a comic catharsis to shake off the horrors of the war years. In the world of public opinion, he was a lovable rogue akin to the congenial uncle who tells clever stories but drinks too much.

"From a very different direction came the unsubtle culture wars. The van Meegeren forgeries opened a vein of class resentment for all to see. With overwrought language and uncompromising certainty, the experts with their semi-mystical powers had blessed the forgeries' authenticity. For the masses, it was delicious to see the pompous, self-important art connoisseurs exposed as frauds. Their humiliation calls to mind the Hans Christian Andersen fairy tale where the child calls out that the emperor has no clothes.

"The trial was, of course, a public spectacle." Bernadette turned to point her clicker at the computer on the podium. The new slide was of a packed courtroom with some of van Meegeren's Vermeer forgeries hung on the walls. The ornate courtroom could have been mistaken for an art gallery.

"The forger's wit during the proceeding enhanced his legend. For instance, when asked by the judge to admit he sold his forgeries for high prices, van Meegeren responded, 'I could hardly have done otherwise. Had I sold them for low prices, it would have been obvious they were fake!'

"In the end, van Meegeren was convicted on the charge of forgery and sentenced to a year in prison. Fueling his growing legend, he died of a heart attack before serving a day of his sentence."

Bernadette clasped her hands together and fell silent. Apparently interpreting the silence as an invitation for questions, hands shot up all over the lecture hall. Bernadette smiled broadly and again clicked the screen to reveal the cover of her book, *Perfect Strangers*.

"I am afraid we are out of time," she said. "But if you want to hear more about van Meegeren, please come to my book event for *Perfect Strangers* this Friday at six o'clock at the American Book Center on Spui 12." She turned to the podium and began packing her leather bag.

Henry waited for the students to leave for their next classes and walked down the lecture hall stairs.

"Bernadette, that was a terrific lecture," he said. "What a story, what a life!"

"Thank you, Henry. The 'evil little man,' as Lola calls him, was terribly clever and energetic," she said while packing her bag. "To me it is a wonder he could balance his addictions, work, and wealth. There is so much more to the story."

"I've neglected my own class preparations because I couldn't get my face out of your book. Congratulations. It's a great read."

"Thank you so much; I am delighted you enjoyed it. Since you are interested in van Meegeren, I have an offer for you." She paused to gauge Henry's reaction. "I will travel by train in two days to Rotterdam to meet with the curator at the Boijmans Museum to examine their forgeries and files. Three of van Meegeren's forgeries are kept in the basement. Would you care to join me?"

Henry fell into step with her as they left the lecture hall. "Absolutely, I'm free all day."

"Very good," she replied with a flick of her arm. "Please meet me in front of our building at eight o'clock. I will bring breakfast. Now we are friends, Henry, and should say goodbye in the Dutch fashion."

Smiling into Henry's eyes, she touched cheeks three times: right-left-right. Pulling back, she said, "Ciao for now."

As their double-decker train pulled out of Amsterdam Central Station, Henry and Bernadette took seats across from each other on the train's upper level. She wore black peg-leg slacks with a matching jacket, a long white silk scarf, and metallic gold Converse sneakers. Henry felt fashion-challenged in his gray houndstooth Armani sports coat.

With the train picking up speed, Bernadette placed a thermos of coffee, bananas, and fresh croissants on the table between them. Pouring the coffee, she asked, "Do you take the train frequently in Texas?"

"Can't remember the last time."

"Such a pity, trains are wonderfully relaxing. Milk and sugar?"

Grateful for the strong Dutch coffee, Henry asked, "Did you drop Lola at school this morning?"

"No. Unless there is something special for me to do at school, Lola gets herself there. She is very fond of school."

"I hope I'm not prying," Henry said, looking at Bernadette over his mug, "but is your husband around?"

"There never was a husband," she replied nonchalantly while peeling her banana. "I was pregnant before I really knew Lola's father. I decided he would never transition from a sweet boy to a reliable man. I was young but not youthful . . . is that correct English?"

"Absolutely," replied Henry. "Have you raised Lola by yourself?"

"Yes. It is best because I have changed in significant ways," Bernadette said as she brushed a finger across the top of her glasses and pulled aside her bangs.

Henry wondered what Bernadette meant by "changed in significant ways." Before he could ask, she said, "Look out your window. See the gardens with little sheds next to the tracks?"

He pressed closer to the train's window and saw row after row of gardens on squared-off plots of land fly past. Most incorporated red mini-structures resembling tool sheds.

"Who owns those plots?"

"They are owned by the municipalities and leased to people living in neighboring flats so they can enjoy a garden. We Dutch love our gardens. In the summer the flowers are fantastic. In Dutch the plots are called *volksuins*. I do not know how to translate that into English. But the reason I point them out is that when I met Lola's father, he lived in one of those shacks, and much of what he ate came from his vegetable garden. We had wonderful times there. Part of the problem is that Lola's father still lives there. Lola and I are fine in Amsterdam center."

Her emotionless logic—almost Spockian—impressed Henry. He could not help but contrast the appeal of her rational approach with Marylou's increasingly emotional state. The more time Henry spent with Bernadette, the more captivating he found her sheer "Dutchness."

"So, since you asked about Lola's father, is it polite to ask whether you have children?"

"Yes," Henry replied with a smile. "Marylou and I have a married daughter, Laney, living in California. As I think I mentioned to you, Marylou was visiting her and our granddaughter last week. She could not possibly make the trip to Holland without first seeing them."

"Do you regret not going with Marylou for the visit?"

Henry, reminded of the Dutch reputation for directness, took the question in stride. "I guess so, but I was pressed for time with my commitment to the University of Amsterdam. Besides, alone time for mothers and daughters is a good thing."

"That is wise of you. I look forward to meeting your wife. Does she have plans for her time in Amsterdam?"

"Excuse me," Henry mumbled, pointing to his mouthful of croissant. He swallowed and continued. "She has enrolled in a painting class she hopes will be therapeutic. She has recently experienced some painful business problems."

"I am sorry to hear that."

"Thanks." Henry was not in the mood to talk about Marylou's issues. He was much more interested in getting to know his travel companion. "Will we go straight to the museum when we arrive in Rotterdam?"

"Yes, that would be best. I think you will find the Boijmans Museum very nice. It was one of the few buildings in Rotterdam the Luftwaffe missed." She held up her thermos. "More coffee?"

■■■

Henry and Bernadette's train pulled slowly into the silver-metallic, spaceship-shaped Rotterdam train station. After exiting on the station's steep escalators, they walked briskly up the esplanade to the barracks-like brick Boijmans Museum. At the museum's entry hall, Bernadette spoke in Dutch with the woman behind the information desk. Five minutes later, a bald, red-faced man with bright green-framed glasses presented himself.

In a vaguely British accent, the thirty-something Luuk van Wijngaarden explained that the curator, Mr. J. A. van Doorn, regrettably had been called away on an emergency, and he would step in as their guide. Bernadette, with a look of mild disappointment, shook his hand and said, "It is not a problem. Shall we go?"

Luuk led them down two sets of stairs to the museum's basement. It was a cavernous space filled with wooden crates of all sizes for shipping and storing art works. The group stopped at a set of floor-to-ceiling steel doors and waited for a security guard to unlock the huge vault door. The door swung open to a musty-smelling room with a series of sliding shelves, twenty feet long and ten feet high, holding paintings. Luuk pulled open one of the shelves, carefully removed three paintings, and placed them on wooden supports preventing them from touching the floor. Luuk stepped to the back of the room and turned his attention to his cell phone.

"These are good examples of van Meegeren's forgeries," said Bernadette. "Look at this one. It was an attempt to forge a seventeenth-century domestic scene."

Henry looked at the painting of two couples playing a card game in the painting titled *Inn Scene*. It incorporated a number of Vermeer cues like the kitchen's open window, a tapestry on the wall, the white water pitcher, and the familiar checkered floor. Although well executed, there was something lacking in the painting's use of light.

"I like the painting," said Henry. "But it doesn't look much like a Vermeer."

"Oh, very good, professor," Bernadette said with wide eyes of approval. "It was sold to this museum as a Pieter de Hooch. I said we would see van Meegeren forgeries; I did not say they would all be Vermeer forgeries. You must have been an attentive student. I only can dream that my students will be so observant."

Bernadette's approval charmed Henry. For the second time in a week, he thought his decision to major in art history might have been more than a sophomoric whim.

"This one," Bernadette said, pointing to a poorly preserved oil titled *The Blessing of Jacob*, "is simply horrible. It is one of those van Meegerens sold as a lost painting from Vermeer's early years."

Henry squatted to take a closer look at the painting. It was torn in at least five places and was peeling badly at the top. In the bottom forefront of the painting, a man leaned over in front of Christ.

"Henry, how do you feel about the man preparing to receive Christ's blessing?"

"I hope this doesn't sound sacrilegious," Henry said, rising stiffly from his squat, "but with his awkward position bent over the table and his grim look, well, he looks like he's preparing for the guillotine."

"I agree. Look here," she said, gently touching Henry's arm. "It is the exact same water pitcher as in the painting of the card game. Oh, van Meegeren was such a lazybones! The light reflecting off the pitcher is in the exact same place as the card game painting!"

Henry bent over to look and confirmed she was correct.

"I have read," she continued, "that when they arrested van Meegeren, they found this same water pitcher in his studio. Of course, Vermeer used a similar pitcher in a number of his paintings, so it was an easy prop for van Meegeren to incorporate."

After a few more minutes moving back and forth among the paintings, Bernadette asked, "Would you like to see the famous *The Supper at Emmaus?*"

"Absolutely," replied Henry. "I remember it from your lecture. Is it in here with the others?"

"No, it is prominently displayed upstairs. Most of van Meegeren's forgeries are concealed in museum basements. The Rijksmuseum in Amsterdam has at least five hidden away. They refuse to let me see them. But here, the museum has kept *The Supper at Emmaus* continually on display. They simply changed the artist's nameplate from Vermeer to van Meegeren. For all the wrong reasons, it is probably the museum's most famous painting."

Henry was enchanted when Bernadette took his arm as they walked up the stairs to the main gallery's entrance. They stopped in front of the infamous *Supper at Emmaus*. The painting had undeniable appeal. The plate of bread in front of Christ incorporated a well-executed punctilio of seeds in the Vermeer style. It called to mind the bread on the table in Vermeer's *The Milkmaid*. Something caught Henry's eye. Keen for Bernadette's approbation, he said, "Look, Bernadette, van Meegeren did it again! He used the same white water pitcher as in the other two paintings with light reflecting off the same exact spot."

"You have made an art discovery!" Bernadette said with a wave of her hand that sent her ever-present bracelets chiming. "I wonder if anyone else ever noticed. I certainly did not. Do you think this painting is nice?"

"I guess the painting is interesting, but it feels flat and lifeless. There's something dull about the three faces."

"Yes, they all have such heavy eyelids. I think they look stoned. After all, it was painted in Amsterdam." Bernadette enjoyed her own joke.

Luuk, who had been hanging back, stepped forward, saying, "Unfortunately, I have another appointment. If you want to see van Meegeren's sketches in the print room, we need to go there now."

"That is fine," replied Bernadette. To Henry, she said, "I think you will enjoy van Meegeren's sketches. They show he was an artist of rare talent."

In the print room behind the museum library, Luuk took off the shelf a large canvas portfolio and placed it on the viewing table. Slipping on white gloves, he opened the book to a pastel sketch titled *Fighting Peacocks*. The drawing's flying feathers were kinetic. One peacock, lethal claws outstretched, was about to pounce on his opponent's neck.

"You can see," Bernadette said, "in this drawing, van Meegeren froze an explosion of motion into a singular moment. Freezing a single moment is quite a trick. He was truly gifted."

They paged through more of the files, thanked the librarian, and walked to the museum's foyer. Henry sensed a shift in Bernadette's usual sunny outlook. "Everything okay?"

"Oh, yes. Would you mind if we walk through the museum gift shop? They sell two of my technical books, but I would like to see what they have done with *Perfect Strangers*."

As they entered the gift shop, Henry spotted on the shop's front table twenty-five copies of *Perfect Strangers*. Propped on a small easel behind the books was a poster of Bernadette and a quote from the London *Times*: "*Perfect Strangers* is a *tour de force* casting an uncompromising eye into a dark corner of the art world."

"Bernadette, you're a star! Why didn't you tell me about the *Times* review?"

"Oh, the excitement will pass quickly," Bernadette said with a shrug. "I think the English word is 'ephemeral.' Besides, despite my publisher's efforts, we cannot seem to generate any interest in the United States."

"Maybe we can help," offered Henry. "Marylou's college roommate stayed in Philadelphia after college and has become a leading figure in literary promotion. Her name is Penelope Smith. Let's talk about her when Marylou arrives."

"That would be very nice," said Bernadette as they exited the museum. She immediately picked up speed walking back to the train station. Fighting to keep pace, Henry asked, "Your book describes in detail van Meegeren's painting of the illicit lovers in *Perfect Strangers*. I spent an hour on Google trying to find a photo of the painting but came up empty handed. Is there a photo somewhere?"

"Not that I have found," replied Bernadette. "In 1950 there was an auction of van Meegeren's possessions to pay back taxes. The auction included many of his paintings. We know *Perfect Strangers* was auctioned to H. A. J. Kok from Utrecht. The description of the painting in my book comes from the auction records. After Mr. Kok paid five thousand Guilders in cash, a very high price for that time, the painting and Mr. Kok disappeared."

"So, no one knows where it is?"

"Correct."

"Any guess?"

"Maybe somewhere in the United States. After van Meegeren's rise to fame as the swindler of Göring, the prices of his own works sky-rocketed, especially in the States. Van Meegeren was an exceptional portraitist, and I have every reason to believe his painting of secret lovers in *Perfect Strangers* was excellent. I hope someday it will surface. Shall we stop for a coffee before the train?"

■ ■ ■

As their train raced back toward Amsterdam, Bernadette closed her eyes and quickly fell asleep. Henry alternately stared at the endlessly flat Dutch landscape and stole peeks at his beautiful companion. He rebuffed thoughts about whether he and Bernadette might someday have something in common with the clandestine lovers in the *Perfect Strangers* painting.

The vague outline of a dangerous plan began to form. The missing painting, *Perfect Strangers*, a painting out of sight since 1950, just might be the key to solving Marylou's issues. Henry's mind went into overdrive.

PART II

STOPPING THE MOMENTUM OF A BAD IDEA

TWO MONTHS EARLIER

5

It had not been Henry Lindon's finest year. While he sat alone in the kitchen, Marylou stayed upstairs, again. The mornings Marylou crawled into bed after sleepless nights had become the norm. The fun-loving and active wife he adored had become a stranger living in the same house. In less than an hour he would teach class at Southerland University. Although he enjoyed the give-and-take of the classroom, this would be his last semester at the university.

On his way to class, Henry parked his car in one of the university's underground garages, shouldered his Tumi briefcase, and turned toward the Southerland University Business School building. On the first Monday in December, Dallas was shrouded in fog snaking like wispy apparitions through the campus's ancient live oak trees. He shuffled along, rehearsing out loud the morning's lecture. Lately, talking to himself had become a habit.

Walking deeper into campus, he spotted movement on the trunk of one of the oaks lining the sidewalk. A gray squirrel noisily chased another in spirals up the tree's trunk and across the branches.

"Must be mating season," he said.

The diminished visibility made the normally bustling campus appear empty. The only person Henry could see was a large student lumbering toward him. The student's hair was cut in a modern monastic crown, a half-inch on the top and shaved on the sides.

As the man came into view, Henry thought, *Must be one of the university's football players and, by his build, probably a linebacker.*

The student carried a gallon jug of spring water, proclaiming to the world that he was a world-class athlete in need of around-the-clock hydration. When the two men were about ten yards apart, Henry saw another pair of squirrels chasing each other around a tree trunk. The terrified female launched herself to a horizontal branch hanging fifteen feet above the sidewalk. In a frenetic effort to escape her impassioned suitor, she scrambled upside down on the horizontal branch. Losing her grip, she fell toward the ground, twirling, turning, tumbling, and twisting through the air, then cat-like, she bounced off the linebacker's shoulder.

"Holy shit!" the linebacker exploded in a high-pitched scream, launching the jug of water into the air. Henry froze in place. It took every last molecule of self-restraint to stifle a laugh.

"Are you . . . ah . . . alright?" Henry finally blurted out as he bent over to pick up the water jug.

The danger passed, the steroid-pumped man, smiling sheepishly, said, "Yeah, of course I'm fine. It was just a little . . . unexpected."

"Okay . . . well, have a safe day," Henry responded as he handed the student his water jug.

Smiling to himself, Henry walked up the path to the business school building. As he pulled open the door, his cell phone rang with the sound of a revving motorcycle—the ring reserved for his lifelong friend Dan Moore in Wichita. Preoccupied with his upcoming lecture, he let the call go to voice mail.

Entering the classroom, Henry sprightly called out, "Good morning" to his students as he shrugged off his jacket and plugged in his flash drive. The students wore disengaged looks and Henry decided to energize them with the story of the morning squirrel incident. As he recounted the events on the sidewalk, the class began to titter, and

Henry erupted into laughter at his own story. With a tear running down his cheek, his hilarity veered alarmingly close to out of control. Wiping his eyes with a handkerchief, he chastised himself to get a grip. With all that had recently happened to him and his wife, Marylou, his emotions were fragile and unpredictable.

Regaining his equilibrium, he was pleased that the class had gotten a kick out of his story. But continuing his lecture, he grew apprehensive. While he was lecturing about the profoundly unfunny antitrust laws, furtive giggles sprinkled the lecture hall. As always, he called for a five-minute break at the halfway mark of the two-hour class.

While the students took advantage of the break to check in with social media, Henry reviewed his lecture notes. Nothing funny there. He spotted a student named Justin approaching the podium. Justin had been in his class the prior semester and the two shared a cordial relationship.

"Hey, Justin, what's up?"

"Professor Lindon," he said, looking discreetly over both shoulders. Waiting a beat, he leaned forward and whispered, "I thought you should know that . . . well . . . you're way south of half-mast."

With the universal male head-bob at the receipt of such news, Henry looked down, seeing his zipper was not only down to the final teeth, but a corner of his white shirttail was peeking through the aperture. With a brisk "thanks," he turned around to correct his sartorial blunder.

"God damn it, get a grip!" he whispered under his breath.

After the break, in uninspiring fashion, Henry continued his lecture on antitrust exotica such as cross-elasticity of demand, conscious parallelism, and predatory pricing. He sensed his presentation was off target. His words were there but the lecture had no music.

When he thought the session had reached its low point, it deteriorated further. He was forced to turn his back on half the lecture hall. The defensive posture was necessitated by the exacerbating sight of a sophomore pulling her fingers through her long red hair in the incessant pursuit of split ends.

Henry was relieved to exit the building. He was scheduled to attend the monthly faculty meeting and turned in that direction. However, after a dozen steps, he did an about-face, concluding that today was not a day he could face the bureaucratic ramblings of lifelong academics. Watching the fog lift from the campus, revealing patches of blue sky, he ruefully hoped he would find some blue sky at home.

6

"Detective Ortiz, walk me through this mess again, soup to nuts," bellowed Captain Johannson from behind his government-issue Steelcase desk. "The Southerland University student's murder has half of Dallas crawling up my butt. I let you take the lead because you said a quick indictment was a lead-pipe-cinch certainty. So where's the indictment? I mean, like what the hell?"

Detective Esmeralda Ortiz pushed her trademark long, thin braid off her shoulder. She recrossed her thick legs and sat up straighter, steeling herself for the inevitable confrontation.

"As you know, we found the victim, Nichole Kessler, in her garage apartment strangled to death. The autopsy confirmed she was strangled with two hands, and post-death, a red Southerland University tee shirt was wrapped around her neck. I interviewed her roommate, her landlord—who's an emergency room doctor—her Southland professors—"

"Yeah, yeah," interrupted Captain Johannson, fiddling with the White Owl New Yorker cigar in his shirt pocket. "I also remember you telling me the deceased was topless . . . and she swung from both sides of the plate—she was doing both her roommate and the emergency room doctor."

"Yes. My interviews revealed—"

"What makes you so sure she was double-gated?"

Ortiz was reminded that this prurient, lardaceous, neckless mound of man in front of her was, by a perverse twist of fate, her boss. As always, his attention was fixated on the salacious details. She took a deep breath.

"The autopsy revealed that Ms. Kessler was two months pregnant and the doctor, her landlord, admitted he was the father. The roommate was very forthcoming about the sexual nature of their relationship . . . "

"What confirms the roommate's assertions?" Johannson shot back in a disrespectful tone as he slid his cigar out of its cellophane wrapper.

What a moron! The only one who can confirm their relationship is the murder victim! Stay calm. Lightly touching the angry scar on her chin with her index finger, Ortiz responded, "Well, the two women had identical dragonfly tattoos on their right butt cheeks. That demonstrates a degree of intimacy."

"So, she had two love interests. They seem like obvious suspects." Johannson pulled the cigar in and out of his mouth and rolled it against his gums to release the nicotine.

"On the night of the murder, the roommate was in Abilene with her parents. The doctor was home alone, asleep after doing back-to-back shifts in the emergency room."

"Home alone asleep don't sound like much of an alibi. Was the doctor's DNA at the crime scene?" asked Johannson, continuing to noisily work the unlit cigar around his mouth.

"Yes. You may recall the doctor found the deceased—he lived in the main house and was the deceased's landlord for the garage apartment." Ortiz had to look away from the cigar mastication to calm her building nausea. The smell of wet tobacco was overpowering. *What a fine form of a man!*

"Have you ID'd all the DNA found at the scene?" Johannson asked, taking the cigar out of his mouth and dunking the tip in his coffee.

"All but one. DNA from the roommate and the doctor were found."

With the cigar back rolling around in his mouth, Johannson asked, "What about the unidentified DNA? What have you done to ID it?"

"We sent a sample to the Department of Public Safety Crime Laboratory in Austin. They came up empty, so we sent it to the FBI's Combined DNA Index System. Unfortunately, there was no match there. As you know, sir, less than ten percent of Americans have their DNA on file."

"Yeah, I know that. So, let me see if I can sum up your progress so far. The doctor's only alibi is that old chestnut 'I was home alone asleep.' What if the doctor found out about his girlfriend's little AC/DC act? Isn't that a strong motive? Plus, you found an unidentified person's DNA at the crime scene. But as far as I can see, you abandoned the investigation of anyone except for this Wheeless, who's serving time in Leavenworth. And, the topper is Wheeless's DNA wasn't at the crime scene. Right? Right?"

Watching the increasingly saturated cigar move in and out of the obese man's mouth, Ortiz's mind's-eye image of Johannson melded into Jabba the Hutt. The role of Jabba's obscene tongue licking his toad-like lips was played by Johannson's sodden cigar. Ortiz found the morphed image comical.

"What the hell are you smiling about, detective?" Johannson's rebuke startled Ortiz back into the moment.

"Sorry, sir . . . it was nothing. What was your question?"

"This may be your rookie year as a detective, but this is ridiculous. Didn't you learn anything at the academy? Why the hell focus all your efforts on one suspect? Wheeless's DNA wasn't even at the crime scene."

"Sir, the main suspect, Guy Wheeless, is the deceased's uncle. Six months after Nichole Kessler's murder, Wheeless was convicted of criminal assault and battery against multiple women and is now doing time in Leavenworth. Violence against women is his calling card. The deceased was estranged from her uncle and their acrimonious relationship is well documented. It was so bad she hired private detectives in Wichita to follow him. Most importantly, we have a copy of his company plane log showing he flew to Dallas on the night of the murder. Also—"

Johannson yanked the cigar out of his mouth and shouted, "Then where's the indictment, Miss Smarty Pants? You have no DNA evidence of

Wheeless at the crime scene. Your only evidence pointing to Wheeless is a copy of a page out of a flight log and his supposedly toxic relation with the victim. Where's the original of the flight log?"

"The original is still in Wichita, I thought . . . "

"Obviously you didn't think!" Johannson shouted, pointing his cigar at Ortiz. "I suggest you get off your ass and find the original. Without it, your copy isn't admissible into evidence. You have viable suspects and leads to run down, but you're doing nothing but chase after a hunch. This is some pathetic piece of detective work. Get out of here, go do your damn job!"

Ortiz waited a beat, stood up, and without a word, turned on her heel. Although humiliated and furious, she also knew her boss had a point. She would reexamine every lead, no matter how small. She knew that Wheeless murdered his niece, and she would prove it.

What she did not know: Wheeless had been released from Leavenworth prison that morning.

7

Edward O'Brian's time in the sun was over. He had basked in his tenure as the Wheeless Strategic Fund's acting chairman. The cavernous office, the doting staff, the unfettered power—all were intoxicating. But, with Guy Wheeless's unanticipated release from Leavenworth, his time was up.

On his hands and knees, he crawled under the desk and around the side tables, removing any hint that he had occupied the chairman's office. With his rail-thin build, all elbows and knees, he looked like a giant praying mantis stalking its prey. If he left any evidence of his stay in the chairman's office while Wheeless served time in Leavenworth, there would be hell to pay.

O'Brian reflected on the turn of events that brought him to his hands and knees. After Wheeless's sentencing on multiple counts of criminal assaults against women, he was expected to serve a minimum of eight years before any opportunity for parole. During Wheeless's incarceration, O'Brian had served as the acting chairman. But, just eighteen months into his sentence, the judge had ordered a new trial and released Wheeless on bail. O'Brian was confident that someone, probably the judge, had been bribed. Having labored under his heavy hand for a decade, O'Brian was well aware of Wheeless's core belief: money solves any and all problems.

Satisfied the office was scraped clean of any trace of his presence, O'Brian closed the office door behind him and headed for Kristen's desk. The heavily made-up receptionist was being chatted up by one of the stock traders from the basement's trading floor. Before Wheeless was incarcerated, there had been almost thirty traders. Now, only four remained. O'Brian remembered the trader was known as "Bud" because of his regard for the Budapest Stock Exchange.

"Bud, what brings you up here?" O'Brian asked.

"Just talking about Mr. Wheeless's return to the office. Pretty exciting, and I guess unexpected too," replied Bud as he straightened up and sheepishly took a half step back from the desk.

"Tremendously exciting," replied O'Brian. "He called to say he's on the way to the office right now. What would Mr. Wheeless think if he found you off the trading floor while the New York Stock Exchange is open?"

Nodding knowingly, Bud skulked toward the door. O'Brian took the trader's place in front of the reception desk and said, "Kristen, the chairman's office is ready for Mr. Wheeless. I'll be in my old office."

"Yes sir," she replied, her smile replaced with a countenance that was all business. "Can I help in any way?"

"Thanks," said O'Brian, reaching into his back pocket for an envelope. "Here's a list of employees Mr. Wheeless wants to talk with when he arrives. As you'll see, you're on the list. There is one thing you can do for me."

"Certainly."

"Remember the copy of the flight log for the company jet we supplied the Dallas policewoman, Detective Ortiz, when she was here investigating the murder of Mr. Wheeless's niece?"

"Yes, of course."

O'Brian stared intensely at Kristen. "Let's remember, we gave the copy of the log's page to Detective Ortiz in response to her specific request. Remember?" O'Brian skirted the truth—he had deliberately brought the log's existence to Detective Ortiz's attention. She had not asked to see it.

"Yes, of course, Mr. O'Brian."

"Good, we should expect Mr. Wheeless shortly. I'll be in my office preparing reports."

O'Brian headed down the long hallway, shouldering a sense of dread. He envisioned Wheeless strolling into his offices, resplendent in one of his double-breasted suits with his perfect, slicked-back vampire hair. He would undoubtedly wear an imperious look intended to intimidate his fiefdom.

Wheeless assuredly knew that the fund bearing his name was nearly insolvent. When he was sentenced for the assaults, the fund was hit by a hurricane of increasingly shrill redemption demands. O'Brian had delayed the withdrawals with every dilatory trick available to him. When the withdrawals became inevitable, O'Brian put in place plans to ensure the transfers benefited him. The opportunity to profit from Wheeless's troubles had been blindingly obvious.

The wind under O'Brian's wings was about to become a choke leash around his neck. His only comfort was the extraordinary action he had already taken to ensure Wheeless's eventual return to prison. He made a mental note to find and destroy the company jet's flight log.

8

Entering his house through the garage door, Henry found the breakfast dishes in the kitchen sink and the empty coffee pot still on. He heard the television in the upstairs media room. In the past, in fact the recent past, Marylou would have been busy with her business partner, Maria Jose, directing their import business. With a sense of foreboding, he headed upstairs to finalize the evening's wedding anniversary plans the couple had discussed the night before. Then, his phone rang. It was again his childhood friend Dan Moore calling from their hometown of Wichita. Henry turned back into the kitchen to answer the call.

"Henry, I began to wonder if you'd ever pick up. I've got news, but first, how's my friend Marylou?"

"Not good. She can't seem to pull out of her tailspin. This whole mess with the yellow ducks has drained the lightness from her personality. She's tormented by it and anything I say makes it worse."

"Has she been able to get back all the tainted yellow ducks she imported?" Dan asked.

"Oh, yeah. The cost of retrieving and destroying them bankrupted her company. Still, she can't shake from her head that some child, somewhere, sometime, put a duck in his mouth and was poisoned. She and her partner spent everything they made over the last eight years on the recall. Marylou can't reconcile that one of her ducks might have poisoned a child."

"Does she still think Guy Wheeless is responsible for the ducks being covered in lead paint?" asked Dan.

"She knows there's zero proof of his role in it, but her women's intuition tells her he did it."

"That makes my news tougher. Henry, Wheeless was released from Leavenworth this morning—the judge ordered a new trial."

"How the hell is that possible?"

"Apparently two witnesses recanted their testimony, and the judge ordered a new trial. I'm as certain as the day's long that Wheeless bought the witnesses' new testimonies. Who knows, maybe the judge as well."

"God damn it! Marylou is going to implode when she hears this," Henry said, firmly pressing down the cowlick on the back of his head. "So, just like that he's out?"

"All I know is the judge made him repost his bail bond and ordered him not to leave the state. If it makes you feel better, I'll have one of my men on him 24/7 for as long as it takes. I'll have more information shortly. My best to Marylou, talk again soon. Bye."

Henry knew Dan's private investigation team in Wichita was world class, but Dan's assurance failed to lift his spirits. The news of Wheeless's release was a disaster. How would he tell Marylou? Starting back up the stairs, Henry quickly decided it was not the right time to tell Marylou about Wheeless.

"Hey, Henry," Marylou said listlessly from the couch. The fact she was still in her bathrobe was not a good omen.

He sat down next to her. "Feeling better today?"

"Oh, I guess I'm feeling better . . . just tired."

Henry put his hand on her knee and said, in a voice he hoped was reassuring, "I know how upset you are. Anyone facing what happened to you would be crushed. Learning that those yellow ducks were covered with lead paint was devastating. How that paint got on them we may never know."

"What are you talking about?" Marylou snapped. "I know damn well Guy Wheeless is responsible for contaminating the ducks!"

"Easy," Henry said, taking his hand off her knee and sitting up straighter. His wife had lost all ability to let even the small things slide, though the contaminated ducks were no small matter.

"Don't tell me 'easy'! I know damn well it was Wheeless. He ruined everything I worked years to build."

"Let's talk about this later," Henry said, getting off the couch. As was frequently becoming the case, the couple's marital harmony had fallen victim to Marylou's anger and Henry's inability to comfort her.

Henry left the room murmuring to himself, "Don't say a word, this is not time to tell her about Wheeless or that she forgot about tonight's anniversary celebration."

■■■

Just past midnight, a nightmare slithered into Marylou's sleep. She saw herself in a kindergarten classroom. The children, sitting in a circle, chattered away while enjoying lemon popsicles. She stepped closer. When she was next to the group, she saw they were not licking popsicles—they were licking the contaminated ducks.

Jolted awake by her pounding heart, she screamed and sat bolt upright.

"What the hell! What's happening?" Henry said.

"Just a bad dream, go back to sleep."

"Want to talk about it?"

"No," she said. "Just go back to sleep."

After recovering her breath and slowing her heart rate, she gently pulled back the sheet and stepped out of bed. Henry was already sound asleep; she envied his ability to sleep. She tiptoed down the stairs and wandered aimlessly around the dark living room, randomly picking up photographs and other memorabilia. She reflected on how she had once been happy—gloriously happy. She had married the only man she'd ever loved, been blessed with a daughter successfully navigating her way in life, and now a granddaughter. She had every reason to be happy.

But happiness was a distant emotion. She was not the woman she had once been and certainly not the one she aspired to be. Her once active and fulfilling life had degenerated into sleepless nights followed by exhausted days. She sat down on the living room couch with a sigh.

Her eye caught a small photograph on the end table. The silver frame held a joyful photo of Henry and her on their wedding day. She picked it up, trying to recall the day's texture. An opaque memory floated past, just out of reach. As her recollection languidly came into focus, an emptiness washed over her as she realized how bad things had become. Yesterday had been her wedding anniversary, and in her doldrums, she had drifted past their celebration plans.

Marylou got up from the couch and moved to a hard, high-back chair to wait for morning. The dawn would bring no relief—it would be just another sunrise without the promise of a new day. Closing her tired eyes, she nodded off for a split second. But it was enough to see the malevolent vision of Guy Wheeless. His cruel, laughing face staring down snapped her awake with a start.

Taking cleansing breaths, she promised herself that not another day would pass without telling Henry the whole truth.

9

Henry brought a glass of orange juice to Marylou in the living room where she had been dozing on the sofa. She whispered thanks but was in no mood for morning chitchat. Knowing she was again functioning on little sleep, he wondered how he would break the news to her about Guy Wheeless's release from prison. After a few minutes of thorny silence, he headed upstairs for his morning shower.

The shower failed to produce the therapeutic effect he hoped for. With a towel wrapped around his expanding waistline, he stood at the sink staring at the hot water-fogged mirror. He used both hands to push his hair straight back from his forehead and said out loud to the mirror's foggy image, "You are one huge asshole! You allowed that stupid revenge game with Guy Wheeless to ricochet onto Marylou and ruin her business and our marriage. You are one jackass!"

He lathered his face and began to shave. Staring into his own eyes, he realized he needed to talk with someone. In the past, that person would have been Marylou. But that was a different Marylou than the one he was now living with. He was left with only one choice—his brother, Marvin. Although Marvin was capable of providing the worst advice known to man, there was no alternative. No one else understood the depth of his devotion to Marylou or his history of animosity with Wheeless. He splashed water on his face, picked up his cell phone, and called his well-to-do, ne'er-do-well brother.

"Yelloo," said a deep, and probably hungover, voice.

"Morning, Marvin. I need to talk."

"Okay . . . shoot."

"No, this needs to be in person."

"It's damn awful early . . . I mean . . . hold on."

Henry could hear Marvin apologizing to his bedmate, whoever she might be.

"Henry, give me a sec . . . I'll call right back," Marvin said.

"No. This is important. Meet me for breakfast at Freshii."

"How 'bout some slack here?" said Marvin. "You're askin' me to jump out of a warm bed way too early for a breakfast of bean sprouts. Get real, I'll meet you at Kuby's—give me thirty minutes."

"Okay," agreed Henry, not surprised by his brother's restaurant choice.

Calling out "goodbye" to Marylou but receiving no response, Henry left the house and drove to Kuby's Sausage House. Dallas's venerable German delicatessen and restaurant sat on a Snider Plaza corner with a giant cuckoo clock protruding from the building's facade like a malformed snout. Entering Kuby's, Henry walked past the racks of German magazines and the scores of sausages dangling like stalactites from the ceiling. They had names like Braunschweig, Grobe Liverwurst, and Weisswurst Beer Bratwurst.

Below the dangling sausages, the deli refrigeration shelves overflowed with huge porcelain bowls of yellow German-style potato salad and white coleslaw. Henry turned right into the restaurant section and settled into the farthest wooden table. The communal tables had been in place since the restaurant opened in the 1950s and bore the scars to prove it.

Henry was growing impatient when Marvin finally arrived with his long, bright white hair askew under a ball cap and wearing an oversized Southerland University basketball sweatshirt. A number of customers looked up from their eggs at the imposing six-foot-six athletically built man. Walking toward Henry's table, he gently took the elbow of a middle-aged waitress in the aisle and said, "Darlin', top of the mornin'. Can you save my life with a cup of java?"

The smiling waitress playfully rolled her eyes and seconds later returned with a steaming mug. Without looking at the menu, Marvin was ready to order. "I'll have the King Ludwig with a double hit of that delicious Hollandaise sauce and a side order of country ham . . . no, make 'er bacon."

Henry opted for dry rye toast and an egg white omelet. He lamented for the umpteenth time why he had been born without his brother's accelerated metabolism. As the waitress left with their order, Marvin leaned back in his wooden chair, taking an appreciative sip of coffee. Smiling at Henry, he said, "There's not another soul in this old world I would have jumped out of a warm bed and lickety-split dragged my sorry ass over here for. You got one hundred percent of my attention. Waz up?"

"I'm really worried about Marylou—"

"Henry," Marvin interrupted, "before you get rollin', can I ask you somethin'?"

"Okay."

"Are you makin' some kinda fashion statement?"

Henry mentally checked his button-down dress shirt, pullover crew-neck sweater, and decade-old khaki pants—no fashion statement there. "What are you talking about?"

"Just wonderin' whether there's some new style thing at the university. Those frat boys just shavin' half their face?"

Henry's fingers flew to both sides of his face. *God damn it! I'm so distracted I can't even shave right!*

"Oo . . . kk . . . ay, no biggie, don't look that bad . . . sorry to interrupt, fire away," Marvin said with a wily smile. "What were you windin' up to tell me?"

"Dan Moore called yesterday with bad news. The judge in Wheeless's case in Wichita has ordered a new trial—he's out on bail."

"Well, shee-it," said Marvin. "Not exactly upliftin' news. I wonder who that prick paid off?"

"At this point, it's all speculation. Dan said two of the women who testified against Wheeless recanted their testimonies. How they can do that without facing perjury charges is beyond me. Dan has one of his investigators trailing Wheeless 24/7, so maybe we'll soon get a clearer picture. But, see my problem?"

"You betcha. When Marylou hears he's out, she's gonna freak." Marvin put down his coffee mug and leaned conspiratorially across the table. "What do ya hear about the murder investigation on Wheeless's niece? What the hell is taking so long to charge him? Obviously the piece of shit killed that beautiful girl."

"Don't hear a thing," Henry said dispassionately. "Haven't talked to Detective Ortiz in weeks."

The waitress interrupted with their breakfast orders. In silence, Henry picked at his food while Marvin inhaled his.

"Damn, I was 'bout half-starved," said Marvin, patting his lips with a napkin. "So, what's goin' on with Marylou? I know it's not good. You think she's dabblin' with depression?"

"'Dabbling with depression'? What the hell does that mean?" Henry's hand pressed down on his cowlick. "Marvin, she is in an absolute, total funk. She's seeing a therapist but doesn't want to talk about it. It's like Wheeless infected her and there's no vaccine."

The brothers sat in silence weighing how to avoid an argument. Finally, Henry said, "But that's not what I wanted to talk about. I've been teaching at Southerland for three years. It's been great, but I need a change of scenery. Maybe it's this mess with Wheeless and the damn ducks, I don't know, it's just time for a change."

"Okay," Marvin said, sliding the saltshaker to the middle of the table.

"Seems you chewed all the flavor out of Southerland University pretty damn quick."

"I've enjoyed the run, but my gut tells me to make a change."

"So, in other words—" while crossing his long legs, Marvin's knee banged loudly against the table's pedestal. "G . . . O . . . D . . . D . . . A . . . M . . . N!"

"That hurt. You alright?"

"Yah, I'll live," Marvin replied, blowing out a breath and rubbing his knee. "Seems to me somethin' is itchin' at you, and you've got no idea how to scratch it."

"Maybe."

"You gonna go back to the corporate world?"

"Done there."

"Back to practicin' law?"

"Absolutely not."

"Okay, so what are you gonna do? You're not the retiring type," Marvin said, drumming his fingers on the table.

"I'm not through with academia. I've been offered a visiting professor spot at the University of Amsterdam for next semester, and I'm going to accept. The change in geography will do us good."

"Amsterdam? Why Amsterdam, of all places?" Marvin asked, rubbing his knee.

"It's a beautifully preserved city—I visited a number of times when I was in business and always thought a stay, long enough to feel a part of the community, would be great. It's easy to get around and everybody speaks English."

"San Francisco meets those qualifications. Why not make it easy on yourself and go there?"

"There's more to it. I've always had a thing for seventeenth-century Dutch painters like Vermeer, Rembrandt, de Hooch, Cuyp, Frans Hals . . ."

"I haven't forgotten you were an art history major—that decision landed you in law school to make a livin'."

"There's some truth there," Henry said, leaning back in his chair and shoving his hands deeply into his pant pockets.

"Whatever floats your boat," Marvin said in the bored tone he reserved to terminate any conversation veering toward the intellectual.

"But I'm worried about Marylou. Given her current state, I'm not sure she's up to it. And I sure as hell can't leave her alone. Should I tell her about Wheeless and postpone telling her about the Amsterdam plan?"

"Probably best not to string it out," said Marvin. "Just let 'er rip in a single blast. Tell you what—if Marylou can't make it, I'll sub in." Marvin sat up straight and histrionically widened his eyes. "Can't yah see it! We'll throw back gallons of Heineken, sample the best smoke in the coffee shops, play pinch and giggle in the red-light district. Hot damn, I'm gettin' all lathered up!"

Henry's hand pressed firmly on his cowlick. *Why do I ask this maniac for marital advice? He's constantly on the prowl for his next ex-wife despite four trips down the aisle.*

"Ah . . . nice offer. I'll get back to you. One more thing."

"Shoot."

"I may head to Wichita in the next day or two to put my head together with Dan Moore—try and get a game plan together about Wheeless. I can't let what he did to Marylou pass. Want to tag along?"

"Henry, you know how I feel about tanglin' with that varmint." Marvin put both elbows on the table and adjusted the sides of his ball cap with both hands. "Let me try one more time—folks don't rotate 'tween smart and stupid. Same's true with evil pricks, they never change their stripes. Some folks are just no damn good! Why can't you just walk on by?"

Henry saw heads swivel from the surrounding tables. Lowering his voice, he said, "Marvin, let's dial it down. Wish I could move on. After what he did to Marylou with the ducks—that depraved hump ratcheted up the game. Are you in?"

"Sorry bro, got a date with a shrink."

"You're seeing a psychiatrist?"

55

"No, not like that," Marvin laughed. "I'm datin' a psychiatrist and she's takin' me huntin' for feral hogs at her family ranch down in East Texas. I want you to meet her—her name is Constance, and I've never met anyone like her."

"I've heard that from you a time or two," Henry said with a tilt of his head and raised eyebrows.

"You'll see. This one's a real Texas twister!"

Getting up from the table, the brothers stood and clapped each other on the back. Exiting the restaurant, they turned in opposite directions on the pavement.

Henry wore a knowing smile. *Marvelous Marvin in love yet again. This time hunting wild pigs with his psychiatrist girlfriend!*

10

While Edward O'Brian printed out Excel spreadsheets reflecting the dismal state of the Wheeless Strategic Fund, the telephone rang. "Mr. Wheeless would like to see you in his office, now," Kristen said. Gathering his papers and slipping on his suit coat, he headed down the long hall. Entering the office, O'Brian was surprised to find another man with Wheeless. The two were leaning over Wheeless's desk, examining spreadsheets.

When Guy Wheeless turned around to greet him, not surprisingly, he was resplendent in a chalk-stripe suit with creases as sharp as a knife. But O'Brian was taken aback by how much he had aged. His hair, always oiled and slicked back to perfection, was dull, graying, and shaggy. He looked weathered. *How had just over a year and a half in Leavenworth aged Wheeless by ten years?*

"Hello, Edward," Wheeless said without extending his hand. "I'd like you to meet my friend Al Starsky." O'Brian had never before heard Wheeless refer to anyone as a friend. Wheeless's short, fit friend had coarse, closely cropped hair the color of gunmetal. He wore a pale prison tan.

As Starsky extended his hand, O'Brian read the silver legend on his black tee shirt: "Karma is an Echo." Around Starsky's neck was a string of blue beads with a red tassel on the end. O'Brian's latest girlfriend, a meditation devotee, also wore one. The necklace, called a mala, with

108 beads, is the Sanskrit equivalent of rosary beads. O'Brian had never before seen a man wear a mala.

With an ambiguous smile, Starsky, in a Michael Jackson whisper voice, said, "Your reputation precedes you."

"Edward," Wheeless said, straightening his necktie knot, "Al and I were bunkmates up at Leavenworth. He got out a few weeks before my release and will be joining us here at the Wheeless Strategic Fund. Let's sit down for a few minutes?"

As the three sat, O'Brian said in his sycophantic voice, "Guy, I'm delighted to see you looking so fit. We've certainly missed you around here!"

"Thanks," Wheeless said insincerely. "Before you arrived, I was taking Al through the state of the Wheeless Strategic Fund before and after I was shipped up on those trumped-up charges. It's painfully obvious the bottom fell out."

"We've had a trying time without your hand at the helm," O'Brian groveled. "Most investors withdrew their funds when they learned you were . . . eh, no longer here leading the charge."

"Edward, when you say 'most' of the investors, don't you mean everyone but me?"

"I guess that's right, Guy."

"And, in fact, I see that despite your position as acting chairman, you acted like a lemming and withdrew your investment. What does that say about your confidence in our strategy? Not exactly the unflagging support I anticipated from the acting chairman."

"Guy, my support never faltered. It's just that I had some unforeseen personal financial issues—"

"Let's not wade into that now," Wheeless said, cutting O'Brian off with a wave of his hand. "We have plenty of time to discuss the business in the coming weeks. One more thing before you leave, starting today, you'll report to Al."

All three men stood and O'Brian moved to the door. The other two leaned over Wheeless's desk. As O'Brian quietly closed the door, he glanced over his shoulder at the two men's backs. He saw Al place a reassuring hand on Wheeless's shoulder.

O'Brian realized an uncomfortable truth. For his plans to succeed, one way or another, Wheeless had to return to prison. He chastised himself for forgetting to secure the flight log. With Wheeless in the office, now was not the right time.

■■■

"The past year has been a fucking unmitigated disaster!" Wheeless shouted, stabbing his finger on the spreadsheet. "That skinny prick O'Brian ran the fund into the ground. Not only were all the withdrawals devastating, the performance was so bad it had to be intentional. Money doesn't just vanish into thin air. I'm going to set meetings with some of our long-term investors and find out where all that cash landed."

"That sounds right. As you said, O'Brian's a world-class bootlicker—we'll deal with him in due course."

"How about right now!"

"Firing him is the right thing to do, but not right now. Guy, something was said during our interviews this morning that got under my skin," Starsky said, fingering his mala beads. "Remember that little twit we talked with earlier? You know, the one made up like a clown."

"Kristen, our receptionist?"

"That's the one," Starsky said with a nod. "I'm thinking she's playing hide the weenie. Remember how she explained, at length, that the Dallas policewoman asked for the flight log from the company jet?"

"Yeah, so what?"

"It's about a lack of responsiveness. You simply asked her whether she met Detective Ortiz when she visited the offices."

"Yeah, so what?"

"Well, she never answered the question. It was a simple yes or a no. She jumped to spitting out that Detective Ortiz had asked for a copy of a page from the company jet flight log. Why bring the log up out of left field? Absence of responsiveness waves a big red flag. Let's run that little chippy through her paces again."

Nodding his head once in agreement as he stood up, Wheeless opened the office door and called out, "Kristen, can we speak with you?"

Moments later, with an apprehensive look on her face, she entered the office. Wheeless signaled her to take a seat at the conference table, where she sat with her hands folded in her lap. Starsky sat across from her looking beneficent and supportive.

"Kristen, I want to make sure you understand how much I appreciate your loyalty and hard work while I was away," began Wheeless.

"Thank you, sir. We all worked hard . . . especially Mr. O'Brian. He was here day and night."

"I bet he was," replied Wheeless with thinly veiled sarcasm. "Kristen, there's nothing I hold dearer than loyalty. And, loyalty requires total candor. As a long-term employee here, you are entitled to a second chance to prove your loyalty. When we spoke earlier, you told us you gave a copy of a page from the flight log to that Dallas policewoman. But you gave it to her only after she asked you for it."

"Yes sir, Mr. Wheeless."

"As I'm sure you know, we just finished speaking with Mr. O'Brian. He told a very different story about the flight log," Wheeless lied. "This is your second chance to prove your loyalty." Wheeless held up two fingers staring silently at Kristen.

Her lower lip began to tremble—a silent tear followed. Starsky reached for a Kleenex box. Putting a comforting hand on her shoulder, he slid the box in front of Kristen and, in his soft voice, said, "Just take your time."

"I'm so sorry, Mr. Wheeless. I didn't know what to do. I'm a single parent with a young child and can't afford to lose this job."

"I understand, Kristen," Wheeless said in a sympathetic voice. "Just tell us the truth, everything will be alright."

"Thank you, Mr. Wheeless," Kristen said, fighting to recover her composure. "Mr. O'Brian told me to say that the policewoman, her name was Detective Ortiz, asked for a copy of the log."

"Did she?" asked Wheeless.

"Not really. Before Detective Ortiz even came to the office, Mr. O'Brian gave me a copy of a page from the flight log."

"Okay," said Wheeless, staring coolly at Kristen. "Then what happened?"

"Mr. O'Brian told me to hide the flight log and keep handy the copy of the one page."

"Did you?"

"Well, yes. After the detective met with Mr. O'Brian, she came to my desk. She said Mr. O'Brian told her about the flight log and she asked me for the copy of the page she was interested in."

"And you gave her the copy?"

"Yes sir, that's what Mr. O'Brian told me to do. Since Mr. O'Brian had already made the copy, I just handed it to her," Kristen explained while looking down at her hands.

"Did this Detective Ortiz ask to see the whole flight log?"

"No, she just put the one page in her briefcase and left."

"Kristen, where's the original flight log?"

"It's in my credenza, Mr. Wheeless. I've kept it there since Mr. O'Brian sold the company jet. He said we couldn't afford to keep it."

"Let's go get the log, shall we?"

Wheeless followed Kristen to her desk. She unlocked her credenza and pulled out the leather-bound three-ring binder and handed it to Wheeless.

"Thanks," Wheeless said with an unkind smile. "While you're here, clean out your desk. You don't need to come in tomorrow . . . or any other day."

"But—you said loyalty meant everything to you . . ."

"Loyalty? Get the fuck out of here," Wheeless snarled as he tucked the flight log under his arm. He walked back into his office and, without looking back, slammed the door behind him. "She's history," he said to Starsky. "Now let's get that emaciated prick O'Brian up here and fire his ass!"

"Let's put that idea on standby for now," replied Starsky with a twinkle in his pale blue eyes. "Wouldn't it be better to keep him close until we figure out what went down around here? I don't get what this flight log thing is all about. Why give a copy to that policewoman? Is there something in the flight log we should be concerned with?"

Wheeless looked his ex-cellmate up and down and gave a little snort. "Not a damn thing to worry about. And, yeah, you're right—we'll keep O'Brian on a real short leash until we figure out what the hell happened around here."

Slipping the flight log into his knapsack, Starsky said, "I'll hold this sucker for safekeeping. Something tells me it's going to be a piece of the puzzle."

11

Detective Esmeralda Ortiz parked her dark blue 1992 Honda Accord in front of her garden apartment on Sylvester Street, just off Dallas's Maple Avenue. Her week had been drudgery, but it was Friday. Exiting her car, she surveyed the area for potential trouble. The neighbor on one side had two abandoned grocery carts on the curb, and there was still a torn mattress on the corner of Sylvester and Lucas. There was nothing she liked about the apartment complex.

She inserted her key in the door while balancing her grocery bag on her hip. In the bag were two bottles of cheap Chablis, a party-size bag of Cheetos, a pound of day-old ground round, and a box of Philly Cheese Hamburger Helper. The door was chained from the inside. She leaned on the buzzer until her aunt Sherrie slid back the chain. Sherrie was dressed in her green floor-length robe, a silver chain wrapped around her head, and huge hoop earrings bouncing on her shoulders.

"Damn it, Sherrie," Esmeralda said, shoving the cat away from the open door. "Why are you always chaining the door?"

"Well, howdy doody to you, Miss Esmeralda. A client's in my room if you don't mind."

"Who is it this time?"

"It's Mrs. Rodriquez from next door. You know, the retired nurse. She's got some issues to work through. We'll be done in fifteen."

Forty minutes later, Sherrie said good-bye to the petite Mrs. Rodriquez while Esmeralda towel-dried her hair in preparation for their traditional Friday night at the Grapevine Bar.

"How's Mrs. Rodriquez?" asked Esmeralda from under her towel.

"She accessed some righteous energy today. The subject of her readings is always her nephew—she thinks he has sugar in his pants."

"Has Mrs. Rodriquez started to pay for her sessions?"

"Not yet," Sherrie said, pushing back a tangled mess of prematurely gray curls from her face. "But when she's aligned with the inter-dimensional universe, she'll know it's the right thing to do. She's also a friend and friends are important."

"So I'm told. Someday I'd like to move out of this dump," Esmeralda said, waving her arm at the living room. "If you could find a way to make a buck or two, it would help the cause. About every joker in the complex has two things in common—they're your clients and none of them pay. At least get Mrs. Rodriquez to turn down the telenovelas; I can hear every word through these cardboard walls."

"Be nice," Sherrie said with a soft smile. "Those telenovelas keep her company. Esmeralda, there's something deep in your subconscious struggling to escape. Letting it go will make you a much happier person. I've got an idea."

"I bet you do."

"Wait right here."

Sherrie returned carrying an ornate wooden box. A pentacle star carved on the box's top was similar to the one Sherrie wore on a long silver chain around her neck. She slowly opened the lid to reveal a four-inch purple crystal atop a tarot deck.

"I've been saving this deck just for my Esmeralda! The crystal has been energizing the deck for two months. This tarot deck is . . . well . . . celestial. Let's see if we can focus in on your prospects. Shall we?"

Esmeralda needed a stiff drink rather than her aunt's new age mumbo jumbo. "Sherrie, it's Friday night. Let's just do what we always do, hit the Grapevine, get some guys to buy us drinks so that you can get picked up and I can go home alone."

"You never know, Esmeralda, this might be your lucky night. Remember the time you met Kenny Turner at the Grapevine?"

"Kenny was over a year ago. Girl, you're tall and thin and can talk to guys about a wide range of topics. Me, I'm just wide. One more plate of Hamburger Helper and I'll be downright fat!"

"Please, Esmeralda," Sherrie said as she sat down on the couch. "You have to reset how you view yourself. You're positively Rubenesque. Men love full-figured women."

"Can't prove it by me."

"This is the perfect night for a tarot card reading. There have been two Mercury retrogrades that caused the planets to realign, which in turn causes each of us to reconnect with our past lives and detox from the experiences causing misalignment in our current lives."

"Whatever, Sherrie. Let's not take all night."

Sherrie removed the seventy-eight-card deck and expertly shuffled the cards three times. She set the deck on the table and asked Esmeralda to cut the cards.

As Esmeralda reached for the cards, she said, "Can we put a timer on this?"

"Patience is its own reward," Sherrie said as she carefully aligned the deck and slowly pulled off the top card and laid it face up on the table. It was the Lovers card.

"What a wonderful start, Esmeralda. The card is facing you, so for divination purposes, it means you will not only overcome your trials, but love is coming your way."

"Can we just stop there?"

"Of course not," said Sherrie as she picked up a second card and placed it next to the Lovers card. "This is remarkable. The Sun card

65

indicates material happiness and contentment. The next card is SOOO important."

Sherrie then turned over the Knight of Wands. "This clearly implies a change of residence."

"Hot dog," said Esmeralda. "We're finally getting out of this dump."

Ignoring Esmeralda, Sherrie turned over the next card. It was the King of Cups. With a look of concern, Sherrie said, "The King of Cups is facing me so its meaning is reversed. It means that there is a double-dealing man coming into your life."

"He already arrived. That toad I call my boss has had it in for me since day one."

The fifth card Sherrie turned over was the Ten of Cups. "Esmeralda, this is startling. This card's meaning is simple—it means contentment. Your future is so bright! Now the sixth and final card for your Pentagram Spread." Sherrie turned over the Eight of Wands.

"The Eight of Wands in this spread means arrows of love are already in the air and flying your way. Esmeralda, your ship's about to come in! This is the most positive reading I have ever seen."

"That can mean only one thing—let's hit the damn bar."

12

Marvin was unaccustomed to rising before dawn. He lay in bed half asleep, propped up on one elbow watching Constance dress. Her back turned to him, she wiggled into her well-worn Levis. Her narrow hips and muscled shoulders gave her a boyish sharpness. Pulling a long-sleeved white shirt over her head, she shook out her long, gray-streaked chestnut hair.

"Can I ask you a question? How did an East Texas gal get a name like Constance?"

As she brushed her hair, Constance's expression reflected that the question had been asked and answered too many times. "Mom was a music teacher in Gun Barrel City. She adored Mozart. Mozart's mother was named Constance. If I had been a boy, I would have been named Amadeus. So, here I stand, Constance Whitcome. You're stalling cowboy, get a move on. Get wet while I call the hospital to check on how one of my patients did overnight. Let's go, today's a hunting day!"

Thirty minutes later they were flying east on Route 175 in Constance's white Range Rover Autobiography. Marvin, trying to shake his cobwebs, switched on the radio. The backbeat of one of his favorite songs filled the car—Roy Orbison's "Only the Lonely." As he was about to tell Constance about the song's backbeat, with a flick of her wrist, she silenced the car.

"Let's talk. Songs about loneliness are depressing."

"Okay," said Marvin. "How 'bout them Cowboys!"

"Is that your protective shield going up?"

"Sorry, just bein' a smart ass. What do ya want to talk about?"

"Your brother, Henry," Constance said, giving Marvin an inquiring look. "When he called the other morning, you jumped out of my bed like there was a five-alarm fire. You abandoned me. I *really* do not like feeling abandoned."

"It's com-pli-cated," Marvin said, pulling his fingers through his thick white hair. "We were Irish twins growin' up on a Kansas wheat farm, all we had was each other. So we've always been as close as fresh paint on an old barn."

"You're still close today?"

"Oh yeah. Sure, like all brothers we fuss and fight. By definition that's what brothers do. As I tell Henry, the two of us are like different fingers on the same hand." Marvin wiggled his fingers at Constance.

"So what's so complicated?"

"Henry's as normal as it gets. He's a both-feet-on-the-floor, two-hands-on-the-wheel kinda guy. But he has this one hunker of a problem."

"When I hear someone is 'normal,' whatever that means, there's always a 'but.' What's his problem?"

"Bet that's right about 'normal,'" said Marvin, nodding. "Henry prides himself on always being in control. But, there's one exception. Forever Henry's had a tit-for-tat thing goin' with a real a-hole named Guy Wheeless in Wichita. Since high school the two of 'em found countless ways to jag each other's wires. The stupid little game spilled over in a serious way onto his wife's business, and she's mad as hell about it."

"What happened to her business?"

"She had a real successful home furnishing business and someone, she's damn sure it was Wheeless, managed to have a slew of baby duck ornaments she imported from China painted with yellow lead paint. She went broke retrieving all of them."

"That's terribly sad for her."

"Addin' to the mess, Wheeless has been in jail for assaultin' women in Wichita. But, now somehow he's out and Henry's worried about what's around the corner. The topper is this Wheeless jackass is under investigation here in Dallas for murdering his niece. Like I said, it's com-pli-cated."

"Wheeless sounds like a real jewel. Is your brother feeling like a piñata?"

"No . . . he's not like that. Henry's not a woe-is-me kinda guy. He's big on staying in control, like I said, two hands on the wheel and both feet on the floor. Since he's so even, some folks underestimate him. When Wheeless got his ass thrown in Leavenworth, Henry thought the door had been permanently slammed on the problem. But like a bad penny, he's back. Henry told me he's just lookin' for closure."

"There's no such thing as closure in the real world," Constance said, gently shaking her head. "It's a word made up by divorce attorneys to justify their fees."

"Amen," Marvin said with a knowing laugh.

"Don't want to play therapist here," Constance said, adjusting her ROKA aviator sunglasses, "but the word 'closure' assumes the past is permanently over. That's a fantasy—memories reset, emotions evolve, and facts transpose. When I hear the word 'closure,' usually someone is looking to avoid responsibility."

Constance turned to smile at Marvin. He loved her crooked front tooth. She had large glowing teeth, but her front right incisor protruded slightly over to the left. Most women Marvin knew would have straightened the tooth years ago. Indicative of Constance's authenticity, she left it in its natural state like the traces of gray in her hair or the delicate lines defining her luminescent face.

"We need to have dinner with Henry and his wife so you can take your own measure of what he's all about."

"Has Henry always been a professor?"

"Oh no, it's what he calls his second act. He started life as a lawyer, but eventually rose to become chairman of a publicly traded food company in

Dallas. A couple of years back, around the time he turned fifty, he decided he wanted to be a professor. Henry's real smart, but, like I said, understated. I'm damn sure you'll like him and Marylou too."

"Great, I look forward to meeting them," said Constance as she maneuvered back into the passing lane. "But please keep in mind I *really* do not like feeling abandoned."

"I got 'er. How 'bout you fill me in on what we're up to today."

"Have you done much hunting?"

"Growin' up in Kansas, all we ever hunted was pheasant. God made Kansas for wheat and pheasants. Been down to Argentina with the boys shootin' doves. Never shot a deer or anythin' like that."

"Today we're going to help the state of Texas reduce a plague. These varmints are ruining our state."

"Always happy to be on the righteous side," Marvin answered a bit tenuously. "But remind me what problem we're tryin' to fix?"

"Let me give you a bit of a history," Constance said as she aggressively accelerated past a slow-moving sixteen-wheeler carrying drilling pipe. "Pigs were brought here about three hundred years ago by the Spanish conquistadors. They got loose, and in a matter of a few years, became feral—with thick skins, bristly coats, and lethal tusks. More importantly, they started reproducing like rabbits. They have two litters a year of up to ten piglets. These porkers can get up to four hundred pounds, can sprint at thirty miles an hour, and supposedly can smell a meal seven miles away. I've read there are four million of them in Texas alone."

"It's a problem," Marvin agreed.

"No kidding. They eat everything, including each other. When we kill one, sometimes we just leave it in the field, and its brothers and sisters finish the job."

"A friend of mine, Chad, he's one of the guys that comes by my office for happy hour on Wednesday afternoons." Marvin hesitated. "By the way . . . are you gonna come by one of these afternoons for a drink so I can introduce you to the boys?"

"I've got enough emotional issues on my plate already," Constance said with her eyes fixed firmly on the road. "I'll leave those therapy sessions to you."

"Fair enough, you got no idea how close you are to the truth about those get-togethers bein' therapy sessions. Well anyway, ol' Chad did an interestin' thing to get rid of the pigs on his place over in Glen Rose. He's got a huge pond at the southeast end of his ranch. He wired the pond with dynamite, threw in a burlap bag full of dead chickens, and then hid up in a deer blind. When about a hundred of those porkers start slopping around in the mud, he blew up the whole lot to hog heaven."

"As creative as that all sounds, this morning we're going after them the old-fashioned way," Constance said in a firm voice. "You, me, and bowie knives."

Marvin wondered how, with the pigs clocked at thirty miles an hour, he was going to run down one of the monsters with just a bowie knife.

Constance turned onto Route 20 and pulled off into the access road. "We've got about fifty miles to Wood County, straight and dull. Mind taking the wheel so I can check in with a couple of patients?"

Marvin agreed and they got out of the car. As they came around the back going in opposite directions, Constance gave Marvin a firm slap on the butt saying, "You're a good man, Marvin Lindon."

Constance's physicality always energized Marvin. Around Constance, he had to be on his toes both literally and figuratively.

Driving down the uninspiring Route 20, Marvin tried not to listen, but could not help hearing, Constance's patient conversations. With a smile on her face, she spoke in soothing, yet firm tones. "Let's focus on issues, not decisions." "I can't speculate about him; I only have access to you." "By definition, relationships are two-way streets." "Energy is better spent on solutions than problems." Marvin was impressed by her confidence and fluidity.

An hour later, Constance was directing Marvin down an unpaved county road. They came to two ten-feet-high stone pillars anchoring a wrought-iron gate with a "CW" logo in the center. Constance picked up her iPhone, pressed an app, and the gate swung open.

"So," said Marvin, "it's just you, me, and the pigs?"

"Probably not. My Uncle Charlie will undoubtedly be hanging around like a mother hen. There was an "incident" during a hunt two years ago and Uncle Charlie has been overly vigilant ever since. He and my dad were partners in the ranch, but now it's Uncle Charlie and me. Shared ownership of property is never easy, especially when it's a family thing."

A half a mile later down a well-maintained gravel road cutting through fenced cattle pastures, they pulled in front of a two-story stone house topped with a sharp-angled steel-seam roof.

"That's some beautiful stone," said Marvin. "What kind is it?"

"Glad you like it. It's called rattlesnake chopped stone. Dad supervised the quarrying down in Granbury. He called the stones his personal mélange. He wanted the house, outside and inside, to look like a mosaic. As you'll see, he overdid it a bit."

As they opened the car doors, an odd couple appeared on the broad front porch. A short, round Mexican woman wore a smile as wide as her bright blue apron. Next to her was a tall, wide-hipped patrician man with tortoise shell glasses. His thinning, wavy hair was brushed straight back from his forehead. He wore a camouflage outfit and knee-high boots. Marvin thought he looked like a Rhodesian Afrikaner ready to defend his domain. In his right hand was a drink garnished with a celery stick—it looked like a Bloody Mary.

The woman hurried down the stairs with her arms extended until they were wrapped around Constance in an unabashed embrace. *"Connie, mi querida ha pasado demasiado tiempo! Mi amor, por favor charlemos en mi cocina!"*

"Please, Gabriella, English," Constance gently admonished. "Meet my friend Marvin Lindon. I told him you're the best cook in East Texas."

Gabriella gave Marvin a quick hug and quickly turned back to Constance. Marvin glanced up to the porch. The man's position and expression were unchanged. In his full-on Labrador puppy mode, Marvin bounded up to the porch with his hand extended.

"This is one beautiful place. I'm Marvin Lindon from Dallas."

The man gave Marvin a firm handshake and replied, "Charles Whitcome, Constance's uncle. I've been expecting you. Come on in."

13

Henry sat in the living room rehearsing how to tell Marylou about Guy Wheeless's release from prison and his plan to teach in Amsterdam. Marvin had been right at breakfast—it was best to get it all out there in a single blast. Procrastination had led him to the end of his runway. He was out of time; today was the day.

Henry grew uneasy when Marylou entered the room. She looked too purposeful. Before Henry could open his mouth, she preempted him, "I need to talk."

"Okay," said Henry. "I'm all ears."

"Yesterday, I had a long conversation with Maria Jose. She wants me to come to Buenos Aires for an extended visit."

"What does she mean by 'extended'?"

"Hold your horses, I'm getting there. For the last two months she's been enrolled in an art therapy program. They paint for ten hours a day and she's learning lots of different brush techniques. The instructors are world class and can paint anything. She said when she's painting she can't think of anything else, especially those yellow ducks."

"That's great for Maria Jose," Henry said, wondering if it was his turn to speak. It wasn't.

"So, she said it would do me a world of good to enroll in the class . . .

help me get back to . . . me. The minimum commitment is one month. I talked it over with my therapist and she says a change of surroundings might be the spark I need. So, what do you think? I could leave right after the New Year—with the new semester starting at Southerland University, you shouldn't be too lonesome."

Henry was elated—Marylou had provided the perfect segue for him to share his plan to teach in Amsterdam. There was no need for Marylou to go to Buenos Aires; Amsterdam, of all places, must have dozens of art schools. A shared new adventure in Amsterdam was just what the couple needed to revive their relationship. Now the only issue was telling her about Guy Wheeless's release from prison. As he prepared to drop the bombshell, Marylou cut him off.

"Henry, there's something else I need to tell you." She carefully tucked her shoulder-length blond hair behind her right ear. It was a gesture that Henry found endearing. "It's something I should have shared with you years ago . . . decades ago. The mess with the yellow ducks makes it impossible for me to hold this in any longer. My therapist agrees."

"Marylou, what in the world . . . "

"Please don't interrupt, this is already tough enough. Henry, I'm so, so sorry. I should have shared this with you forever ago. It's so hard. We've been together since lightning struck when we were teenagers; since then we've had no separate life experiences. Our lives are so completely intertwined, there's never a story about the time before we met."

"Yes, and that's one of the things that makes our marriage so special. Just the other day I was saying—"

Marylou cut off Henry with a gentle hand on his thigh. "Please let me get this out." Marylou sat up straighter in her chair. "The year before we met, I had my first date . . . it was to a prom. I was sixteen and so excited. I hadn't met my date, but agreed to go with him because my friends told me he was cute and had a great car."

"Do I know your date?"

"Please, please just let me finish. If you keep interrupting, I'm not sure

75

I can get through this. The evening started fine, but it was not only my first date; I also had my first drink. My date had a silver flask of sloe gin he passed around. I thought he was so cool, I felt all grown up. By the end of the night I was more than a bit tipsy."

Marylou stopped talking, took a deep breath, and stared at the hands in her lap. "After the prom, he drove me home and when he turned into our cul-de-sac, he parked away from our house under some trees, and we began kissing. It was my first date, first drink, and first kiss."

Henry's face began to grow numb.

"I liked it. But suddenly, he was on top of me yanking down my panties. I begged him to stop and tried to push him off . . . but then I just froze, body and mind. It was like my whole being just locked down . . . I felt I wasn't part of what was happening. Henry, he raped me. When it was over, he laughed in my face and said I loved it."

The ripple of numbness spread down Henry's body, triggering a sensation of helplessness. He tried to get up but couldn't. He wanted to wrap his arms around Marylou but was frozen in his chair.

"I told my sister Susan the next morning what happened. Back then there was no language to describe date rape. We sat in her room crying— we were both embarrassed and confused. She told me to pretend nothing happened and that before long I'd forget all of it. I love my sister, but after all these years there's been a cone of silence about what happened that night. That's maybe the saddest part of all.

"I should have told you long ago . . . I could just never find the right time. I wasn't a virgin that night at your parents' farm. But, emotionally I truly felt I was."

"Marylou, it's totally irrelevant . . . "

"Let me finish," Marylou said, wiping tears from both eyes. "My therapist told me that for a time I might have convinced myself that it really didn't happen. But after he poisoned the yellow ducks, it's like he raped me all over again. That hateful man is back in my life, our life. I never thought I could say this about anybody . . . I want him dead! My only small comfort is he's in prison . . . it's like . . . it's like some kind of deferred punishment for what he did to me."

Marylou's lethal desire shocked Henry. He finally moved to her side and they embraced silently—saying the rapist's name out loud would have cloaked him in undeserved affirmation. Henry felt as helpless as a punched-out boxer. With a tear running down his cheek, the opportunity to finesse his news was long gone.

"Marylou," Henry blurted out. "He's out . . . out on bail two days ago. There's going to be a new trial."

14

When Marvin followed Uncle Charlie into the ranch house, he understood Constance's comment about her father overdoing the stone. The house's floors and walls were constructed of the same rattlesnake chopped stone as the exterior. Narrow floor-to-ceiling lead-glass windows, skylights, and vibrant Mexican throw rugs brightened the home's interior. With one arm already locked with Gabriella's arm, Constance took Marvin's arm and pulled the trio toward the kitchen.

Uncle Charlie turned in the opposite direction and called out over his shoulder, "The truck will be out front in five."

The kitchen was no show kitchen. Years of dedicated cooking had permanently splattered the burners and splashboard. Gabriella and Constance sampled with a wooden spoon the pozole simmering in a large iron pot on the stove. Marvin guessed most everything concocted in Gabriella's kitchen at some point passed through that iron pot.

After a few minutes, Constance turned to Marvin and said, "We best get a move on or Uncle Ants-in-His-Pants will leave us behind."

Stepping onto the porch, Marvin saw Uncle Charlie at the wheel of a decades-old Suburban with its motor running. The Texas sun had long ago baked off the vehicle's shine and the rear cargo door was missing.

Through the open space, Marvin saw a cage holding two large and excited golden retrievers.

Constance came out of the house with an enormous canvas bag slung over her shoulder, the sturdy type favored by mothers with infants. She yanked open the truck door, making a metal-on-metal screech. Making room for Marvin, she scooted across the front bench seat next to Uncle Charlie. The passenger door was still wide open when Uncle Charlie hit the gas. "Which way we headed?" Constance asked as Marvin pulled the door closed.

"With all this damn December heat, I figure the best chance is they'll be rooting and wallowing down in Green River. Billy's down that way checking traps, we'll touch base with him."

The ride across the ranch around cattle and over their patties was jarring. After twenty minutes, Constance turned to Marvin. "You're looking a bit pale. I got just what this doctor ordered." Reaching deep into her bag she pulled out a foot-long sausage wrapped in cellophane. She unwrapped it and cut a piece for Marvin with a yellow pocketknife.

"Dare I ask?" said Marvin.

"It's wild hog sausage à la Gabriella—it's her Italian recipe. She throws in a ton of fennel, coriander, anise, garlic, and of course a bottle or two of cheap Zin. Wild hog sausage has a ton of iron—just what you need."

Marvin reluctantly bit into the sausage and found it tasted more like beef than pork. He finished and asked for another piece, which Constance handed to him as Uncle Charlie pulled to a stop on a bluff overlooking Green River. Marvin laughed to himself about the name: the Green River was a nearly dry arroyo.

Uncle Charlie stepped out of the truck and onto the rusted running board to survey the terrain. Ducking back into the truck, he drove a few hundred yards upstream near some cottonwoods. He parked again, came around the back of the truck, and shouted at the excited dogs to pipe down; remarkably, they sat quickly and silently.

An enormous man waved and climbed up the gentle creek bank to greet the new arrivals. With his OshKosh overalls, tuft of hair, and narrow head, he looked like a chessboard bishop. Constance stepped forward and stuck out her hand, "What a pleasure to see you! Marvin, meet Billy. Billy knows more about feral pigs than anyone in these parts."

After a round of handshakes, Uncle Charlie said, "These two are hankering to chase down a hog. Can you point them in the right direction?"

"With this heat, them critters are lookin' for some mud to roll 'round in. If you jump off here and head upstream, you might jus' find what you're lookin' for," said Billy. "I'll be workin' downriver with our traps. Give me a call if you need some help."

Constance reached into her canvas bag, this time pulling out two eighteen-inch, bone-handled bowie knives. As Marvin attached the knife's sheath to his belt and Uncle Charlie unloaded the dogs, the hunt's methodology became clear. He felt a ping of anxiety.

Uncle Charlie fitted the retrievers—Dirk and Evie—with protective harnesses around their chests. Handing Dirk's leash to Marvin, he said, "The vests protect the dogs from the hogs' tusks. Getting gouged is no laughing matter. Careful, Marvin—hogs can smell fear."

Marvin gave Uncle Charlie a sarcastic grin. Laughing, Uncle Charlie said, "Just keeping it real." An excited Constance pulled her hair into a low ponytail and pushed on a straw cowboy hat. Taking Evie's leash from Uncle Charlie, she shouted, "I'll lead with Evie. Okay, hit it!"

As Constance turned upstream in a near sprint, Marvin grasped that the hunt would not be a casual affair. He was grateful that, at Constance's suggestion, he had exchanged his cowboy boots for running shoes; he second-guessed his choice of Versace jeans. He began to sweat as Dirk pulled him straight across the dry arroyo bank. Looking over his shoulder, he was pretty sure Uncle Charlie and Billy were sharing a laugh at his expense. Despite growing up on a Kansas wheat farm, in this group, he was the urban cowboy.

Fifteen minutes later, Constance, running at a steady gait, was a hundred yards ahead and Marvin was breathing hard. Reminding himself that he had once been "Marvelous Marvin," the star of the Southerland University basketball team, his ego-driven adrenaline generated a second wind. Another mile later, Evie began to bark urgently, and Constance made a hard left turn into mesquite brush. As he followed her into the bramble, vines tore at Marvin's face and arms and he quickly became covered with thin red lines from the wild rose and blackberry vines. He wiped the blood off his arms and pulled his ball cap more firmly onto his head.

Ahead, Constance unchained Evie; following her lead, Marvin unleashed Dirk. With full-throated howls, the dogs dove into the prickly shrubs. As Constance ran at full speed circumventing the bramble, Marvin heard an unworldly squeal so high and desperate that it froze him. The cacophony of howling dogs and the hog's shrill screams of mortal fear steadily built in intensity. The sounds were primeval and overwhelming. Suddenly the sound changed—the intermittent squeals became an unending scream, like a short-circuited security alarm.

Snapped back into the moment when Constance shouted his name, Marvin circled the bramble, wanting to cover his ears. He spotted Constance standing behind the hog desperately fighting for its life as the dogs tore at its flesh. Constance grabbed the hog's rear legs while the dogs dove onto its head. She hoisted the kicking legs two feet off the ground. Struggling to hold on, she shouted for Marvin to grab the legs. He came behind her, and with sweat pouring into his eyes and stinging the scrapes on his face, he grabbed the hog's frantic legs as the dogs continued to rip the head.

As Marvin hung on for dear life, Constance unsheathed her knife and, with surgical precision, calmly plunged it through the hog's shoulder into its heart. The squealing abruptly stopped but the growls continued as the dogs gnawed triumphantly on their prey.

Marvin was exhausted and incredulous. Had this sensational woman actually done what he witnessed? Having spent a lifetime as the alpha male in any group, he had landed in alien territory. Had he been a willing participant? Had he enjoyed it? As the dogs continued to gnaw the carcass, Marvin felt drained.

"You alright?" asked Constance, holding her hat in one hand while wiping her brow with her shirtsleeve. "That was pretty darn intense. But you did good, real good. We'll let the dogs enjoy themselves for a bit, they earned it. Why don't we move under the trees?"

Marvin followed Constance to the base of an Osage orange tree. As they sat, she pulled a red bandana out of her pocket and gently dabbed Marvin's facial scratches. "I hope I didn't lead you down an unwelcomed road. I grew up with this stuff. You okay?"

"I'm fine, but I've got to say that was a rollercoaster—not sure when I'll jump back on 'er."

"And that's just fine. Tasting something new is what life's all about. Don't like it, spit it out. Fancy it and you've opened a new horizon. Being willing to try is the key."

Marvin wasn't sure he understood what Constance was talking about. There was a lot about her that left a shadow of a doubt. After a few minutes, Marvin caught his wind. He picked up one of the dense and dimpled hedge apples scattered under the Osage orange trees. Weighing it in his hand, he ran his finger over the wart-like surface. Drawing back his arm, he flung it as far as he could, shouting, "Hot damn, Constance, that was a pisser!"

Jumping to his feet, he took Constance by both hands and pulled her up to give her a long kiss. Helping her to her feet made him feel more secure about his status with the unique woman.

After dusting off the seat of her jeans, she put both hands on Marvin's cheeks, saying, "You've got a bit more to do. Make a decision: leave the carcass for the coyotes, vultures, and pigs . . . or carry it back to Billy. He'll dress it and give the meat to Gabriella to make her sausage. Your call."

Thinking that eating what one killed was the manly thing to do, Marvin chose sausage. "Great," said Constance. "Since it weighs over a hundred pounds, no way I can lift it. I'll show you the best way to carry it back."

After shooing away the dogs, Constance instructed Marvin on the best carrying method. Minutes later, Marvin had hold of the hog's rear legs again. But this time, he held the legs over his shoulders to steady the dead hog draped over his back like a backpack. The still-warm hog was a difficult carry, but the overwhelming smell of urine and feces was far more problematic. Constance led him through a shortcut back to the Green River. By the time they arrived, Marvin had sweated through not only his shirt but his jeans as well.

"Drop it here," said Constance. "I'll call Billy. He'll drive over and pick it up. Uncle Charlie will take us back to the house."

Marvin wondered why Billy didn't come pick up the pig where it was killed. *Is Constance testing me?*

Ten minutes later, Billy's truck appeared with a large cage on the back. In the cage were half a dozen squealing feral pigs. Billy opened the truck door and his huge body oozed out. "Well, lookie, lookie! On your first hunt you bagged you a nice one. Congratulations!" After handshakes all around, Billy gave Constance and Marvin cold bottles of water. Marvin could not remember anything ever tasting so good.

As they loaded the dead hog, Uncle Charlie's Suburban pulled up in a cloud of dust. Stepping out to load the dogs, Uncle Charlie looked the soaking-wet Marvin up and down. "Welcome to East Texas, Marvin. You done good."

15

After Gabriella's pozole lunch, Marvin retreated upstairs to rest for a few minutes. His head reverberated with the counterpoint of the day's sounds—from Constance's soothing patient consultations on the drive down Route 20 to the hunt's dissonant clamor of barks and squeals. His "rest" turned into a two-hour nap.

Marvin's infatuation with Constance was growing. Instead of resting after lunch, she quickly showered and, fresh as a daisy, retreated to her study in the room next door to their bedroom. It was becoming abundantly obvious—Marvin was falling head over heels for a woman he barely knew. Given his marriage record, he could ill afford another failed campaign. He vowed to understand far more about Constance before drifting past the point of no return.

His thoughts turned to Henry and his wife, Marylou. They were in a tough stretch, but really, how hard could it be? They shared everything in life, in all ways they were a dyad. They traveled to the same places and knew all the same folks. His history with Constance was diametrically different. Was he falling in love with a total stranger?

Constance had asked Marvin to be downstairs by five-thirty for drinks and an early dinner to accommodate Uncle Charlie's weekly poker game at the next-door ranch's bunkhouse. She gratuitously added that Uncle Charlie had a reputation as a poker cheat.

Marvin dressed in his only clean clothes—jeans and a dark blue silk shirt covered with tiny white sharks swimming at divergent angles. He wished he had packed something more country.

Leaving the bedroom, he wandered into the house's main room where he heard George Strait's "Amarillo by Morning" playing softly. Uncle Charlie was sitting on a brown leather couch wearing a khaki outfit—shirt, pants, and belt. He resembled a pudgy General Douglas MacArthur.

"Evening," Uncle Charlie called out, tipping his glass at Marvin. "Join me for a pick-me-up? Constance told me you're a Pabst Blue Ribbon man. I loaded in some for you."

Uncle Charlie was quickly and agilely out of his chair and to the bar. Moving further into the room, Marvin spotted two photographs in identical bright-silver frames on the fireplace mantel. One was Constance's smiling college graduation photo. Next to it was a photo of a boy in a full baseball uniform, posing with a fist firmly thrust into a fielder's glove.

Charlie joined Marvin in front of the fireplace with a frosted beer mug etched with the "CW" insignia. Handing the mug to Marvin, he said, "Don't cotton to a lot of rules around here, but there is one. I serve the first drink, and then you're on your own. Rest assured, no one's counting."

"My kind of place. I love the graduation picture of Constance. Who's the boy in the baseball getup?"

Charlie shot a querulous eye at the mantel. "That's no boy; that's Constance age ten. She had one hell of an arm. My brother desperately wanted a son; he did everything possible to mold Constance into one. That effort had some unfortunate long-term consequences."

"This is one beautiful spread you got here," Marvin said, seeking to redirect the conversation away from Constance. It felt wrong to be talking about her behind her back. "How long y'all been out here?"

"I'll give you the *Reader's Digest* version." Uncle Charlie stopped to take a healthy pull of his drink. "Built it back in '93, me and my brother, David. We were partners in the oil and gas business. We were a good team—Constance's dad loved being out in the field and I had the big picture, if you know what I mean. I saw an opportunity out in the Permian Basin for some horizontal drilling. After a ton of hard work, good luck stung us. We took some chips off the table and built this place to kick back and escape Dallas's sorry-ass pretentiousness."

"Well, you certainly did a bang-up job," said Marvin. "You spend a lot of time down here?"

"After my brother passed, it took me a good chunk of time to wind down the business and take care of the mess of an estate he left behind." Uncle Charlie stood to refill his scotch and said over his shoulder, "I've got a lot going on back in Dallas, but I try to get down as often as I can to make sure the business end is running smoothly."

"Does Billy, the pig expert we met with down by Green River, work on the ranch?"

"Sure does. He lives on the property with his wife and son. Good country folks. He'll be at the poker game tonight. Interested in playing?"

"Hell yeah, but I better check in with Constance. Say, why did Billy have all those pigs in his truck?"

"That's our little give-back to the community," Uncle Charlie said with a self-satisfied smile. "I pay to have the pigs butchered and turned into sausage, and then Billy trucks the meat up to a food bank in south Dallas. No big deal, just a way to say thanks for all we have."

"Nice gesture," Marvin said. He poked his nose in the air making a sniffing sound. "Smells like Gabriella's cookin' up somethin' mighty tasty. Is she here full-time too?"

Uncle Charlie deflected Marvin's attempt at small talk. "So, you made a solid opening appearance today. There's been more than one abject failure."

"Folks didn't find a hog?"

"No, most always the dogs can hunt down one of those devils. Billy puts out feed for them when Constance is coming down for a hunt. Odds are pretty high that she and whatever friend she brings down will bag one."

"Sorry," said Marvin, taking a sip of his beer. "What do you mean by 'abject failure'?"

"It's about the reaction to Constance's choreographed kill routine. When she sticks her knife in the hog, more than a couple of her friends have blown cookies, and one passed out cold. But you, you did good. Has Constance told you about what she calls the 'incident'?"

"Matter of fact, she mentioned it as we were pulling into the house. But she didn't have time to tell me what went down."

Uncle Charlie gave Marvin a lopsided grin. "Let me give you some background. My brother, Constance's father, was one hell of a man. But he also had his fair share of peculiarities, especially when it came to raising Constance. One of the things he drilled into her was that any man who shies away from ranch activities, like a pig hunt, isn't worth his salt and certainly not worthy of her. Daughters tend to take their father's advice to heart. Constance took it far too literally. She takes the measure of men by her father's standard."

"Was that what was goin' on today?"

"Correct. In the past, some of Constance's friends have not been as successful as you. What Constance refers to as the 'incident' happened when one of her friends, as part of Constance's little test, was carrying a dead pig on his back. I assume you did the same dance step?"

"Afraid so."

"Well, while that poor sap had the stinking hog over his back, he went into cardiac arrest. He recovered but sued Constance, the ranch, and me. It was damn ugly."

"Sorry about that."

"We lived through it." Uncle Charlie took another deep drink and asked, "What's up with the tattoo on your forearm? What's it say?"

"The tattoo was a fumble," Marvin said, staring disapprovingly at the underside of his forearm and wishing he had worn long sleeves.

"Is it fair to assume a woman was involved?"

"What else?" Marvin said, pulling fingers through his hair. "It says what the ghost said to Scrooge: 'I wear the chains I made in life, I forged them link by link.'"

"That's a gloomy sentiment. Don't know any man who hasn't screwed up royally trying to curry favor with a woman. Getting a tattoo certainly isn't the worst I've heard."

Marvin was about to ask about the past hunts when Uncle Charlie fixed eyes with him and asked, "How well do you know my niece?"

"We've been seein' each other for two months and havin' a damn good time. She's good company and easy on the eyes."

Uncle Charlie pursed his lips and nodded slowly in agreement. "Has she told you about her sabbatical?"

Before Marvin could respond, Uncle Charlie said, "Well, speak of the devil," as Constance glided into the room.

Marvin's face lit up at the sight of her. She wore a mid-length skirt with wide yellow stripes as bright as the house's Mexican throw rugs. Her hair, with a single tortoise shell barrette over her left ear, bounced on her dark blue satin blouse. She looked simultaneously elegant and casual.

"Hope you boys are talking about me," she said, winking at Marvin. "Gabriella's cooking smells heavenly and yes, I'd love a glass of wine."

As Uncle Charlie worked to uncork a Californian sauvignon blanc, Constance put her arm around Marvin and said, "Gabriella's excited about tonight's meal. She's awful impressed by you—I think we're talking crush."

"Well, al . . . right, I guess," Marvin said giving Constance a squeeze. "Whatever it takes to tuck into a great meal. What's cookin'?"

"I know the *entrada* is a citrus queso salad, then a Mexican-style *picadillo* with chorizo, potatoes, and peppers, followed by a white chicken chili with *agris* and *queso fresco*. What else is anyone's guess. You two relax while I help Gabriella. Uncle Charlie, please pour a second glass for the chef."

As Constance left for the kitchen, the two men sat back down. Giving Marvin a quizzical look, Uncle Charlie asked, "You aren't from Texas, are you?"

■ ■ ■

Thirty minutes later, the four sat at a table covered by a bright red tablecloth. Gabriella smiled sweetly to compliments and was clearly a fan of her own cooking. Uncle Charlie dominated both the wine and the table conversation. He strutted articulately through topics far and wide: the health-care system's failure to focus on immunotherapy, a country of hopeless dependents, and the inscrutable habits of millennials. He then turned to pig hunting.

"You did good today, Marvin, for a rookie and not even a native Texan. Our neighbor next door has made a business of getting rid of these varmints."

"How's that?" asked Marvin.

"Our neighbor, Dustin, where I'm going to play poker tonight, bought a helicopter he christened his 'Porkchopper.' He takes up Japanese businessmen, arms each of them with an AK-47, and they plow the pigs down from the air. One time they killed nearly two hundred. And, best of all, he charges ten thousand a pop for the privilege. Great business model!"

Marvin was surprised that Constance, rarely at a loss for an insightful comment, had nothing to add to the dinner conversation. She seemed content to enjoy her meal and whisper in Spanish with Gabriella.

Continuing his domination of the conversation, Uncle Charlie described at length the ranch's diverse cattle herd. He then excused himself from the table and went to the kitchen. He returned with a bottle of ketchup. Sitting back down, he splashed ketchup on his picadillo and methodically rescrewed the bottle cap. The women were visibly peeved.

Apparently oblivious to his dinner mates, Uncle Charlie asked, "Now where were we?"

Without a word, Constance and Gabriella rose in unison, cleared the table, and retreated to the kitchen. Ten minutes later, the women returned with a deep-dish peach cobbler. While Gabriella cut the cobbler, Uncle Charlie turned to Constance.

"The cards are calling my name. We need a fifth player tonight. Can Marvin get a hall pass for a couple of hours?"

"If that's what Marvin wants to do, it's fine by me. Gabriella and I are in sore need of some girl talk." The two women smiled at each other.

Not confident of which way the wind blew, Marvin caught Constance's eye. She silently conveyed "yes."

"Sure," he said. "Let's play a few hands."

16

Henry sat at his desk reviewing his Amsterdam plans. He was convinced that getting out of Dallas was the key for Marylou and him to put their problems behind them. The opportunity to immerse themselves in the city was the perfect solution.

He clicked WhatsApp on his phone to see if he had received the housing information he requested from the University of Amsterdam. The video began with nothing more than a woman's voice. "Hello, Professor Lindon. I am Professor Bernadette Gordon. The university asked me to give you a brief tour of the apartment you will be staying in. I will be your neighbor, since we live in the apartment directly above yours."

Henry hit the pause button to consider Bernadette's voice. Her Dutch accent with slightly rolled "r's" and throaty "g's" was delightfully European but free of the sharpness of many European accents. He wondered who were the "we" he would be living below. He hit the play button again.

"I am standing in the main room of your apartment. As you can see, past the chair and couch is the kitchen. It is small but has everything you need. I believe you will find it quite nice. Turning back to the main room, you see two lovely French doors. When I open them you will see the bedroom. Let me show you."

The camera bounced as she opened the French doors and Henry got a brief glimpse of the apartment's parquet wood floors and Bernadette's black Converse shoes. When she opened the doors to a bedroom, Henry saw a room dominated by a ceiling of ornate nineteenth-century plaster molding. It was wonderfully un-American.

"Here is a window seat for you to view what is happening in the street below as well as the university directly across the street. It is very nice to get out of bed for such a short walk to the classroom. That is all for now. When you arrive, ring my apartment, I have keys for you. Ciao."

Henry played the video a second time and was disappointed it did not show the woman behind the enticing voice. He was curious about his future neighbor. He had read that Dutch directness could be off-putting. She had been polite but certainly not warm.

He opened his computer and Googled Bernadette Gordon. The photos revealed a woman as enticing as her voice. There were multiple photos of her standing at a lectern and one of her receiving some sort of award. She was not just a professor; she was the head of the university's prestigious art department. He noted that there were no other people included in the photographs and she did not wear a wedding ring. He wondered again about the "we" he would be living below.

Henry had conceived the Amsterdam semester as a chance for Marylou and him to leave their problems behind. However, maintaining a sympathetic veneer in the face of Marylou's dark moods was increasingly exhausting. Although feeling the sting of guilt for his thoughts, he could not help weighing the newly discovered benefit of a solo stay in Amsterdam.

17

With a red Solo cup of whiskey in hand, Charlie drove Marvin to the neighboring ranch in the beat-up Suburban. They drove a half a mile past the expansive main house to the barn-like bunkhouse. In preparation for the night's activity, a round wooden table draped with a green felt blanket had been set up in the middle of the bunkhouse. There were five chairs around the table with three men already sitting with cans of beer and various forms of tobacco in front of them.

As they entered the room, Marvin spotted the massive Billy still in his overalls. Billy stood and greeted Marvin with a warm handshake. "Good to see ya again. You got rode hard today, tonight will be a whole lot easier. It's a friendly game, we don't play for no beaucoup bucks."

It was instantly clear to Marvin that Charlie was the group's lead dog. He introduced Marvin to the ranch owner, saying, "Meet Dustin Wright. Dustin is the proud owner of the 'Porkchopper' I told you about. And this old dog over here is Jimmy Ray Johnson, who's the brains behind this spread."

As the men made their way to their chairs continuing their introductory conversation, Uncle Charlie grabbed the box of chips and began making five stacks. Charlie pushed a pile of chips to Marvin on his left and said, "We start with $500 of chips. Ten buck ante."

Marvin had less than fifty dollars in cash with him. Before he could say anything about his financial state, Charlie grabbed the deck of cards from the middle of the table and said, "Girls, we here to gab or play cards?"

"Kiss my ass, Charlie, deal the cards," Jimmy Ray said while lighting a cigarette.

"We'll start with Texas Hold 'em," Charlie said, passing the deck to Marvin.

Cutting the cards, Marvin said, "As we used to say in Kansas, trust your mother and cut the cards."

"A lot of truth there," Charlie said as he started dealing two hole cards to each player. "Marvin, as the 'little blind,' you need to throw in ten bucks."

Peeking at his three of clubs and seven of hearts, Marvin concluded he would need to quickly fold. After Charlie burned a card and then dealt three community cards face up, Marvin folded. The betting grew more vigorous through the turn card and the final river card. In the end, Charlie's two queens were enough to take the pot.

Pulling the chips toward him, Charlie said, "Your deal, Marvin. What's the game?"

"Let's go with seven-card stud," Marvin said as he dealt each player two cards face down and one up. As Marvin dealt three additional cards face-up to each player, the betting accelerated with each card. With two jacks and two fives, Marvin decided to stay in the game. When he dealt the final card down to each player, his card was a third five. He held a full house—fives over jacks. The betting continued at an accelerating pace and Marvin estimated there was at least two thousand dollars in the pot.

Dustin called the bet. With a grin, he laid down three tens. As he reached for the chips, Billy interrupted, "Just a minute son, read 'em and weep," spreading out three kings.

As Billy gleefully looked around the table, theatrically rubbing his hands together, Marvin interrupted, "Beginner's luck," and laid out his full house.

"Charlie," said Jimmy Ray. "Did you bring you a ringer?"

"Seriously, just beginner's luck," said Marvin. Knowing he now had more than enough money to cover his buy-in, he decided to play defensively for the rest of the evening.

The next deal was Jimmy Ray's. When he announced five-card stud, Charlie put up both hands, saying, "You've been hanging out with your great-aunt Annabel! Five-card stud? Why don't we play hearts!"

"Your deal will come. I called five-card stud."

Marvin spent the rest of the evening observing the players. All of them drank steadily through the games, but Charlie led the pack. Marvin reached two definite conclusions: Charlie only wanted to play Texas Hold 'em; and every time he dealt, he won.

■■■

Marvin slid under the covers just after midnight with an extra eight hundred dollars to show for the evening. Constance rolled over and gently kissed him. "I hope you had a decent time. Gabriella and I had a good old-fashioned chat. She gets lonely and needs company. You probably have lots of questions. We'll talk on the road tomorrow. We need to be in the car at sunrise. Sweet dreams."

Marvin's head spun. *Somethin's not feelin' quite right 'round here. Do Constance and Uncle Charlie have a problem? What's the deal with Uncle Charlie? Is he on a first-name basis with the bottom of the deck? What was with the ketchup at dinner? The pig hunt was for sure some kind of very weird test, but what kinda test? What's Constance's sabbatical all about?*

After hours of tossing and turning, Marvin drifted off to an edgy sleep.

18

At dawn Constance's white Range Rover Autobiography was headed back to Dallas. "So," Constance said, "what do you think about Uncle Charlie?"

"He's an interesting guy with a good line of bullshit, and he's real clever with the cards. Looks like the bottle might be an issue for him. He cracks 'er open early and corks it late."

"Not to worry, he's had plenty of practice," Constance said dismissively.

Watching the treeless pastures fly past the car window, Marvin asked, "Does he always dress in costume?"

"Yeah, a lot of the time. Having spent half his life as an actor, he accumulated quite a wardrobe. Be happy he didn't feel in a *King Lear* mood. What did he have to say?"

"He said he worked alongside your dad in the oil patch, your dad favored bein' out in the field, and, if I'm recallin' right, Uncle Charlie was the big-picture guy. They eventually got lucky and took some money off the table to build the CW ranch."

Staring straight down the road, Constance smiled sadly. "Dad was successful in the oil business for decades while Uncle Charlie failed at acting. I suppose he also told you he heroically wound down Dad's business and his estate?"

"Yup, he said it was a bit of a mess."

"Sad," said Constance, gently shaking her head. "I was the executor. Other than the money Dad left Gabriella to make sure she'd be comfortable for life, I was the sole heir. I took off a year from my practice to get everything in order. It wasn't all that hard, as Dad was a meticulous man. In reality, I used the time off to grieve. Uncle Charlie spends most of his time at the ranch because he doesn't have much of a place to call his own. Did he say anything about Gabriella?"

"No, don't recall him sayin' anything."

"Good," Constance replied over the screech of tires as she turned too aggressively off the ranch driveway onto the county road. "Gabriella raised me. My mother died of a brain aneurysm when I was six. With my dad being away so much of the time, I don't know what I would have done without Gabriella. Uncle Charlie have anything else to say?"

"Yeah, he told me about how he traps pigs with Billy and they contribute the meat to a Dallas food bank. Damn nice gesture."

"Would be if it were true . . . can you grab the wheel?" When Marvin reached over for the steering wheel, she pulled her hair back with both hands and fastened it into a high ponytail.

"Thanks," Constance said, retaking the wheel. "The truth is less magnanimous. They do make some sausage for the less fortunate. But, Billy carries most of the pigs to Van Zandt County and frees them on an unsuspecting rancher's land. Then, a few months later, after the critters have had a chance to reproduce and become a problem, Billy has the sheer chutzpah to stop by the rancher's house and offer to get rid of the hogs for a price."

"What a lying dog!"

"I'm not so sure," Constance responded with a grimace. "There's a difference between a liar and a delusional person, and that difference is belief. A delusional sincerely believes in what he says, whereas a liar knows he's not telling the truth. I'm pretty sure Uncle Charlie is clinically delusional. In the current nomenclature, he lives in a world of alternative facts."

"How do you deal with it?" asked Marvin.

"I don't. He's family and I choose to ignore most everything. I wish he'd leave Gabriella out of it."

"What do you mean?"

"Last night that stunt with the ketchup? Uncle Charlie will gladly tell anyone willing to listen that he's a big shot in some highfalutin gourmet society in Dallas. Pulling out the ketchup bottle was his way of letting Gabriella know her cooking was not up to his pompous standards."

Marvin ran back through his conversation with Uncle Charlie. At least the question about Constance's sabbatical had been answered. He wondered why Uncle Charlie even brought it up. It seemed like the right time to ask about the hunt.

"Constance, we're havin' a damn good time and I love what a straight shooter you are. But, I gotta ask—the pig hunt, was it just for fun or did ya have somethin' else in mind?"

She shot him a quick sideways glance. "I'm forty-three years old. Obviously, you're not the first man to visit the CW with me. Is that what's on your mind?"

"No, don't believe that's what I was gettin' at. Was the pig hunt some kinda test? I mean, was that some sorta manhood throw down?"

"No. But it was a test." Constance loosened and then retightened her grip on the steering wheel. "I had a different kind of childhood. My dad wanted a boy and did about everything he could to turn me into one. Pig hunting, fishing, riding, cow herding—we did all the guy stuff, and I loved it. Until college, I lived on the ranch and had a tutor. Don't remember owning a dress until I was twelve. I loved spending time with Dad and felt so lonely when he took off on some business trip with Uncle Charlie. In many ways the ranch defines me. So, I wanted to give you a taste to make sure you didn't gag on it. Some men find the ranch and what goes on there . . . disenchanting."

"Fair 'nough," Marvin said, playfully rolling his shoulders. "So, you and me, we're good?"

"Right as rain. I got to ask, did you enjoy the hunt?"

Taking a moment to gather his thoughts, Marvin said, "I'm not exactly singing yippie ky yay, but I gotta admit I'm lookin' forward to tellin' the boys about it. They're gonna love the story. And, I think my brother, Henry, will get a kick out of it too."

"Speaking of Henry, when do I get to meet that brother of yours? And his wife, I think you said her name is Marylou."

"Marylou's her name and you'll like her, everybody likes Marylou. I'll get us together for dinner or somethin' real quick. Recently she's had a hard run and she's seeing a therapist, in fact a female therapist."

"Humph," Constance responded neutrally. "I have an appointment with a patient in an hour and I need to check over my notes. She's a police-woman with anger-management issues. Mind taking the wheel again?"

Before Marvin could respond, Constance pulled off onto the access road to the clatter of wheels on gravel.

19

Detective Esmeralda Ortiz sat in the psychiatrist's waiting room scrutinizing the other patients. Clearly the balding thirty-something man with residual acne was a recidivist child sex offender. The woman sitting across from him with her disorganized knitting strewn over the floor was a life-long schizophrenic who had, at best, a passing familiarity with reality. Analyzing the rest of the waiting room population, Ortiz took a fair measure of self-satisfaction at being the only normal person in the room.

She was confident that her altercation with a fellow police officer had been nothing more than a brief and totally understandable aberration. Anyone who knew the little twit recognized who was at fault. If he had simply kept his thoughts about her bra size to himself, there would have been no problem. Nevertheless, the police department leadership had decided both combatants needed anger management therapy. As much as she disagreed with the decision, she enjoyed her sessions with the doctor, who was, all things considered, a good egg.

"Ms. Ortiz," the receptionist announced, "Dr. Whitcome will see you now."

Entering the office, Esmeralda walked directly to the comfortable beige accent chair across from Dr. Whitcome and fell into it. "Afternoon, Constance. Everything good? As always, you look great."

Ortiz wondered why such an attractive woman always wore her hair in a schoolmarm's bun.

"Thanks," responded Constance, sitting across from Esmeralda and opening her notebook. "Anything new with you since our last session?"

"Same old same old. That toad I call my boss has his head up his ass, I can't get laid, and my ex is hopelessly behind on his piddling alimony. Other than that, everything's peachy, just peachy."

"Let's focus on you," Constance said, making a note in her book. "What do you think you need to be happy?"

"Don't know," Esmeralda said, pushing her thin braid off her shoulder. "Is any woman really happy?"

"It's, of course, a matter of degree. I've asked you that question before. Have you given it any thought?"

"No, not really."

"Esmeralda, the more you resist thinking about something, the more the mind focuses on it. So . . . be honest, it's just the two of us here."

"You're right," Esmeralda admitted with a sigh. "I've thought about it. I'd really like to have a friend . . . a friend like you."

"That's nice of you to say, but remember, I can only be your doctor. But friends are enormously important. How was work this week?"

Did Constance just brush me off? Or is there some sort of professional stricture against shrinks befriending their patients? It's best, as Constance always says, to assume good intentions.

"I'm still investigating the murder of the Southerland University coed. There's a ton of heat to solve the case. If she hadn't been a beautiful white girl, I'm betting there wouldn't be such over-the-top interest."

"Do you believe there are racial overtones to the case?" asked Constance, staring nonjudgmentally into Esmeralda's eyes.

"Hell's bells, this is twenty-first-century America. Is there anything that doesn't have racial overtones?"

"Is it important to you that there is a racial aspect to the case?" Constance asked, recrossing her athletic legs.

"No . . . I suppose not. Either way, I have to get to the bottom of it. As I told you before, I know who the killer is—a monster named Guy Wheeless in Wichita. The victim was his niece, and they had a terrible relationship. The only thing new is he's been released from Leavenworth, where he was serving time for assaulting those women in Wichita, crimes he obviously did. Have I told you what he did to those poor women?"

"No, I don't think you did."

"Well, this cretin had a whole closet full of dog costumes made of human hair, every kind of dog imaginable. God only knows what they cost. He'd get the women to put on a dog costume and then proceed to beat the bejesus out of them. A real sweetheart. What's the definition of a psychopath?"

"It's easiest to think of a psychopath as a person incapable of guilt who consistently exhibits aggressive, disinhibited behavior, often of a serious criminal nature."

"Bingo," said Esmeralda. "Fits this creep to a T."

"I take it you believe he also committed the murder here in Dallas?"

"Without a doubt. Now I've got to drag myself back to Kansas supposedly to find what I missed the first time."

"Do you think the trip will be a good use of your time?"

"Absolutely not. There's no question who killed the girl."

Constance paused before asking her next question. "You've told me in the past that you love your job. Has your perspective changed?"

Esmeralda unconsciously touched the scar on her chin. "The job's all I got. I go home to nothing but an unaffectionate cat, suspicious neighbors, and of course my crazy-ass cousin . . . I mean my aunt."

"I'm sorry," said Constance, placing her pen against the side of her face. "Do you live with your cousin or your aunt?"

"Like my life, it's all screwed up. Mom had me when she was eighteen and then five years later her mother, well into her forties, had a surprise—my aunt Sherrie. She's like my younger cousin but really's my aunt. Like I said, it's all screwed up."

"I understand," said Constance. "Let's go back to why you're here, your job. How's that going?"

"Yeah, I like my job, but not the dipshits I work with. Sometimes I think they are intentionally dumbing down the police force."

"Esmeralda," Constance paused. "There's something personal we've never talked about."

"What's that?"

"The scar on your chin. Is it painful physically? Emotionally?"

Here we go! It always comes down to my scar. It's the same shape and in the precise place as Harrison Ford's famous scar that makes him look so good. Yet another example of gender inequality—a facial scar accentuates a man's looks but destroys a woman's.

"So we're going to get down to it today!"

"If you're uncomfortable, we don't have to talk about it," Constance said, turning a page in her notebook. "You seem keenly aware of it, and I think it may bother you."

"My ex-husband, the Catholic priest, gave it to me."

"I'm sorry," Constance said, slightly cocking her head. "You were married to a Catholic priest?"

"Like anything that favors men, there's exceptions to the celibacy vows for Catholic priests. When I married him, he was an Episcopal minister. We were an interesting couple, a minister and a cop. Somewhere along the liturgical line he decided the true church was Roman Catholic. You can imagine how hard up the Catholics are for priests that have any idea how to run a church. So, they make exceptions for ordained ministers willing to change teams—they let them bring along baggage—their wives."

"That's interesting," said Constance. "How did you feel about that transition?"

"I thought it would be great," Esmeralda said, opening both arms. "I was raised Catholic and excited about returning to the church. Given the way the church has consistently taken anti-female positions, I was incredibly naïve. I didn't think through the implications."

"What were the implications?"

"A Catholic priest's wife is like a turtle with tits." Esmeralda smiled conspiratorially as she leaned forward in her chair. "I was useless. No one knew what to make of me or how to treat me. I was invisible in the parish."

"Did the way you were treated have a role in your scar?"

"Yeah, I'll say." Esmeralda touched her scar with two fingertips. "My ex was always abusive, but early on it was emotional stuff. I've come to learn that abusive ministers are far too common. But when we got to his Catholic parish, it jumped to a whole new level. I was a humiliation to him and the rest of the parish. I mean . . . what the hell's the role for a Catholic priest's wife? I was an embarrassing intruder they ostracized in every way possible. We were relegated to separate worlds—and he began to drink . . . heavily." Esmeralda paused to gather her thoughts.

"In my ex's mouth, liquor was the devil's right hand. One night I came home after a double shift to find him rip-shit. I said I'd put on some coffee, and in response he threw his tumbler at me for a perfect strike. It took twenty-eight stitches to close."

"I'm so very sorry," said Constance. "Is it something you think about every day?"

"Hell yes! Would you want to look into a mirror and see this thing staring back at you?" Esmeralda pointed at her chin. "Constance, have you been married?"

"No, close a couple of times, but no."

"Do you want to marry?"

"Esmeralda, these sessions are not about me. This is a good point to close today's session." Constance put her pen in the middle of her notebook and closed it. "I'll see you same time next week."

Walking through the reception area, Esmeralda surveyed the new group of patients. She concluded that, although the faces had changed, the same old problems were manifest.

20

Edward O'Brian sat in melancholy contemplation. Toast at the Wheeless Strategic Fund, he needed to complete his move away from Guy Wheeless, who would undoubtedly become a dangerous enemy. The ring of his desk phone startled him. The new receptionist said, "Mr. Wheeless wants to speak with you."

Predictably, Al Starsky was also in the chairman's office. He wore his usual uniform of a black tee shirt, jeans, and a mala necklace, this one with yellow feathers on the end. O'Brian read his latest tee shirt slogan—"Closer to Enlightenment." Wheeless, dressed in a dark blue pinstriped suit and vibrant blue tie, sat at his desk on the phone. Although Wheeless's hair was back to its glowing form, prison had thinned his face giving him a foreboding look. Wheeless signaled with his hand for the two to take a seat at the imposing chrome and glass conference table.

Trying to gauge Starsky, O'Brian asked, "So, how long have you been practicing yoga?"

Giving O'Brian a blank stare, Starsky responded, "I don't. Why do you ask?"

"Every time I see you, you're wearing a mala and a yoga shirt."

"My sister manages a yoga studio in Florida and sends me the stuff she can't sell. After prison, I don't exactly have a closet full of clothes."

O'Brian's next question, about whether Starsky was enjoying his time in Wichita, was met with a stony stare.

After hanging up the phone, Wheeless moved to join them at the table. He began talking before he sat down. "Edward, Al and I have been thinking long and hard about the future of the Wheeless Strategic Fund. The fund had a remarkable run of success until my recent misfortune. In deciding how to reinvigorate the fund, Al has been indispensable."

Starsky gave O'Brian a little head waggle.

"The fund is named 'Wheeless,' and that alone inextricably ties the fund's fortunes to me. The key to resurrecting the fund is to reestablish my reputation first here in Wichita and then across the country."

"Guy," O'Brian interrupted, emphatically nodding his head, "that's some very sound thinking."

Ignoring O'Brian's comment, Wheeless continued. "What do my hometown people really think of me? Do they think I'm a secretive, rich hedge fund asshole? Do they believe I'm capable of committing those alleged assaults? As completely unfair as it is, my name, my reputation, and my fund need total rehabilitation. Al, walk Edward through the plan."

Wheeless leaned back in his chair and relaxed his shoulders. Starsky stood and walked to a flip chart next to the conference table. He picked up a marker, dramatically pulled off the cap, and began. "With Guy's release from prison, we're obviously winning big in the court of law; we now need to do the same in the court of public opinion.

"There are three pillars to the plan." He wrote the word "Heritage" on the page. "First, Guy is the scion of the man who singlehandedly built the biggest bank in the state of Kansas. As the son of that great man, Guy could have retired to a life of leisure. But no, he chose to build on that heritage by forging one of the most successful hedge funds in America, and with that success brought a new sense of pride to his hometown. We will hammer home the message of multigenerational contributions to the city of Wichita."

O'Brian was having a hard time hearing Starsky's hushed tone and debated asking him to speak up. He concluded silence was his best strategy.

"Second, we will wage a campaign I call 'Disrepute and Exile.'" With his mala swinging back and forth, he wrote the words on the chart. "The marginal women who perjured themselves at Guy's trial will be totally discredited. They deserve nothing less. Anything and everything in their lives will be uncovered and exposed—they will be disgraced. And, because their lies besmirched the Wheeless name, they will promptly leave Wichita for good."

O'Brian was confident the planned "nuts and sluts" campaign would be neither voluntary nor painless.

"The final front of our campaign is where you come in, Edward." Starsky wrote the words "Community Largess." "In an unprecedented demonstration of commitment to his hometown, Guy has set up a ten-million-dollar fund to make charitable contributions in Wichita over the next year. We have retained a public relations strategist who will ensure each contribution gets the publicity it deserves. Her name is Janet Lancing, and she knows how to get results. Half the fund is ear-marked for the Wichita Museum of Art. Guy, do you want to fill Edward in on what you have in mind?"

"It's pretty simple," Wheeless said, putting his elbows on the conference table. "I'll underwrite the museum's acquisition of the type of paintings they never dreamed possible. I'll make the selections to be placed in a new wing that will, of course, be named 'Wheeless.' This will be the most talked-about collection in the country. Edward, this is where you come in. I want you to locate and retain the most discerning art experts in the world to pull together acquisition targets. I want the initial target list two weeks from today."

"I'm honored to be any part of this historic effort," said O'Brian. "I'm already thinking how I can best balance my responsibilities here at the fund."

O'Brian was wary of the way Wheeless was looking at him. It was the look of an executioner who enjoyed his job. O'Brian wondered if Wheeless practiced the look in front of a mirror.

"Edward," Wheeless said sternly, "from this minute on, you have one job and only one job. Get me the list of acquisition targets. Spend whatever is necessary on consulting fees, but get the list and get it quick. Keep one thing top of mind—this is not about acquiring great art; this is about acquiring art that will garner the most publicity to bolster the Wheeless name. Understand the goal? This is all about publicity."

"Got it, Guy."

The meeting was over. O'Brian got up and thanked both men for including him in the campaign.

Before he could get out the door, Wheeless said, "By the way, Edward, a detective from Dallas named Esmeralda Ortiz called. She wants to talk with us about her investigation into my niece Nichole's murder. Didn't she already talk to you?"

"Yeah."

"Any idea what she wants?"

"None."

O'Brian hurried out the door.

■■■

Lightly scratching the side of his face, Wheeless said, "Al, sure hope you're right about including that patronizing prick in our plans. Look how badly he screwed up the fund when I was inside. I still think I ought to fire his skinny ass."

"Guy, Guy," Starsky said softly. "We've been through this. Having him here is the best way to keep a close eye on him. His phone is tapped and his computer hacked. We'll figure out exactly what he's done. Patience."

Wheeless, pushing himself up from the table, spat out, "Okay, but if this falls apart, it's on you! Now get out of here, I've got some real work to do."

"One more thing," Starsky said, remaining in his seat. "How do you propose to pay for all this? The Wheeless Strategic Fund is essentially broke."

"Leave that to me," Wheeless replied. "Like I said, I got real work to do—just execute the plan."

Walking down the hallway, Starsky concluded nothing had changed. Wheeless was the same bombastic charlatan he had been in prison. Wheeless might be able to fool himself into believing he was on the road to prosperity, but he wasn't fooling Starsky. Hitching his wagon to Wheeless's would ultimately be a train wreck. It was time to look for an alternative solution.

21

Friday night found Detective Esmeralda Ortiz and her aunt Sherrie dressing for another night at the Grapevine Bar. Ortiz ruefully looked around their drab apartment, realizing she had allowed another week to pass with zero progress on finding a new place to live.

"Sherrie, we're in a rut. We live in a dump, and the only thing we look forward to is spending every Friday night in a dive bar. There's got to be something more."

"Lighten up, Esmeralda. As soon as you walk into the Grapevine, your spirits will lift. Maybe we should do a tarot card reading before we head out?"

"Absolutely not."

The women arrived at the Grapevine Bar at just past nine o'clock. Sherrie read out loud the front door's inscription:

Check Your Attitude at the Door.

"Pretty sound message, don't you think, Esmeralda?"

"You're awful free with advice," Esmeralda said, pulling open the door. They waved to Jake, the enormous bartender who wore his long hair in a man bun. Without being asked, Jake started mixing their Greyhounds.

Nodding hellos to the regulars, they squeezed through the crowded bar and past one of the last cigarette machines in Dallas. They settled in at a cheap metal table next to the worn pool table, a perfect spot to see and be seen.

"Esmeralda, your hair looks great down. You should wear it that way more often."

"Thanks. Do I have on too much makeup?"

"Not at all, you look SOOO cute!"

"Probably not. Looks like there's some opportunity tonight."

"Agreed. Just look uninterested."

Halfway through their first Greyhounds, a fit forty-something in a size too-small tee shirt appeared at their table. Esmeralda instantaneously tagged him as a cop.

"Evening, ladies. I'm Richie here with my buddy Billy Ray, the handsome one at the end of the bar. Well . . . we were wondering if y'all might let us buy you a drink?"

"That's sweet," said Esmeralda. "But we're waiting for our dates."

Watching Richie skulk back to the bar, Sherrie said, "I know rule number one is never say yes to the first ones that ask, but Lord have mercy, those two had possibilities."

"For sure Richie's a cop, I can smell 'em a mile away. So, saying yes would also violate rule number two—no cops. Besides, the night's young."

Before long two tall men with micro-length facial hair made their way to the table. The one holding two Greyhounds said, in an Eastern European accent, "Looks like you ladies might be thirsty. I am Jordan and this is my cousin Davit."

Davit, the far better looking of the two, made a theatrical bow from his trim waist.

"Grab a chair, guys," said Esmeralda.

After obligatory introductions, Sherrie said, "I just love your accents. I could listen to you talk all night. Where did you say y'all are from?"

"We are Georgians," answered Davit, flashing a radiant smile. "Georgia is the most beautiful part of the old Soviet Union. We are here to open an import office in Dallas. It is a beautiful city, maybe we stay."

"What are you planning to import?" asked Sherrie.

"Hazelnuts. Georgia has a surplus and Americans love them in chocolate," Jordan answered. Then he asked, "Esmeralda, what do you do?"

"In the banking business," she lied.

"And you, Sherrie?"

"I'm a psychotherapist. I help people get in touch with their emotions and values."

"How do you do that?" asked Davit.

"With tarot cards. They are wonderfully insightful. The cards speak to me."

"Sherrie serves a unique class of clients," said Esmeralda, giving Sherrie a raised eyebrow.

After another round of drinks and an easy-going conversation about the contrasts between life in Georgia and Dallas, Davit leaned over and whispered in Sherrie's ear. A smile spread across her face and she nodded.

"Davit thinks it would be fun to head over to Double Wide in Deep Ellum. You wanna come, Esmeralda?"

Having decided early on that Jordan did not measure up, Esmeralda replied, "Thanks, but I need to go into the office early, so I'll pass."

"You two go ahead," said Jordan. "I'll stay here with Esmeralda."

While Ortiz fended off Jordan's string of propositions, both awkward and unwelcome, Sherrie sped in Davit's BMW 325i toward the Double Wide Bar.

"Davit, why do you have Kansas license plates?"

"Ah . . . it is to save on sales tax. Here in Texas sales tax on cars is too high. I hope you like the car."

"I do. I also like your aura, it's so bright!"

"What is aura?"

"It's the energy field your body emits, it's your very essence. We all have gifts. My gift is I can see people's auras. Your aura is remarkable."

"Thanks. I wish I could see yours, I bet it is warm and soft. You said earlier you read tarot cards. Can you do a reading for me and my aura?"

"I'd love to. How about right now? Want to turn around and head back to my apartment?"

Without a word, Davit violently yanked the steering wheel, throwing the car into a power slide that ended in an illegal U-turn.

■■■

Two hours later, Esmeralda turned the key in her front door only to find it, once again, chained from the inside. Annoyed that Sherrie must have brought Davit home with her, she pulled out her phone to call her aunt. Before she could dial, she heard an accented female voice from the other side of the door. "Who's there?"

"It's Princess Meghan. Open the damn door."

A teary-eyed Mrs. Rodriquez opened the door. Looking past Mrs. Rodriquez, Esmeralda saw Sherrie on the couch holding an ice pack to her left cheek.

"What the hell's going on?" Esmeralda bellowed.

"It is so terrible, so terrible," Mrs. Rodriquez replied, dapping a handkerchief to her eye.

"I had an awful night," wailed Sherrie.

"Will someone please tell me what happened?"

"At the Grapevine there were happy auras blinking all around the room," Sherrie sniffled. "But Davit's was by far the brightest. I thought . . . he was a kind and gentle man." Tears choked Sherrie while she pressed the ice pack against her cheek.

"It is terrible, so terrible," Mrs. Rodriquez again chanted like a Greek chorus.

With a piercing stink eye, Esmeralda silenced Mrs. Rodriquez. Turning to Sherrie she said, "Take a deep breath and tell me what happened."

After a few minutes of breath-catching sniffles, Sherrie said in a halting voice, "It happened . . . when we got back here . . . "

"Sherrie, please, what happened?"

"We decided to come here to read the cards for him. It was going so well . . . he appreciated all my insights . . . but then I turned over the Lovers card. He jumped up and said, 'The minute I saw you I knew you'd be the one. Let's hit the sheets.' His accent disappeared and his aura . . . his aura went dark like someone had switched off a table lamp. I've never seen anything like it."

Sherrie covered her face with her right hand. Esmeralda waited silently. After a few moments, she recovered and began again.

"When I said no, he told me I'd be missing a once-in-a-lifetime experience. I said . . . I said I needed more time to get to know him. Then he . . . he stood up, called me a bitch tease, and slapped me, hard. I screamed and—"

"Yes, I heard Sherrie's scream through the wall," interrupted Mrs. Rodriquez. "So I banged on my side and ran out of my apartment to help. It is so terrible, so terrible."

"Give it a rest, Mrs. Rodriquez! Sherrie, is that all?"

"No, it got much worse. He yanked me by the hair and gave me a message for you."

"For me?"

"Yes, a message for you from Guy Wheeler."

"Do you mean Guy Wheeless?"

"Could be. I was so scared I couldn't think."

"Sherrie, pull yourself together. What was the message?"

"He said to tell you to stay the hell out of Wichita or . . . "

"Or what?"

"He said I'd never touch a tarot card deck again because . . ."

"Because what?"

"He said . . . he said he'd come back and cut off my fingers. Christ, Esmeralda, what have you got us into?"

As Esmeralda searched for the right words, she spotted a black camera bag on the floor. She pointed at it, saying, "Is that your bag, Mrs. Rodriquez?"

Sherrie lowered the ice pack from her cheek to look at where Esmeralda was pointing. "No, Davit brought that in with him."

Esmeralda picked up the bag, opened it, and pulled out a Sony HXR movie camera. "Sherrie, that son of a bitch was up to no good! He was planning to take a compromising video of you!"

With both hands on her head, Mrs. Rodriquez again said, "So terrible, so terrible."

22

Henry and Marylou sat across from each other at Henry's desk. After a few uncomfortable moments, Henry asked, "You sure you're up for this call?"

"Yes, let's do it."

Henry put his iPhone on the desk, dialed Dan Moore, and pressed the speaker button. Before it rang, Marylou said, "Hold it a minute, Henry."

Pressing the off button, Henry said, "Yes, is there something else?"

"I already spoke to Dan about Wheeless. We talked last week."

"I thought we agreed to talk with Dan together?"

"I know, I know. I was just getting impatient. Go ahead and call him. Let's get this over with."

Giving his wife a wary look, Henry redialed the call. "Hey, Dan. Sorry we couldn't make the trip to Wichita, but with me heading to Amsterdam in two days and Marylou on her way to San Francisco to visit Laney and our granddaughter, schedules got crazy."

"Hello again," Marylou added. "We promise to make the trip real soon."

Henry was annoyed that his wife said hello "again."

"No problem, but I'm holding you to your promise," said Dan.

"Thanks Dan. So, we might as well dive in. What's going on with Wheeless?"

"We've got a pretty good read on what he's up to. He returned to

Wichita with his bunkmate from Leavenworth. His name is Art Starsky, and he's a piece of work. He's carved out a unique reputation for a lifetime of gratuitous violence. For instance, we were told that in his first week in Leavenworth he sat down for breakfast and drove a fork deep into the knee of the inmate sitting next to him. He had never before seen, much less spoken to, the dude."

"Lovely. What's his connection to Wheeless?"

"Apparently Starsky provided an umbrella of protection for Wheeless inside in exchange for a job on the outside."

"A match made in heaven," said Henry. "What are these two charmers up to?"

"Word on the street is Wheeless is pretty much broke. He had to sell his Bentley Mulsanne and fired that creepy chauffeur of his. Without the chauffeur for protection, he's taken to carrying a .38."

"That has to be a violation of his bond agreement. Should we report him?"

"Since carrying an unlicensed gun would land him back in Leavenworth, that's a card we may want to play at some point. But first, here's what he's up to. My source tells me he's got a grand plan aimed at resurrecting his image. He just announced an eight-figure charitable fund targeted at building an eye-popping collection at the Wichita Art Museum."

Looking with exasperated eyebrows at Marylou, Henry asked, "So he's not lying low in Wichita?"

"Hell no. He's got a bare-knuckle publicist named Janet Lancing working it 24/7. She's got a columnist at the *Wichita Eagle* in her pocket pumping out weekly stories on Wheeless's civic largess. Last week she wrote about Wheeless's unselfish efforts to bring an NHL hockey team to Wichita. Talk about fake news—gag me with a freaking spoon!"

"Americans always embrace reformed sinners," said Marylou. "Is that his pitch, you know, he sinned, he's sorry, and wants a second chance?"

"Not him," responded Dan. "This piece of garbage is incapable of acknowledging a mistake no matter how big or small. His position is he did nothing wrong, the women perjured themselves, and he's the inno-cent victim."

"We've all known Wheeless since high school. Does that surprise you?" asked Henry. "Anything else?"

"He plans to make the women who testified at trial disappear. By the time the retrial is on the docket, there'll be no witnesses and the only evi-dence will be the affidavits withdrawing the original testimony. Bottom line, he thinks he'll walk scot-free."

"Will he?" asked Henry.

"Not if I can help it. Our investigators are busy rounding up victims who didn't testify at the first trial. We have some promising leads. But, I've had it with this lowlife—he deserves his final judgment day, like right now."

Henry was alarmed by his friend's choice of words and tone. He looked across his desk at Marylou; his wife's eyes were glacial. She inched forward on her chair closer to the desk. Avoiding eye contact with Henry, she spoke directly into the iPhone.

"I agree. He's an unreconstructed predator who never pays the price. As long as he's alive, he'll continue to destroy women's lives over and over. He needs to be eliminated."

Henry wondered if he had heard his wife correctly. On the night she described the rape, she said she wanted Wheeless dead. He had optimis-tically dismissed it as emotional hyperbole. His hand went to his cowlick.

After a moment of silence, Dan said, "Henry, as I'm sure Marylou told you, we talked this over last week and I've given it a fair amount of thought. There's a man I know real well, who can handle it using a combi-nation of calcium gluconate and potassium chloride. It'll look like a heart attack. The Wichita medical examiner's chromatographic equipment can't possibly pick it up."

"Whoa, time out!" Henry shouted, jumping out of his chair while making the time-out signal with his hands. "I thought you were talking metaphorically. I can't believe you two already discussed this! We're all upset here, but what the hell, this is crazy talk."

"Why crazy?" asked Marylou in a controlled tone. "Wheeless is an animal and our vaunted criminal justice system has failed. It can't hold him for all those assaults in Wichita and he still hasn't been charged with killing his niece in Dallas. He's on a lifetime crime spree against women, which will continue until he's stopped. If not us, who?"

"Have a better idea, Henry?" asked Dan.

Henry fell back into his chair. "Any idea is better than this insanity."

"Okay," said Dan. "Whatcha got?"

"Hell, I don't know . . . give me a break. Let's all think on it . . . I'm sure we'll come up with a better solution. This phone call alone is sufficient to get us indicted on multiple felony counts."

"The time for pussy-footing around is over. It's time to drop the hammer on this prick," Dan said emphatically.

"Dan, just give me some time to think. To say the least, I didn't expect the conversation to go like this. I'll call you."

Henry clicked off the phone and gave Marylou an open-armed "what the hell" gesture.

"It's been going on since the night Wheeless raped me," Marylou said, pushing both hands under her blond hair, her fingers lightly touching her temples. "Everywhere I go there is an ugly, unloved black cat looming beside me. For decades it's been at my bedside whining to be fed. It whines at my feet when we have dinner with friends or when I try to enjoy a movie. After Wheeless poisoned the yellow ducks, the cat has grown fatter and louder. I've talked it over with my psychiatrist—she says comforting things and I like her, but the cat is here and growing. The only way to get rid of it is to eliminate Wheeless. I can no longer live with that hateful cat curled up next to me."

"Why call Dan? Why not talk with me first?"

"One more thing, Henry," Marylou said with a composed look on her face. "My psychiatrist says I've got to be honest with you about my feelings. I never told you about the rape because I was afraid of shaking your famous equanimity. Well, sorry, I'm out of time. Wheeless has to die."

"Marylou, we can work this out."

Rising from her chair, Marylou said, "I just told you. You never understand what I try to tell you. I can't understand why you don't understand."

Henry knew arguing about his wife's garbled logic would be counterproductive. Glued to his chair, he watched Marylou rise and walk toward the study door. With her hand on the doorknob, she stopped and turned back to Henry.

"One more thing. I'm not sure about this whole Amsterdam thing you've cooked up. Maybe it's best I just come home after San Francisco."

Henry had learned long ago how difficult it is to stop the momentum of a bad idea. He needed to come up with a plan, quickly.

23

Charles Whitcome sat alone in the MM Enterprises reception area questioning whether he was doing the right thing. He and Marvin had struck up a nascent friendship at the ranch and over the poker table. But should he insert himself into Constance's personal business? The last time he had done so did not end well. Would it be better to just wait for the inevitable end of their relationship to tell Marvin about her history?

Marvin's offices looked more like a well-appointed men's club than a place of business. The walls were painted different vibrant pastel colors, and the reception area was dominated by a well-stocked wet bar and an enormous fish tank filled with phosphorescent tropical fish chasing each other. The offices appeared empty but for a woman who had introduced herself as Phyllis.

It was now ten o'clock and Whitcome had been waiting for over thirty minutes. Marvin had promised to be in the office no later than nine-thirty. Phyllis came back into the reception area. "Just spoke with Marvelous. He'll be here in five minutes. Can I get you anything? Coffee, water, something stronger?"

"A Bloody Mary would be perfect, thanks," Whitcome responded. He sat down and began to leaf through a copy of *Golf Digest*. He wondered why Phyllis had referred to Marvin as "Marvelous."

Ten minutes later, Marvin barreled into the room. "Charlie, top of the mornin' to ya. Sorry I'm a bit late gettin' here but I've got a real good excuse. Glad to see Phyllis got you a little somethin'. Come on back to the conference room."

The conference room, bereft of a conference table, was decorated with deep, well-worn leather sofas and photos of boys-only golf and fishing trips. Whitcome's suspicions were confirmed—it was not a serious place of business. He again questioned his decision to reach out to Marvin.

"Sorry I'm late gettin' in this mornin'," Marvin said cheerfully. "But Monday mornin's I play racquetball with my buddy John-O. He got lucky and forced a third set. He may stop by after he recovers from the beatin' I laid on 'im. Glad you stopped by, everythin' good?"

Whitcome considered declaring defeat and retreating. He liked Marvin but didn't owe him anything. But . . . he had come this far and leaving without discussing Constance felt wrong. He took a pull of his drink and decided to wade in slowly.

"What does MM Enterprises stand for?"

"That goes back to my playin' hoops at Southerland University. Back in the day, before gravity got the better of me, I had some serious ups. I got tagged with the name 'Marvelous Marvin' for the way I could hang in the air, and the name just stuck on me."

"From these digs it looks like MM Enterprises has done pretty good."

"Don't miss many meals."

"Is MM Enterprises still active in business?"

"Not really," said Marvin with a broad smile. "We were in the industrial tape biz forever but sold out a few years back. These days I watch my investments and do a little of this and a little of that—emphasis on a little. I'm big on keep'n in mind the difference between havin' somethin' to do and havin' to do somethin'."

"That's good, I'll file that one away. Marvin . . . you seem quite taken by Constance and there are some things I feel obliged to tell you about my niece."

"Well . . . okay, shoot," Marvin replied.

Whitcome put his hands between his legs and stared down at his shoes. He reached down to retie one of them. "How much has she told you about her . . . condition?"

"What condition?"

Whitcome locked eyes with Marvin. "When Constance was in college on the West Coast, she majored in drugs, all kinds of drugs. That unfortunate dalliance triggered the schizophrenia she has suffered from ever since."

"What?" Marvin said with a grunt. "I've seen exactly zero indication of schizophrenia. What are ya sayin'?"

Whitcome had anticipated Marvin's response and knew he needed to tread carefully. "The diagnosis was not a surprise. Her mother, bless her soul, committed suicide while Constance was in sixth grade at the Hockaday School. As long as she takes her olanzapine and stays away from recreational drugs, her symptoms are under control. If she doesn't toe the line, she's . . . well, she's not herself—she does irrational things. Did Constance tell you about her year off?"

"Eh . . . why don't you tell me?"

"Three years back, she went off the rails and her practice was in disarray. It got so bad that she regularly drove to south Dallas to buy handshake drugs. She was reported to the Texas Medical Board. I interceded with the board and she was suspended for inadequate patient care rather than having her license yanked."

"Does Constance know you're here?"

"I didn't tell her."

"Charlie, you're my kinda guy and I know your intentions are righteous. But, I'm already late for an appointment with my tax advisor—he can't even spell good news. I gotta skedaddle."

Marvin rose from the couch and led Charlie to the door. As he was about to exit, Charlie said, "You did good at the poker table the other night. We have a game at the Adolphus Hotel every third Tuesday of the month at four o'clock sharp. Interested in playing?"

"Why the hell not? Let me throw one back at ya. Every Wednesday afternoon the boys get together here to lie to each other about all sorts of stuff. Sometimes there's eight, sometimes twenty. Phyllis makes the finest margaritas in Dallas. I'd love to have you join us."

Nodding appreciatively, Charles replied, "Alright, I'll see you back here on Wednesday."

■ ■ ■

Marvin retreated to his office and propped his sneakers up on the desk. His tax advisor could wait. He had to think. *Is Uncle Charlie on the level? Why did he say Constance's mom was a suicide? Hell, Constance told me her mom had died from an aneurysm. And, what was that about Hockaday School? Constance's no 'Hockadaisy,' she was homeschooled till college. One thing's for sure, there's no way Uncle Charlie will tell Constance about his comin'. I'll just deep-six this whole episode. But . . . Uncle Charlie seems like a stand-up guy. What if it's all true? Maybe I need to get Dan Moore's investigators to take a look at Uncle Charlie's pedigree. Yup, I'm gonna call ol' Dan right now.*

Marvin reached into his pocket for his phone and dialed Dan Moore's number in Wichita.

24

Detective Ortiz paced around Wichita's Dwight D. Eisenhower National Airport arrival room. Her designated local police liaison was Lieutenant Will Klepper. He had told her on the phone she would have no problem recognizing him—he'd be the big guy in a green wool coat.

Five minutes before the agreed-upon meeting time, Detective Klepper appeared at the other end of the waiting room. Ortiz watched him reach into his green coat pocket for a tin of Copenhagen and push a healthy dip under his lip. As he placed the tin back in his pocket, Ortiz made eye contact with him and smiled. At six-foot-four and twenty pounds overweight, he was a large, imposing man. Walking over to Ortiz, he stuck out his huge hand, saying, "Detective Ortiz, it's a pleasure to meet you. At your service."

"Thanks, Lieutenant. As we discussed over the phone, I'm here to do interviews at the Wheeless Strategic Fund offices. But first I'd like to make a quick stop at Ewing's Camera on East Douglas. I need to talk with them about this camera." She reached into her attaché case and removed the Sony HXR movie camera left in the apartment by her aunt's assailant.

"Are you a camera buff?"

"No, not at all. This is a personal matter—I need to find out who owns this camera."

"No problem, let's head that way."

"I'd love to compare notes with you about Guy Wheeless."

"That's easy," said Klepper, using his tongue to move his dip. "He's a total dirt ball."

"Agreed. Let me tell you what I'm investigating in Dallas."

Klepper drove silently while Ortiz methodically ran through the specifics of the murder of Wheeless's niece in Dallas. When she finished, Klepper said, "Sounds like you've got some solid leads. Their terrible relationship coupled with the fact the flight log places Wheeless in Dallas on the night of the murder is powerful stuff. Also, Wheeless's conviction in Wichita for assaults on women is great background music. But you seem to have a one-two punch working against you. The combination of Wheeless's DNA not being found at the scene while an unidentified DNA was there is troubling."

"You're right. That's what I'm trying to figure out. Can you tell me more about how Wheeless secured his release and a new trial?"

"Money talks. We're here. That's Ewing's Camera on the left."

At Ortiz's request, Klepper parked his black Ford Crown Victoria at the far end of the strip mall. Although the car was unmarked, it screamed "cop."

Walking into the sparsely shelved store, Ortiz decided to play civilian with her inquiry. She walked to the store's lone counter and placed the camera on the glass top. The man standing behind the counter did his best to ignore her. Finally, peering over his glasses, he said, "Lady, we don't fix Sony cameras. You'll need to send it back to Sony."

"It's not broken. Someone left it at my aunt's apartment and she wants to return it to him. The problem is, she can't remember his name."

The man behind the counter raised a disapproving eyebrow.

"Using the identification number on the back of the camera," Ortiz pushed on, "I was able learn from the Sony distribution company that the camera was sold in this store. I was hoping you could tell me who you sold it to."

"Lady, I'll get that for you in a month or two. Maybe."

"I was hoping I could get the name today."

"Look around you," he said with a flinty squint. "Lady, you have no idea how bad the camera business is. Notice that there are zero customers in here? The iPhone put the camera business on life support. I'm barely keeping afloat, and you want me to drop everything to chase down a name for you?"

"Would this help?" Ortiz said, sliding a fifty-dollar bill across the glass.

"Just might," he said, slipping the bill into his pocket. "Give me the camera, I'll check what's in the back."

Five minutes later, he returned with a piece of paper with a name handwritten on it.

"This is all I have from our warranty record. He never left an address."

Ortiz looked at the paper. The name was Edward O'Brian.

Back in the Crown Victoria, Klepper asked, "Got what you were looking for?"

"I did. The camera belonged to none other than Edward O'Brian."

"The guy that works for Wheeless?"

"One and the same." Ortiz stole an appraising glance at the large man sitting beside her and decided he just might be her type. She liked his straight-ahead attitude devoid of BS. Her firm rule against dating cops didn't apply. It wouldn't be a date, just coffee.

"I don't need to be at Wheeless's office for another hour. Why don't we grab a cup of java and I'll take you through the whole mess with the camera."

25

Starsky's blasé attitude was wearing on Edward O'Brian and his damn clothes were making matters worse. As always he was dressed in a black tee shirt and a mala necklace. The tee shirt read: "Fully Meditated."

O'Brian's research on prospective art purchases for Guy Wheeless's donation to the Wichita Art Museum had proven more difficult than anticipated. What's more, he had a cold and felt like crap. And now, Starsky wanted him to waste time with the detective from Dallas.

"Like I said, Al, I spoke with Detective Ortiz a year ago. I've got nothing new to say. Excuse me." O'Brian pulled a tissue from the box and blew his nose. "Besides, she's way out of her jurisdiction and has zero power to compel any sort of interview. This is a colossal waste of time."

"Might be," Starsky said in his whisper voice while fingering his mala necklace. "But voluntarily making ourselves available to the police is another piece in our PR battle to resuscitate the Wheeless name. I've already talked to her. Doing little things like this will pay off over time."

"What did she ask you about?"

"Mostly where I was the night Guy's niece was killed in Dallas. That was easy—I was doing time in Leavenworth."

"Anything else?"

"She wanted to see the flight log for the company jet you unfortunately chose to sell."

"We've already been over this. I had to sell the jet to pay taxes. What did you tell her about the log?"

"Never seen it, know diddly about it."

O'Brian watched Starsky's eyelids contract and his lips purse. He thought he was lying. "Okay, fine, I'll talk with her. I assume she's in the conference room. Just give me ten minutes."

As soon as O'Brian was sure Starsky had left the floor, he turned in the direction of the new receptionist's desk. As he walked down the hall, he started through the alphabet in his head in an attempt to remember the new girl's name. There it was in the M's—Mandy.

"Hey Mandy, you're doing a great job."

"Thank you, Mr. O'Brian. Can I help you?" she said, looking up from her chair.

"Maybe. Back before . . . well, you know, before Mr. Wheeless returned, I had to sell the company jet. But I was thinking that Kristen, your predecessor, stored the jet's passenger log in the credenza behind her . . . I mean . . . your desk. Do you know if it's back there?"

"What's with this flight log?" Mandy said shaking her head. "Detective Ortiz from Dallas asked about it earlier today. I got to tell ya, never seen the thing."

"That's fine, no problem. Nice chatting with you, Mandy."

O'Brian walked to his office for a fresh Kleenex box.

■ ■ ■

Ortiz sat at the Wheeless Strategic Fund conference table lost in a daydream. She envisioned herself sitting at a candlelit table dressed in her low-cut, red satin dress. Her amorous companion, Lieutenant Will Klepper, gently held her hands on the middle of the white tablecloth. As he mouthed the words "I love you," the sound of a phone ringing in the adjacent office jolted her back to reality.

Her apprehension was growing. The assault of her aunt Sherrie and Wheeless's warning to stay out of Wichita had shaken her more than she wanted to admit. But what could she do? Tell her boss about the threat? How would she explain being picked up in a dive bar by two strange men with fake foreign accents? That her aunt had left with one of them after knowing him for all of forty-five minutes? The shabbiness of the whole episode would only fuel her boss's growing contempt.

As she had discussed over coffee with Klepper, learning that the camera left in her apartment belonged to O'Brian helped solve at least one question: Wheeless must have ordered O'Brian to scare her from coming back to Wichita. The interview with O'Brian could clear up a few things.

Reviewing her iPad notes from her first interview with O'Brian, she confirmed her recollection about the flight log—O'Brian had not only informed her of its existence but also said the receptionist would make a copy of the relevant page for her. Her notes further confirmed that when she approached the receptionist, the copy had already been made. O'Brian clearly wanted her to have a copy of the page.

She silently rebuked herself for sloppy police work; she should have secured the original. Without it, the copy was undoubtedly inadmissible into evidence. In other words, useless. She had done extremely well on the evidence section of her criminal justice course. She scolded herself for making such a fundamental mistake.

So far her interviews had been futile. Wheeless had refused to see her because of the ongoing investigation of his niece's murder. Starsky was an elusive ex-con who knew nothing from nothing, much less the location of the flight log. Mandy, the new receptionist, at least made a search of her credenza but came up empty.

Ortiz reached into her aluminum briefcase for the copy of the log she had been given on her last visit. It set out a month's worth of trips including a flight to and from Dallas the night of Nichole's murder. There was only one passenger listed on the Dallas flight—Guy Wheeless. She shook her head at the slipshod police work. *Why the hell didn't I secure the original log? Was it because all the evidence pointed to Wheeless as the murderer? Did I jump to the conclusion that I had a slam-dunk case? Will that leap end my career? No, Wheeless is the murderer. Hell, he even sent those goons to scare me off . . .*

Ortiz was jarred out of her introspection by an aggressive knock on the conference room door.

"Good morning, Detective Ortiz, nice to see you again."

Ortiz stood to shake hands but O'Brian held up both hands. "I suggest you keep your distance; I have a whopper of a cold."

"Sorry about that. Thanks for agreeing to meet with me. This shouldn't take long."

O'Brian placed three thick file folders and a Kleenex box on the conference table, loudly blew his nose, and discarded the tissue in the wire wastepaper basket under the table.

"Mr. O'Brian, I'd like to start with a few questions about my last visit. You told me about the flight log the receptionist kept in her credenza. You offered to make me a copy of the dates relevant to the Dallas homicide I'm investigating, the murder of Mr. Wheeless's niece Nichole."

"Yes, I remember you asked me if there was a log, and we made a copy available to you."

O'Brian was moonwalking the facts. He, not Ortiz, first mentioned the log.

"Here's what I got from the receptionist on my last visit," Ortiz said, holding up the Xeroxed page in a protective plastic sheath. "I talked with Mr. Starsky and Mandy about the location of the original flight log this copy came from. Neither of them knows anything about it. I thought you might be able to help me out."

"Let's make sure we're talking about the same thing." O'Brian paused to again noisily blow his nose and throw the tissues in the wastepaper basket under the table. "The flight log reflects the plane's maintenance record and it stays with the jet. So the folks who bought the plane have it. The passenger manifest, a separate document, is a historic list of who was on various flights—that's what we retained. Is that what you're talking about, the passenger manifest?"

Ortiz wondered what game O'Brian was playing. Trying to differentiate a flight log from a passenger manifest was a smoke screen. He knew exactly what she was asking. Making matters worse, blowing his nose with that honking noise was driving her up the wall.

"Okay, so the page that was copied was from the passenger manifest, not the flight log. Everybody else calls it a flight log, so let's stick with that name. It shows Mr. Wheeless flew to and from Dallas the day of the murder."

"I don't know what you have," O'Brian said, touching the tissue to his nose. "The receptionist who helped you is no longer with us."

"Do you have any idea where the original passenger log might be?"

"If it's not in the credenza behind the receptionist's desk, I'm afraid I can't help you."

"Do you know if there is a digital record of the flight log?"

"There's none, we never got around to that. Look, detective, I feel like crap. If there's nothing else, I'd really like to crawl into bed."

"Yes, one more thing," Ortiz said, opening her attaché case. "I believe that this camera belongs to you."

O'Brian took the camera from Ortiz and turned it around in his hands. "This sure looks like mine. This is great . . . it was . . . stolen out of my house by burglars a year and a half ago. I've missed it, thanks."

He sure the hell wouldn't play that lame burglary fairy tale to a man!

"I'm sorry to hear that. How long have you lived in the burglarized house?"

"Going on five years."

"And what is that address?"

"Why do you need that?"

"All of police work is details."

"It's 3133 Arnold in Eastborough. Can I have my camera back?"

"Sorry, but I'll have to hold on to it for now. It's evidence in an ongoing investigation."

"What kind of investigation?"

"Excuse me? Obviously the burglary ring here in Wichita. Is there some other investigation you have in mind?"

"No . . . of course not. I understand," said O'Brian, handing back the camera. "If there's nothing else, I really do need to crawl into bed."

"Alright, hope you feel better."

O'Brian grabbed his tissue box and exited the conference room, leaving his file folders behind. Waiting a few minutes to ensure O'Brian would not return, Ortiz leafed through the documents. On top of each page in bold letters was the word "confidential." Some of the documents were spreadsheets; others, memoranda.

After running through her head the rules of evidence from her criminal justice class, Ortiz made a decision. She put on plastic gloves, picked up a piece of paper, and placed it in a plastic evidence bag. It was a long shot, but she no longer had the luxury of taking anything for granted.

26

The weekly conclave in Marvin's conference room was at full throttle. Charles Whitcome, making his first visit, comfortably joined eight of Marvin's friends sprawled out on the room's leather couches and armchairs. Well lubricated by Phyllis's famous margaritas, the discussion rotated from bass fishing, to oil prices, to the future of artificial intelligence. Lane Hamilton, an investment banker from Arkansas, tried to put the artificial intelligence debate in context.

"We're getting way ahead of our skis here. What I'm talking about is some sort of robotic device capable of machine learning to do housework and maybe play a few hands of gin. What you're talking about is a Terminator ready to kick your neighbor's ass."

"Okay, Lane," answered David Black, an orthopedic surgeon. "What does your mild-mannered, domesticated robot look like? Is it going to be canine? Teddy bear? Humanoid?"

"I haven't thought that all the way through," responded Lane. "Maybe it will look like R2-D2. But think about it, having it look human is downright creepy."

"I disagree," chimed in John Rigau, an old-line oilman. "If we're honest about where our society is headed, most folks would be perfectly happy to live alone with a humanoid companion programmed to meet our every need and not give us any lip."

"No lip is damn appealing," said Charles Whitcome with a laugh. "As I understand machine learning, these machines could have infinite learning capacity. So at some point their use of binary script will make them smarter than us. Being lippy may be the least of our problems—what if they decide to take over?"

"That's bleak," replied John. "But back to my point. Do we assume they'll be human form?"

"Of course," David declared. "Think about it—if these humanoid robots are perfected, it will be the next frontier of human sexuality."

"If that's where we're headed," said Lane, "it will be great news for you, David. You can finally get rid of that Japanese companion doll!"

Over the hoots and good-natured recriminations about an inflatable doll, Marvin heard a knock on the conference room door. Opening the door, he found Phyllis.

"Sorry to interrupt, Marvelous, but Marylou's on the phone. She says it's important."

Wondering what his sister-in-law might want, Marvin walked down the corridor to his office and picked up his phone. "Marylou, I was hopin' you'd call. How you feelin'?"

"Feeling better, trying to stay busy while Henry's in Amsterdam. Sorry to interrupt your Wednesday brain trust, but I wanted to make sure you've got everything you need."

"Well, I think so. I'm lookin' forward to the whole deal and especially the chance to finally introduce you to Constance. Let me ask you somethin'. This afternoon, me and the boys been talkin' about this artificial intelligence thing. What do you think about it?"

"You mean like asking Alexa to look up a recipe?"

"No, further down the highway. More like a full size, human-like Alexa that can hang out with you, kinda like a friend."

"Not sure where you guys are going with this, probably don't want to know. But, the thought of some impassive, anthropomorphic thing hanging around the house is . . . disturbing. I'll let you get back to your friends. See you in three days."

PART III

THE PLAN

27

With a bouquet of bright sunflowers under his arm, Henry stood in the pack of limousine drivers holding signs with the names of passengers arriving at Amsterdam's Schiphol Airport. He felt trepidation about Marylou's arrival. Would she import anxieties and gloom and darken his Amsterdam experiment?

Seeing her walk through the doors, his excitement surged. As fast as that emotion soared, it crashed. Right behind Marylou, clownishly waving his arm over his head—Marvin.

"Henry, that's sweet," Marylou said, wrapping her arms around his neck. "Sunflowers are so happy. I told you I had a big surprise for you!"

Marvin came from behind Marylou and gave Henry an unwanted bear hug, saying, "The look on your face when I walked through the door was priceless. Now don't start frettin'—I'm not bunkin' with you lovebirds. I got us a suite at the Pulitzer hotel and we'll only be here for five days."

"Is there a 'we'?" asked Henry.

"My friend Constance arrives tomorrow. She was supposed to be on our flight but got hung up with some problem at the hospital. Says it comes with the territory. I can't wait for the two of you to meet her. I'm tellin' ya, she's the one."

Henry and Marylou exchanged knowing glances. During the span of four marriages and endless girlfriends, Marvin had christened numerous women as "The One." Henry characterized Marvin's many relationships as his personal catch-and-release program.

"Let's grab a taxi and hightail it into the city," said Marvin.

"I've got a better idea," replied Henry. "I've learned how to take the metro, despite the Dutch making it about as difficult as possible. It's a whole lot quicker."

Cradling her sunflowers as they walked to the metro station, Marylou talked enthusiastically about her trip to San Francisco to visit their daughter, and the painting classes that would start in Amsterdam the next day. Henry was relieved that, at least for the moment, she seemed to be her old self.

■■■

After reaching the Central Station by metro, the trio piled into a taxi and dropped Marvin off at the Pulitzer on Prinsengracht before heading to Henry's apartment in the Plantage district. Henry pulled Marylou's modest-sized bag out of the taxi's trunk and placed it on the sidewalk next to a massive bike rack.

"Here we are," he said, unlocking the building's front door. "Check out the stairs."

"You weren't kidding," said Marylou. "I've seen ladders that aren't this steep."

After Marylou showered, Henry set out teacups and, in the Dutch fashion, put cookies on a plate. "How are your new friends upstairs?" Marylou asked, pointing to the ceiling.

"Terrific, you'll love Bernadette. I went to one of her lectures; she was fantastic. Her book *Perfect Strangers* was published recently and she's invited us to her book event tomorrow night."

"What fun. Shall we invite your brother and his new love interest?"

"Sure. Marvin told me she's a shrink. It's probably a good idea she'll be with him. Marvin footloose in Amsterdam is a scary prospect."

"You're right, some adult supervision is good," she said, reaching for a cookie. "And, Marvin did say she's 'The One.'"

They shared a smile at the inside joke.

"So, tell me more about your plans for painting school."

"I've enrolled in a studio called Atelier Molenpad. It's in an old school-house near the Leidseplein. I think I'll be able to walk from here. Their website says they always have two instructors and the classes are very hands-on. That's exactly what I need."

Henry got up and crossed the narrow room to sit on the couch next to Marylou.

"Since that call with Dan Moore about Wheeless, I've been on a roiling dance floor. But when I met Bernadette, something clicked. I realized there's a way to handle Wheeless. It'll be real tricky to pull off, but the potential payoff is huge. Here's what I have in mind . . . "

28

On Friday evening, Marylou and Henry left their apartment to meet Marvin at his hotel. Looking down the stairs, Henry said, "I'll go first. If you stumble, I'll break your fall."

"How gallant!" Marylou responded as the two tentatively crab-walked down the apartment's vertical staircase.

"We made it," said Marylou when they were safely on the sidewalk. "How far is it to Marvin's hotel? Can we walk it?"

"It's a clear evening," Henry said, checking the sky. "It's only a thirty minute walk past the Hermitage museum, across the Amstel and into the Jordaan neighborhood. You up for it?"

"I have no idea what you're talking about. Lead on," Marylou said, taking Henry's arm.

"Marvin said to meet him and 'The One' in the Pulitzer bar. I've been there a number of times when I was here on business. It's lovely."

The couple cautiously waded into the Amsterdam rush-hour scrum. The relentless stream of bicycles of every size and shape were driven by an eclectic group—businessmen in suits, mothers with multiple children aboard, and insouciant free spirits with rock-and-roll hair flowing behind them. The swarm of bicycles resembled a video game. In the Dutch tradition, no one wore a helmet. Henry wondered if the lack of helmets was a statement of Dutch derring-do or the manifestation of faith in the abilities of their fellow citizens.

Henry took Marylou's hand to cross an intersection with a confounding mingling of foot traffic, streetcars, automobiles, motorcycles, and the dominant bikes. The whirl of the trams and the bone-rattling sounds of ramshackle bikes added to the street's chaotic energy.

They arrived at Prinsengracht and stopped on a humpback canal bridge to admire the view. Waving his arm over the canal, Henry said, "I love the way the house lights shimmer on the canals. And just look at the neck gables on the townhouses—they look about ready to fall into the canal."

"It's beautiful," said Marylou. "It's fun to think how much of this view would have been the same three hundred years ago. In our first class at the art studio, our teacher Yara said to look carefully at the faces you see on Amsterdam streets."

"Why's that?"

"Because you see the same Dutch faces today as those in the seventeenth-century paintings."

Henry took a new interest in each passerby. A few hundred yards on, Henry pointed discreetly across the street and said, "How about the tall guy with the Vandyke beard?"

"Too easy," said Marylou. "Clearly one of the figures in Rembrandt's *The Night Watch*."

As the couple came around a corner, a man stepped tentatively out of a bar and onto the sidewalk. Marylou whispered to Henry, "Check out the tipsy Dutchman with the splotchy red face. Name the painter."

As the man passed, Henry ventured, "I don't know. Ah, how about Jan Steen?"

"Very good. I'll tell you who I had in mind—one of Frans Hals's famous red-cheeked drinkers."

Marylou's little game delighted Henry. A playful wit was core to her personality and one of the things that first attracted Henry. He hoped that the plan he had shared with her about Wheeless was working as an elixir.

Looking at his watch, he said, "We need to step lively. I told Marvin we'd meet him in the Pulitzer bar ten minutes ago."

■■■

Entering the Pulitzer, the couple moved quickly through the lobby, unwrapping scarves and unbuttoning coats as they went. They crossed through a glass tunnel cutting the courtyard in half. The tunnel connected the amalgamation of twenty-five converted seventeenth-century town-houses, warehouses, and a brewery that make up the Pulitzer hotel. They climbed up and down short staircases to the bar painted a green so dark it looked black.

Henry spotted Marvin. He had commandeered the bar's premier position—a tight corner with a street-level view. "The One" was talking animatedly with her back to the room.

As Henry and Marylou approached, Marvin stood. "I thought you forgot about us! Henry, Marylou, meet—"

Before Marvin could complete his introduction, the women excitedly shouted together:

"Marylou!"

"Constance!"

While the women laughingly embraced, Henry's brain hit overdrive.

Marvin's new friend is a Dallas psychiatrist; Marylou's Dallas psychiatrist is a woman. Is she Marylou's shrink? This is awkward!

Marvin interrupted Henry's musing. "Well, Henry, looks like you're the only one out in the cold. Meet Dr. Constance Whitcome."

After Henry and Constance shook hands and exchanged pleasantries, they sat down on the purple and green plush velvet seats under the portrait of a smiling seventeenth-century woman. The endless stream of bicycles flowing past the window completed the atmosphere's intoxication.

As the women discussed their plans for Amsterdam, Marvin ordered drinks. Henry was delighted to see Marylou so ebullient and didn't want to interrupt her conversation. When the drinks arrived, Marvin raised his glass, saying, "Here's to a damn big time in The Dam!"

Henry allowed himself to enjoy the moment before finally asking the question weighing on him.

"So, how do you two know each other?"

"We have a long and intimate relationship," Marylou responded and both women laughed.

"Couldn't have said it better myself," added Constance. "For years the two of us have parked side-by-side at a Pilates class Wednesdays at noon. But, Marylou, I haven't seen you for weeks—I've missed you!"

"I so miss our class," replied Marylou. "I've had a . . . business issue that's kept me from a number of things I'd rather be doing. Maybe we can find a class here in Amsterdam?"

Henry heard the Westerkerk Tower chime in the distance and checked his watch. "Sorry to interrupt," he said. "But we need to head over to the American Book Center on Spui for my friend Bernadette's presentation. We need to allow some extra time to get lost!"

Walking out of the bar, Henry was relieved his jump of logic about the women's relationship had proven wrong. His eye landed on a pillow propped up on a brown leather Chippendale chair. The embroidered eyes under the blue turban of Vermeer's *Girl with a Pearl Earring* stared up at him. Henry took it as a good omen.

Rebundled in their scarves and coats, the couples headed farther into the city center. With Google Maps guiding them through the narrow and twisting alleys, they found Spui. The American Book Center took up an entire block. In the long, well-lit window to the right of the entrance was a poster of a smiling Bernadette Gordon. A dozen copies of *Perfect Strangers* were lined up below the poster.

As the group entered the bookstore, Constance said, "Look at the number of books in here. There's not an inch of wasted space."

"The Dutch are masters at space utilization," commented Henry. "Looks like Bernadette's event's on the third floor."

The group climbed the spiral staircase that, for three floors, wrapped around a huge tree trunk. The staircase's curving walls were neatly lined with books from every conceivable genre. The third floor opened to a spacious room set with folding chairs, a projection screen, and a coffee kiosk. Bernadette was bent over a computer with a store employee trying to unravel a snag in the presentation technology. She looked stylish in her black sheath dress and a bright purple neckerchief knotted at the side of her slender neck. As always, she wore Converse sneakers, this time pristine black.

Leaving the technology problems to the store employee, Bernadette greeted audience members filling the space. The room hummed with conversations in Dutch and English. Out of the corner of his eye, Henry saw Bernadette heading his way.

"Henry, thank you for coming!" While he and Bernadette kissed in the Dutch fashion, Henry noticed Marvin giving him an amused look.

"Bernadette, let me introduce my wife, Marylou, my brother, Marvin, and our friend Constance. We're looking forward to your presentation."

"My pleasure," replied Bernadette. "I will start as soon as we get the technology working. Is it a universal truth that all presentations are preceded by a technical problem?"

As Bernadette walked away, Marylou whispered to Henry, "You didn't tell me our new neighbor is so attractive."

"Ah . . . yeah, I guess so. She's real smart."

Marylou gave Henry a knowing smile and slid into the row with Constance, followed by Marvin, leaving Henry on the aisle. Henry surveyed the room's eclectic gathering. Typical of Amsterdam, the attendees were people of varying ages, colors, and ethnicities in clamorous conversations. He recognized a group of students from Bernadette's class. Most of the attendees held paper coffee cups.

Bernadette went back to the projector and said something to the store employee, who, in frustrated response, threw up her hands. Bernadette patted her on the shoulder and headed to the modest wooden podium.

"Good evening, and thank you all for coming tonight. I love this book-store and the role it plays in our community. In this digital age, stores like this are essential to maintaining the role of books in our culture.

"Before someone asks, I will tell you why an art history professor dedicated to the techniques of Dutch masters decided to write about a notorious forger." She was interrupted by polite laughter.

"First, Han van Meegeren was an accomplished painter in his own right. At this point I intended to show you some of his paintings, but we have technical issues—so you will need to use your imagination."

Stepping out from behind the podium and closer to her audience, she stared at the floor, seeming to need a moment to recover from the loss of her multimedia presentation.

"As many of you already know, van Meegeren at the end of World War II transformed himself from despicable to national hero. He remains an enigma because he was secretive, manipulative, and a genius. Let me give you an example that illustrates all three traits.

"In his infamous Vermeer forgery, *The Supper at Emmaus*, once and now the pride of the Boijmans Museum in Rotterdam, he used a blue paint that had become a Vermeer signature—ultramarine. In Vermeer's time, ultramarine was compounded from lapis lazuli, a sulfate found only in Afghanistan. The mineral was and is extraordinarily precious. In the eigh-teenth century it was discovered that synthesizing clay, soda, and sulfur created a cheap and visually indistinguishable ultramarine blue."

Henry glanced down the row to ensure his group was paying atten-tion. Constance looked tired.

"In the painting *The Supper in Emmaus* forged by van Meegeren in 1936, he used ultramarine as an indicator of an original Vermeer. Without knowing more, one would conclude that he, of course, used the synthetic version. But, he did not. Somehow, in some way, he connived to find a supply of the paint made from lapis lazuli. To this day, no one knows how he procured the paint. But, it was this type of technical dedication to his craft, forgery, that drives my fascination with van Meegeren."

As Bernadette provided background of van Meegeren's dissolute years as a wealthy scoundrel in Amsterdam, Henry felt a nudge on his leg.

"Yo, Henry, Constance's doin' the funky chicken."

Henry leaned forward, looked past Marvin, and saw Constance struggling to keep her eyes open as her head, chicken-like, bobbed up and down. He couldn't help but smile—the transatlantic flight had gotten the better of her.

"I'm gonna slip by you and get her a cup of java," Marvin whispered before getting up and making his way through the tightly packed folding chairs.

"*Perfect Strangers* is historic fiction," Bernadette continued. "I tried to stay close to the facts of van Meegeren's documented history as an artist and a forger, but I had a wonderful time filling in my own version of his day-to-day life. I will read a few pages from *Perfect Strangers* to give you a flavor of the book. But first I need to give you a little background of the book's title.

"The title comes from a van Meegeren painting in his own name. The painting, *Perfect Strangers,* was sold, along with van Meegeren's other possessions, at an auction in 1950 to pay taxes owed by his estate. We know a man named Kok, from Utrecht, bought it. Immediately after the auction, the painting and Mr. Kok vanished. We have a detailed description of the painting from the auction catalogue but no photograph. In my book, I took a fair amount of literary liberty in describing the painting and its origins."

Bernadette opened her copy of *Perfect Strangers* and smiled at her audience. "The passage I will read is about the night van Meegeren unveiled his painting *Perfect Strangers* to a group of friends. I wrote this passage in van Meegeren's voice." Pulling her hair off her glasses with her index finger, she began to read.

> *Dinner with my wife, Jo, was dragging on and on. Knowing what awaited me, I grew restive. I had spent the day in the studio on Keizersgracht ensuring everything was in place for the night's*

celebration. The attendees had undoubtedly started to arrive, and in my head I could hear the discordant sounds of the jazz trio. I did not want to miss a minute of the festivities. As usual, Helda was taking her time clearing the table.

"Jo," I said, "thank you for a lovely dinner, but I really must get back to work. I have already spent too much time on that canvas."

"But Han," she said, "you ate so little. You need fuel for your work. Besides, I want to talk with you about an idea. My mother says that in Haarlem one hardly ever sees a Nazi. Here there seems to be a Nazi lurking on every corner. Helda told me that just yesterday one of those hideous green and gray military vehicles pulled up in front of our house and two of them demanded to know if any Jews lived here. Amsterdam is just too sad. Maybe this weekend your driver could take us to Haarlem. I could ask my mother . . ."

My wife's voice was blessedly drowned out by the scream of a Gestapo siren. So it went for yet another evening. I pretended to go to my studio to paint, and my wife, knowing better, acts as a co-conspirator in my deception. Our tacit agreement was the linchpin of our marriage. The pillars of a good marriage are a blind wife and a deaf husband.

"I will finish my work as quickly as possible but these things take time. You and Helda can enjoy a hand or two of cribbage."

I kissed my seated wife on the top of her head and gathered my coat, checking that the loose jewels still filled one pocket and my knife the other. The jewels were party gifts for the ladies and the knife for the increasingly dangerous streets of a hungry Amsterdam. Stepping outside, I pulled on my black beret, a look I have long favored. I felt good and looked better.

Striding briskly down Keizersgracht, my anticipation grew. Tonight I unveil my masterpiece, Perfect Strangers. *My forgeries have brought me material wealth; this painting will secure my artistic reputation for all time. The painting's majesty will ignite an evening of intense sensuality. The ladies are the finest and most expensive in all of Holland, and the gin straight from the Nazis' own cellar.*

I wonder how Jo could even think of leaving Amsterdam. The Nazis have been a boon for my business. With the Nazis' endless cash and the bourgeois Dutch intent on keeping Holland's masterpieces in Dutch hands, it has been the ideal marketplace for my special paintings. Everything I forge sells quickly, quietly, and expensively.

Putting my key in the door, I heard the excited sounds of the jazz trio. My butler bowed deeply and closed the door behind me. "How many guests have arrived?" I asked.

"Seven of the women are upstairs putting themselves together. Ten men are at the bar, including Mr. Beversluis."

Moving to the bar, I hoped that bag of hot air, Beversluis, would avoid ruining another evening by insisting on reciting one of his banal poems. I was relieved to see police commissioner Stijn DeVries standing at the bar. His presence ensured the party would be uninterrupted. Securing a glass of cold gin, I headed up the stairs to my private room for a bit of stimulation.

Standing in front of the mirror, I wiped the remnants of cocaine from my nostrils. I emptied the jewels in my coat pocket onto a silver tray and walked down the hall to the ladies' door. Cheap perfume permeated the room, and as always, the ladies were delighted to see me. My current favorite, Jasmijn, was particularly enthusiastic. After paying them in coveted US dollars, I allowed each to take a few jewels from the silver tray. As with any guest, they were enthusiastically grateful for my thoughtful gifts. I gently kissed each of them and invited them downstairs for my special surprise.

My stage was set. On the parquet dance floor next to the bar stood Perfect Strangers *on an easel draped with a white sheet.*

After securing another glass of gin, I was ready to unveil the painting that would secure the name Han van Meegeren in the pantheon of the twentieth century's greatest painters.

"Ladies and gentlemen, tonight I will share with you the painting I have been working on for three years. Although I have painted café scenes in the past, this one has a depth and message unlike anything you have ever seen. Jasmijn, if you will take the other corner of the sheet, we can reveal Perfect Strangers *to our guests."*

As we theatrically pulled the sheet up and over the painting, I saw wide smiles and heard multiple "oohhs" and "ahhs." Like an amoeba, my guests moved as one closer to my creation and then oozed back. Slowly, back and forth, back and forth. As I stepped to the bar to refresh my drink, the group spontaneously broke into enthusiastic applause. Jasmijn wrapped her arms around my neck and gave me a deep kiss of admiration.

Graciously accepting congratulations, I joined the group inspecting the painting. The two married couples sitting at adjacent tables in a French café were hypnotic. The couples were elegantly dressed for a night on the town. No one could miss the look of nervous recognition on the woman's face nor the man's eyes telegraphing the unmistakable message: "We share no past, act as perfect strangers." The man's eyes were exquisite. The whites were lit with anxiety-filled adrenaline. I perfected the creation of light by painting pointillé with a small, round-tipped brush. My hours studying Vermeer had served me well.

My genius was manifest. No other painter could have seized the instant that I captured for all time—the torrent of emotions shared by illicit lovers in their moment of profound disquietude.

Bernadette theatrically closed the book and gave a nod of appreciation to the gathering's applause. "Thank you. I am happy to answer any questions. But first a sip of coffee . . . there, now I am ready." She pointed to a portly man near the back of the room.

"Was it difficult to construct van Meegeren's dialogue? To find a voice for such a corrupt man?"

"Oh, what a good question! With his enormous talents and total lack of an ethical compass, von Meegeren was a complex personality. From my research I found one trait that was always on display. It was his bottomless self-confidence. When he speaks in the book, I tried to capture that trait."

Bernadette pointed to one of her students, saying, "Good evening, Christa."

"Good evening, professor. Do you think the *Perfect Strangers* painting is hidden somewhere in the Netherlands?"

"It is possible. But it could be in the United States, Germany, France, no one knows. As you can imagine, I hope someday it will resurface, I would love to see it! We have time for two more questions." Bernadette pointed to a middle-aged man in the back of the room.

"Professor, most novels are grounded on the author's life experiences. Can you tell us what percent of your book is fact and what part is fiction?"

"What part of a novel is fact and what part is fiction is impossible to answer. In my mind the answer to your question is this: none of what I wrote happened, but all of it is true!"

Bernadette's evasiveness amused her audience. Saying, "Last question," she pointed to an elderly Dutch woman in the front row.

"Your book is very nice to read, congratulations. It paints a lovely and sympathetic portrait of van Meegeren's long-suffering wife. Can you tell us what happened to her?"

"Certainly. Van Meegeren's second wife was the beautiful actress Johanna Oerlemans, who was known as Jo. Years before his forgeries were exposed, von Meegeren transferred half his wealth to Jo. He did it to dodge taxes and currency control issues rather than out of generosity, but nevertheless, Jo became quite wealthy in her own right. She lived a quiet life of great comfort until passing away here in Amsterdam in 1977 at the age of ninety-one. Thank you, all, for your time. I would love to sign books for those of you who are interested."

Marvin and Constance quickly excused themselves—Constance clearly needed sleep. Henry and Marylou joined the book-signing line. When they arrived at the front of the queue, Bernadette said, "Thanks so much for coming. I hope I did not put you to sleep."

Henry made eye contact with Marylou. He wondered if Bernadette had noticed Constance's head bob.

"Absolutely not," replied Marylou. "I'm halfway through Henry's copy of your book, but I need my own copy. I find Mr. van Meegeren to be mesmerizing. How long did it take you to write the book?"

Signing Marylou's book, she said, "From start to finish it took me four years, but it was a labor of love. I find the degenerate van Meegeren endlessly interesting."

"Bernadette," Henry said, "there's something Marylou and I would like to discuss with you. It's kind of . . . personal. Will you be in Amsterdam this weekend?"

"Yes, I look forward to it," Bernadette said, handing the signed copy of *Perfect Strangers* back to Marylou.

29

In Wichita, Edward O'Brian was preparing for his own art presentation. Wheeless's charge was clear: target art that will generate the most positive publicity for the Wheeless name. He was emphatic that publicity, not fine art, was the goal. O'Brian was chronically distracted from the task; he could not stop his brain from shadow boxing with Detective Ortiz. *Why is she sniffing around? What does she know? Where is the damn flight log? Did she accept my story about the camera? Why the hell doesn't she arrest Wheeless for the murder of his niece?*

Selecting art to meet Wheeless's goal had proven difficult. Some choices were prohibitively expensive while others, although fantastic works of art, lacked the requisite cachet. The task was complicated by the bickering and conflicting opinions among the half-dozen art experts he had retained. Internecine backbiting was the art world's sport of choice.

O'Brian's choices were hemmed in by Wheeless's prejudices. Artists like Frida Kahlo, Jackson Pollock, and Georgia O'Keeffe had been eliminated from consideration. Wheeless's distaste for artists with outspoken political views made them unacceptable. Others like Andy Warhol, David Hockney, and Jasper Johns were eliminated based on Wheeless's rejection of their sexual preferences. In the end, O'Brian

had decided to present Wheeless with five potential acquisitions covering a wide spectrum of time and styles.

When O'Brian entered the conference room, he found Starsky already
seated. He was dressed in his usual mala and black tee shirt uniform.
Today's slogan was "Ego Is No Amigo."

As O'Brian set up for his presentation, Wheeless entered the room,
trailed by an attractive woman with long scarlet hair of a color not known
in nature. Wheeless, rarely out of a suit, was casually dressed in a blue
blazer and slacks. The two sat at the far end of the fifteen-foot-long glass
conference table, as if to put distance between themselves and O'Brian.

"Before you get started, Edward," said Wheeless, "meet Janet Lancing.
Janet is directing all PR efforts for the Wheeless Strategic Fund."

Lancing gave O'Brian a tepid nod.

Wheeless ended the awkward moment by circling his index finger in
the air and saying, "Okay, let's go. Dazzle me, Edward."

"Guy, this is a first cut at what's available for purchase that meets your
well-chosen publicity criteria. By way of background, here is a list of the
art experts I consulted, their published books, and the universities where
they teach." The list lit up the screen.

"Interesting list, I guess," said Starsky slouching in his chair. "But don't
you think it would make sense to talk with an actual artist or two rather
than just academics?"

O'Brian burned at Starsky's ambush. The day before he had painstak-
ingly taken Starsky through the entire presentation. Seemingly satisfied,
Starsky had not offered a single comment. O'Brian decided to keep his
powder dry and not allow Starsky to derail him. He responded, "I'll make
a note of that."

O'Brian continued, "You will see five paintings by prominent artists
that have been identified as available for purchase. Some are publicly available while others are vest-pocket listings that the owners are not ready to
publicly acknowledge. The art world loves secrets. And, there's a school
of thought that publicly acknowledging a painting is for sale diminishes

its market value. I've put the five in alphabetical order. The first up is this painting by René Magritte, the Belgian surrealist renowned for his use of derby hats and pipes."

On the screen flashed a photo of a man standing in front of a mirror. The mirror eerily reflected the man's back rather than his front. O'Brian let his audience digest the image before moving on.

"The second is from Edvard Munch. As you know, Guy, he is famous for his work *The Scream*." A small painting of a portly gentleman flashed on the screen. Wheeless looked indifferent and Janet was engrossed in her phone.

"The third is from an artist we all know, Mark Rothko. Since his death in 1970, Rothko's reputation has skyrocketed. This example is quintessential Rothko and would have a prominent place in any museum in the world."

On the screen flashed a tri-colored canvas with two rectangular boxes. Wheeless, turning to Janet, shrugged his shoulders.

"Fourth is from the French impressionist Georges-Pierre Seurat. His pointillist painting *A Sunday Afternoon on the Island of La Grande Jatte* is priceless. In addition to being a world-class painter, he was also a renowned sketcher." On the screen appeared a drawing of a boy trying to whistle through his hands. O'Brian saw Wheeless whisper something to Janet.

"Finally, we have this wonderfully vexing painting from Grant Wood, celebrated for his painting *American Gothic*. This Wood painting is titled *Death on Ridge Road*." O'Brian had saved the Grant Wood painting for last, thinking it would be the only one that might pique Wheeless's interest.

On the screen appeared a surrealistic painting of a truck barreling down a hill. A caterpillar-like car oozed up the hill in the incorrect lane accelerating toward an inevitable collision. The scene's fences and telephone poles gave it a foreboding sense of motion. The painting was greeted by silence.

After Janet whispered something in his ear, Wheeless snarled, "Is that all you got?"

"Ahh . . . as I said . . . these are preliminary, and I've only been at it for two weeks. Guy, your feedback is, as always, of paramount importance."

"Edward, you've confused effort with results. Nothing you presented is close. Maybe they'd stir up some good press for a day, but nothing near our goal. Fucking unacceptable! Al, what do you think?"

"Candidly, I think there's a lack of creativity," Starsky said, fingering his mala beads. "A sophomore in Wichita State's art history program could have made the presentation."

O'Brian's pulse rate soared. Starsky had set him up for a fall.

"I've got no time for this," said an agitated Wheeless. "Al, you and Janet get way down into the weeds on this. I'll see all of you in ten days. Bring viable options. No more horse piss!"

Wheeless and Janet bolted upright in synchronized fashion. Wheeless violently shoved open the conference room door, banging it against the wall. Passing through the door, Janet shot O'Brian a chastising look over her shoulder.

O'Brian stood at one end of the conference table and stared at Starsky, who returned the stare with a look of pleasure bordering on triumph. O'Brian made a decision. His days at the Wheeless Strategic Fund were over. His final act would be to kick Starsky's ass.

O'Brian's rage sapped any ability to think logically. Although he had committed one incredibly violent act in the past, he had never engaged in a fistfight. Devoid of any plan of attack, his hostility took total control. Pumping up his shallow chest, he walked slowly toward the other end of the table and said, "You duplicitous little piece of shit. That's the last straw!"

Starsky did not move. Looming over him, O'Brian cocked his fist; but before he could deliver a blow, Starsky's left hand sprang up like a cobra and grabbed O'Brian's testicles in a paralyzing grip. O'Brian could not even scream. Starsky, maintaining his vise grip, rose slowly out of his chair. O'Brian's attempt to grab Starsky's neck was met by an excruciating ratcheting up of his grip. O'Brian could not breathe.

"You skinny, boot-licking twerp. The next time I see you around here will be the last time. You hear me?"

O'Brian could only nod in affirmation.

"I'm getting a good idea about what happened while Guy was in the big house. You listening?"

O'Brian again nodded.

"If you show your face here again, it'll end badly."

Giving a final crippling squeeze, Starsky shoved the gasping O'Brian to the floor. As O'Brian tried to get to his knees, Starsky took a step back and, with the precision of a penalty kick, landed a vicious blow to the ribs. As O'Brian groaned and clutched his ribs, Starsky stepped toward the door. He looked back, gave a little shoulder shrug, and with a running start, delivered an even more powerful wallop to the ribs. In his incongruous whisper voice, Starsky said, "Been a real treat knowing you, Edward."

30

On Saturday morning, Henry and Marylou crab-walked down the treacherous apartment stairs. Henry said over his shoulder, "Bernadette asked to
meet her for coffee at the T Café, a few doors down the street. I've never
met anybody with such a taste for coffee."

Pulling open the door of the T Café for Marylou, Henry saw Bernadette
and Lola sitting at the table directly under a life-sized black-and-white
photograph. Pictured was a fierce woman, her bottom torso naked, holding a sign saying "Make War." Apparently unaffected by the image above
them, mother and daughter cheerfully stood to greet Henry and Marylou.

After exchanging three kisses with Bernadette, Henry said, "Lola, nice
to see you again. I'm pleased to introduce my wife, Marylou."

Lola shook Marylou's hand brightly and said, "I knew you would
be pretty."

Sitting down in the inexpensive metal chair, Henry could not avoid
glancing at the imposing nude woman hanging overhead. He was well
acquainted with the Dutch affection for the shock value of human bodies,
but was confident that Marylou, unaccustomed to Amsterdamers' sense
of humor, felt awkward.

"Lola, how was your week in school?" Henry asked.

"School is school. It is always the same. But Mother and I had some great fun last night."

"Tell us."

"We went to the Kriterion Theater up the street with mother's friend Alex and saw a most American film."

Henry felt a pang of jealousy at the news there was a man named Alex in Bernadette's life. He asked, "What film was that?"

"It was called *Weiner*."

Wondering if he had heard Lola correctly, Henry asked, "The film about the ex-Congressman Anthony Weiner?"

"Yes, his wife, Huma, is Hillary Clinton's best friend. He likes to show people his thing, his weiner," Lola said with a giggle.

"I do not hide the uncomfortable realities of the world from Lola," Bernadette interjected unapologetically. "The Dutch audience found the movie enormously amusing."

"I think Mr. Weiner should go on *The Jerry Springer Show*," suggested Lola.

Bombarded by the huge nude staring down at him, the banter about "weiners," and even Jerry Springer, Henry was relieved when Bernadette directed the conversation to the morning's plans.

"I know you have a matter you want to talk about, and I thought we could do that while I show you Amsterdam's most unique museum. It is a place not everyone has heard about. It is called the Six Collection. The collection is housed in the Six family home on Amstel, a palazzo with fifty-six rooms. Lola has her piano lesson around the corner on Herengracht, so we can all walk together that way. Would that be nice for you?"

"Sounds wonderful," answered Marylou. "Any chance we can hear you play, Lola?"

"I am not very good . . . yet," answered Lola. "Maybe by springtime I will be ready."

Henry insisted on paying the bill, and the four rebundled themselves for the trip into the city center. As they walked in the clear, dry winter day, Bernadette gave them some background on their destination.

"The patriarch of the family was the first Jan Six, a wealthy textile merchant and a mayor of Amsterdam in the seventeenth century. Three hundred years later, Jan Six X lives in the family house. The original Jan Six was a friend and patron of Rembrandt, and the artist's famous portrait of him hangs in the living room. Some believe it is the most beautiful portrait ever painted."

"This sounds wonderful," said Marylou. "But I'm confused—are we visiting someone's home or a museum?"

Before Bernadette could answer, the group turned the corner of Herengracht, and came face-to-face with a dozen fit, highly caffeinated women literally bouncing up and down on the sidewalk. On their feet were shoes that looked like ski boots. Attached to the boots were eight-inch ovals with treads on the bottom. Saying, "Excuse us," the pack cheerfully stepped off the sidewalk and bounded down the street calling out to each other.

Henry and Marylou stared as the group went up and down like human pogo sticks.

"Those are kangaroo shoes," Lola said. "All my friends have them except for me. Mother says I would break my leg and maybe my neck."

"Kangaroo shoes are the latest craze in Amsterdam," Bernadette said cheerfully. "Two of my students at the university have broken their ankles. Lola, you are better off with your piano."

After dropping Lola at her piano lesson, Bernadette returned to Marylou's question. "Now, where was I about the Six Collection? The direct answer to your question is that it is both a home and a museum. Over the centuries, the family built a remarkable collection of art with paintings by Rembrandt, Albert Cuyp, and Frans Hals. Until the twentieth century, Vermeer's *The Milkmaid* and *Little Street* as well as Jan Steen's *The Oyster Eater* were part of the family's collection. The Six family sold them to raise money to pay inheritance taxes. Then the government made a deal with the family. They would no longer have to pay inheritance taxes, provided they do not sell any more art, keep the collection in Holland, and open it to the public."

"They open their house to the general public?" Marylou asked.

"Oh no, public access is extremely limited."

"So, we get to go because you're head of the university's art department?" asked Henry.

"You might say that," answered Bernadette with a demure smile.

As they walked in front of the Hermitage museum, Bernadette stopped and pointed across the Amstel River. "There it is," she said, pointing at an enormous wine-colored brick townhouse with a double front stoop of ten steps up each side to the grand entrance.

The three entered the house at ground level below the grand entrance and were greeted by a young, purple-haired, tattooed docent who helped them sign the guest book with a quill pen. The docent led them up the carved wooden staircase into the main house. With its ornate stucco ceilings, gold-colored leather walls, and elaborate crystal chandeliers, the house was from a different time. Henry was pleasantly surprised to see a well-maintained English garden in the back complete with symmetrical privet hedges. Four magpies stalking in the backyard completed the scene.

The house was crammed with centuries of art and family memorabilia. In a room overlooking the Amstel River was Rembrandt's magnificent portrait of his friend Jan Six. The redheaded Baron Six posed with a radiant red cloak draped jauntily across his left shoulder. Disjointedly, across the room on a pedestal was an illuminated lamp. The lamp's luminous globe was not glass but rather a fully inflated blowfish. In the next room was a Frans Hals painting of the famous Dr. Nicolaes Tulp. Under the portrait sat an Egyptian statue from 1700 BC.

The docent moved the group from room to room, enthusiastically describing the scores of paintings by Rembrandt, Albert Cuyp, Jacob van Ruisdael, and other seventeenth-century luminaries. In one room was a large painting including two boys with sticks preparing to hit a small white ball.

Pointing to the painting, the docent proudly announced, "This painting from 1624 is titled *Het Golfspel*, in English *The Game of Golf*. Many believe this painting proves that the Dutch invented golf."

Bernadette leaned in close to Henry's ear and whispered, "We Dutch may be modest people but we love to take credit for inventing a great many things."

While the docent showed Marylou a display of pig bladders that had served as Rembrandt's paint tubes, Bernadette again whispered to Henry, "Would this be a good time to talk about what is on your mind?"

Taking in the wonders surrounding him, Henry knew the Six family home was definitely not the place to discuss his plan.

"Let's wait on that until after the tour. Is that okay?"

"Oh, of course, coffee is always nice for me. I know just the place."

■■■

Seated at a table by the window in the Bake My Day café on Amstelstraat, Henry, in a lawyer-like fashion, described the couple's issues with Guy Wheeless—from high school rivalry, to Wheeless's assaults of multiple women, to the recanting witnesses leading to his release, to the poisoning of the yellow ducks that destroyed Marylou's business, and to the murder of Wheeless's niece, Nichole.

Henry described what he had been told about Wheeless's plan to resurrect his name by funding an art collection in Wichita. Although trying to be as clear as possible, he found himself falling into the trap of extraneous details. As he shared his plan for Wheeless's humiliation, Bernadette's discomfort grew palpable.

"Let me try to summarize what you are saying," said Bernadette finally, unwinding her long orange scarf. "You two have a bad history with Mr. Wheeless. In order to revenge his wrongs—is revenge too strong a word?"

"No, not at all," said Marylou. "We're not talking about some run-of-the-mill grudge. This runs deep."

"You want my help to create and then sell to Mr. Wheeless a forgery of van Meegeren's *Perfect Strangers*? In other words, you want my help to sell the forger's forgery?"

"Sort of . . . yes, that's correct," answered Marylou.

"Please," Bernadette said gently. "This sounds like something I should stay very far away from."

"Bernadette, let me try to explain," said Henry. "From what I read in your book, *Perfect Strangers,* and in my own internet searches, to make a forgery credible it's crucial to have a provenance, the story explaining where a painting has been when it emerges after being out of sight for many years. We're not only clueless about what might be a believable backstory for our planned painting but at a loss on how we communicate that story in a believable way. So, what we are asking—"

"Wait," Bernadette broke in again. "Please, understand my situation. My professional life is as an art historian and author. If even a whiff of what you are talking about touched me, my career would be over, forever."

The three sat in strained silence.

"We certainly understand your concern," said Henry. "But all we are asking is for you—"

Bernadette held up her hand. "Please, we should not discuss this any further. I like both of you very much. I enjoy telling my Dutch friends about my new friends from America. But the role you are asking me to play is impossible. It is made all the more troubling that you are not only talking about forging a van Meegeren painting, but it is the very painting that is the title of my book! Please, understand my position."

Henry looked over at Marylou. Detached from the conversation, she was staring out the window at the snowflakes feathering up the canal. He was relieved that Marylou was not going to persuade Bernadette with the core reason for their plan. She was not going to share the story of Wheeless's rape.

"We of course understand," said Henry. "Bernadette, we regret if anything we said put you in a compromised position. We're sorry for even bringing it up."

"It has been quite a day. My friend Alex is waiting for me in the apartment, probably playing a video game with Lola. It would seem best to forget all of this and return home."

As the three walked home in the fluffy snow, the women talked casually about the joys and issues of raising adolescent girls. Henry shuffled along in silence. He feared that Dan and Marylou might follow through with their plan for Wheeless if his forgery strategy fell through. Time was running out.

■■■

"Well, that idea went over like a lead balloon," Marylou said as she locked the apartment door.

"I see Bernadette's point. Why should she get involved with this Wheeless craziness? I'm grasping at straws to come up with an alternative to what you and Dan cooked up. From Bernadette's perspective, the idea was too close to the bone. She's been awfully accommodating. I guess I just presumed too much."

Henry retreated to the kitchen, took two bottles of water out of the refrigerator, and, returning to the living room, held one out to Marylou.

"No thanks," said Marylou with hands on her hips. "What do you mean by 'accommodating'? I saw the two of you whispering at the Six Collection. Is there something you think you should tell me?"

"About what?"

"About you and our beautiful neighbor," Marylou said, pointing at the ceiling.

"Don't be ridiculous."

"Really? You two seem thick as thieves. Henry, I've known you since you were eighteen. I can read you like a book and I don't like the latest chapter."

"You're being ridiculous. All I did was reach too far to find something, anything, to derail your insane idea. Good night. I'll sleep on the couch."

■ ■ ■

Marylou lay wide-awake waiting for the sound of Henry's snoring from the couch. She was agitated. Her issues with Wheeless left her frayed and making irrational decisions. Was her anxiety pushing Henry away?

She was deeply ambivalent. Bernadette's expertise would be invaluable for execution of the *Perfect Strangers* plan. Marylou was confident that she knew exactly how to secure Bernadette's help. But what if something was going on between Henry and Bernadette? She needed to know.

When she heard Henry's snoring on the couch, she pulled a sweater over her pajamas and silently opened and closed the apartment door. She headed up the stairs to Bernadette's apartment.

She knocked lightly on the door, but no response. She had decided to turn back around when the door opened. Bernadette, in a light blue silk robe and furry slippers, stood in the doorway. Before Marylou could speak, Bernadette put her hands over her mouth with a look of horror and said, "Oh no, it has happened!"

Marylou was discombobulated. What did she mean had "happened"? Was Bernadette talking about Henry? All she could say was, "Excuse me?"

"The heat! Your heat in your apartment has gone out."

"No, no, the heat is fine. Can we talk? Am I disturbing anything?"

"I wish. I am just reading. Please come in."

"We can talk tomorrow."

"No, it is fine. Alex left thirty minutes ago and Lola is sound asleep."

After Marylou sat down on the coach and Bernadette on a chair, Marylou asked, "Have you and Alex been together for a long time?"

"Almost five years."

"Is Alex also a professor?"

"No, Alex is an attorney."

"Henry used to be an attorney. He loves to tell people that he has reformed himself and is now a professor. What kind of law does he practice?"

"Alex is a trademark attorney. Also . . . Alex is a woman."

Marylou's head gyrated with this new information. Her unfounded suspicion about Henry was the latest example of her irrationality. Politely accepting Bernadette's offer of a glass of water, she silently berated herself for her continued senselessness. Wheeless was driving her to the edge of rationality.

"This whole mess with that hateful man Wheeless has left me unhinged. This afternoon, we didn't tell you the whole story. Please humor me for just a few minutes. I need to tell you the entire truth. But first, promise me that what I say tonight will never be repeated, especially to Henry."

"Is this something Henry does not know?"

"Henry knows . . . but only learned it very recently. We had been married for nearly twenty-five years before I told him. Bernadette, Henry's a good man. He's smart, funny, and committed. Most importantly, for a man, he has a feeling heart. But he's also fragile. If he knew I shared with you this story after withholding it from him for so many years, there's no telling about his reaction."

"All men are fragile."

"That's the truth. Do we have a woman-to-woman deal?"

"Absolutely. If women cannot trust each other, who can we trust?"

"Amen to that," Marylou said, nodding in agreement. She then methodically told the whole story, starting with Wheeless's fateful phone call asking her to the prom and the evening's devastating conclusion. She included a description of Wheeless's ignominious attacks on women in Wichita, his release from prison, and the black cat of depression perpetually at her side. She concluded with her death wish for Wheeless and Henry's forgery idea to derail Marylou's murder plan.

When Marylou finished, Bernadette came across the room and sat down on the couch, taking Marylou's hands into hers.

"I am so sorry. His crime cannot go unpunished. I do not like this forgery idea, but it is certainly better than the alternative. Give me a day or two to sort things out. I will get back to you directly."

The women warmly embraced in the hallway and returned to their apartments. Marylou tiptoed past Henry sleeping on the couch and slipped quietly into bed. Lying on her back, she felt better than she had in months. She was bolstered by the fact Bernadette would be an invaluable ally in the forgery plan and hopeful about the possibility of friendship.

She debated waking Henry to apologize for her unfounded accusations and share with him the news about Bernadette's change of heart. Exhausted by the day's whirlwind of events, she decided good news could always wait for morning.

31

The following morning, Marvin quietly closed his hotel room door to ensure Constance's much-needed sleep went undisturbed. Heading to the Pulitzer's exercise room, he was careful to note the many hallway turns in order to successfully navigate the return. Finally reaching the lobby, he headed into the micro library to check his emails. He nodded and said "good morning" to a bird-like, white-haired woman reading the morning's *De Telegraaf*.

Logging in to the library's computer, he scrolled down to see an email from his old friend in Wichita, Dan Moore.

> Yo! Hope you're behaving yourself in Amsterdam, well kind of anyway. As you requested, attached is our report on Charles Whitcome. Derk is one of our best investigators. Be assured he has verified any statement of fact with at least two reliable sources. Whitcome sounds like a ton of fun—our kind of guy. I've sent our bill to your Dallas office.

Marvin quickly opened the attached PDF:

Moore & Co.
Date: 2/5/18
To: Dan Moore
From: Derk Alexander
Subject Name: Charles (Charlie) Whitcome
File Number: XTg6CW
Investigation Type: Background verification
Date Assigned: 1/21/18

Subject and his brother, David, grew up in Lockney, a speck on the West Texas map. Subject graduated *summa cum laude* from the University of Texas, Austin, in 1975 with degrees in theater and civil engineering. Subject was a member and president of the SAE fraternity.

Subject has consistently shown a proclivity for hijinks, skating close to, and sometimes past, legal boundaries. For example, while in college, his action as president of the SAE fraternity led to discipline by both the university and SAE national. Funds were sent by SAE national to the Austin chapter to refurbish the fraternity house's common rooms. Rather than using the money for its intended purpose, subject diverted the funds to build an elaborate bar with multiple beer taps in the house's basement. Subject's actions led to a semester suspension but also made him a campus legend.

Following graduation, subject relocated to NYC to pursue a theater career. He supported himself with jobs waiting tables and later as a sommelier. Subject appeared in minor roles in three different Broadway plays during the five-year period following graduation.

Subject left NYC for Dallas to join his brother, David, in an oil exploration business called CW Exploration. Subject spent most of the 1980s and '90s commuting back and forth between Dallas and Midland, Texas. In the Midland community, subject established a reputation as a shrewd negotiator willing to bend the rules.

In 1997, DW Exploration made a major strike in the Permian Basin's Edwards Field. After drilling forty-six wells, CW Exploration sold its rights to Marathon Oil. The sale price was rumored to be in excess of $300 million. For nearly five years following the sale, the parties were embroiled in litigation. Marathon alleged subject had intentionally misrepresented the field's reserves. The parties settled pursuant to a confidential agreement.

Following his exit from the oil business, subject purchased the first of what would become three art galleries he owns in Texas. Subject has a reputation for a keen eye for art value and a willingness to make complicated trades of paintings. Subject settled a lawsuit in 2011 that alleged his Dallas gallery traded a forged Modigliani sketch.

Subject is an active gourmand. In 1992, he was initiated into the Dallas chapter of Chaine des Rotisseurs and eventually rose to Bailli Provincial, the local chapter's title for the society's leader.

Subject currently lives in a three-bedroom Ritz-Carlton apartment on McKinney Avenue in downtown Dallas. The apartment is said to contain a number of world-class modern paintings. He also spends time at the CW Ranch in Wood County, Texas. Wood County land records list the ranch at 3,276 acres, just over five sections of land. The ranch's title is held by a Panamanian LLC named CW Ranch, Ltd.

Subject plays poker at least three times a week at different venues in Dallas and at the CW Ranch. He has played for the last fifteen years at a high-stakes game held every Tuesday afternoon at Dallas's Adolphus Hotel. Subject is a frequent invitee to restaurant and gallery openings throughout the Southwest. He daily consumes large amounts of alcohol.

Subject has been married and divorced twice and has no known children. Subject has no recorded convictions or debt.

Marvin read through the report two more times. Constance's description of her uncle and the investigator's report were out of sync. *Constance said Charlie had no money. So how the hell does he live in the Ritz-Carlton and own multiple art galleries? She described him as a lifelong acting failure who limped back to Texas to work for her father. Charlie sure don't strike me as willin' to ride sidecar for nobody. Was what Charlie said about Constance's year suspension from practicin' medicine true? Things aren't addin' up.*

Rattled, Marvin wanted to scream but, looking at the white-haired lady next to him, managed to stifle himself. As he stood up to leave the room, the woman looked up from her *De Telegraaf* and said, "Have a good day, young man."

Hurrying out of the tiny library, Marvin headed to the hotel fitness center. He closed the door, made sure the room was empty, and screamed, "Well, fuck me to tears!" To burn off his frustration, Marvin sprinted on the treadmill and boosted barbells. While doing bench presses, he committed to confront Constance immediately. Not another minute would go by without wrestling down the inconsistencies.

After making his way back through the hotel's warren-like hallways, a determined Marvin put the key in his door. Opening the door, he found Constance sitting in the room's only chair. She was dressed in one of the hotel's terry cloth robes. Before Marvin could get a word out, she closed her copy of *Perfect Strangers* and said, "I've been waiting on you. I was hoping you might help me wash my hair."

She stood, unfastened the robe's sash, and walking into the bathroom, let the robe fall to the floor.

Marvin's decision was instantaneous. *The Uncle Charlie discussion can wait. What's the rush?*

32

Pressed together in affectionate afterglow, the couple stepped onto the sidewalk in front of the Pulitzer. Deeply inhaling the cool winter air, Marvin whispered, "Lovin' the sunlight playin' through your hair."

"Thanks, I had some expert help," she said, giving her hair a playful toss. "I know you've got plans for today, but there's a spot up the street I think would be fun. Now I need to remember which direction to turn."

As the couple walked north on Prinsengracht, the street bustled with tourists enjoying a Saturday in Amsterdam. As they discussed the day's potential adventures, Constance spotted two violin players enthusiastically blending their instruments on the Berenstraat Canal bridge. "Marvin, this is incredible. Do you recognize the song they're playing?"

Marvin was clueless. Reaching for an answer, he remembered Constance had been named after Mozart's wife. "Sounds like . . . maybe . . . Mozart, but I can't quite place it."

"Wow, aren't you clever! It's Mozart's Symphony No. 40, my favorite piece of music. I love this city!"

The couple stopped to listen to the violinists and moved closer to the bridge's railing to get out of harm's way from the relentless flow of bicycles. The musicians finished in a crescendo and were rewarded with the appreciative applause from the gathered tourists. After Marvin dropped a twenty-euro note in their upturned fedora, the musicians bowed their thanks. Marvin felt totally at ease; thoughts of Uncle Charlie had evaporated.

Three blocks up Prinsengracht, Constance stopped in front of La Tertulia. The coffee shop was located in a poorly preserved canal house adorned with amateur Van Gogh–themed murals. With plants and flowers inside and out, it could have been mistaken for a florist.

Entering at street level and walking down four stairs bordered by more plants, they were cordially greeted by two middle-aged sisters standing behind the small linoleum counter displaying tea packets. Soft electronic music and the sweet smell of cannabis set a serene mood. They took seats at a small aluminum café table with a lit candle at its center. The only other patron was a millennial obliviously bent over his sketch pad. Constance ordered two herbal lemon teas.

Marvin was bombarded by conflicting thoughts. *Should we be doing this? Charlie said Constance needs to stay away from recreational drugs. Maybe Charlie doesn't know what he's talkin' about?*

"Constance, you sure this is how you want to start the day?"

"Of course, we're in Amsterdam. It's okay to step out a bit, don't you think?"

"Hell, yeah. You're a surprise a minute!"

The tea arrived with the marijuana menu. The listing for joints was replete with fanciful names like Amnesia, LA Confidential, Maui Wowee, Hoot N' Holler, JJ Flash, and Gorilla Glue. Marvin's eye caught a selection near the bottom of the page.

"Hot damn, here we go! This baby's right up your alley—it's called Hog Wild!"

"Perfect for me. You sure it won't spark unwelcome memories of your CW Ranch pig hunt? You know, we never really talked about the hunt."

"Like I told you, I had a great time." Issues with Uncle Charlie darted into Marvin's head, dampening the moment. *Should we be doin' this? Forget Charlie! Life's short, why ruin an adventure?*

Their order arrived in a blue-plastic tapered cylinder topped with a white cap. Marvin slid the perfectly rolled joint out and was impressed with the stiff paper filter at the tip. Handing it to Constance, he said, "Ladies first."

"Always the gentleman," she said, leaning over the candle in the table's center and expertly turning the joint as she puffed it to life. Once lit, she took an aggressive hit, then another, before passing it to Marvin.

"Not your first rodeo, huh?" Marvin said with a smile. He took a pull, inhaled deeply, and immediately convulsed into coughs.

Catching his breath, he said, "Whoa, Toto, we're not in Kansas any-more!" Passing the joint across the table to Constance, Marvin caught the sisters looking with knowing eyes at him from behind the counter.

Constance took an energetic hit and then another. Exhaling a cloud of smoke at the ceiling, she looked like a film noir actress. "Tastes good. Bet it's some type of Kosher Kush. Take care, Marvin, it'll hit home like a sledgehammer."

Constance took an additional hit before passing the joint back to Marvin. Taking a second, more modest pull, Marvin managed to avoid another coughing attack. How Constance could even guess at a mar-ijuana strain danced through Marvin's mind, but the thought quickly blew away. Articulating a coherent thought was like raking leaves in a swirling wind.

They ordered more tea and sat absorbing the experience. Constance relit the joint, took an enthusiastic pull, and said, "Marvin, there's some-thing we need to talk about."

"Shoot."

"I feel bad about some of the things I said about Uncle Charlie."

"How so?"

"My dad adored Uncle Charlie and I think I resent Uncle Charlie for it. I craved my dad's attention and Uncle Charlie was always in the way . . . I felt alone and abandoned. Now he's playing some kind of surrogate father role—for him, just another acting gig. If he heard I was coming to Amsterdam, he probably would have tried to, I don't know, ground me. It's been like this for so long, I'm just tired of him . . . "

Marvin recognized that Constance's pot-fueled harangue was rapidly descending into an unhappy soliloquy. When she stopped to catch her breath, he stepped in.

"Constance, speakin' of Amsterdam, this city pumps me up. The women are stylish no matter their age, and I love the way they fly around town on bikes. Everybody seems to be lovin' life. And, I've never seen so much hair . . . This town makes me stand taller . . . women on bikes are inherently sexy, don't ya think? There's an edge here that, that . . . ah . . . what was I saying?"

"Marvin," she interrupted with a different look in her eye, her Doc eye.

"Yes?"

"What do you say to a walk, clear our heads a bit?"

"Solid thinkin'," Marvin said, standing up and pulling on his coat.

■■■

Stepping out on the sidewalk, the couple turned south on Prinsengracht, content to walk the streets silently and directionless. Marvin's brain was attacked by paranoid thoughts. *Was Uncle Charlie right about Constance? Am I walking with a total stranger? Is the Constance I think I know the real Constance?*

"Are we lost?" Constance asked.

"We're wanderin'. Just cause we're wanderin' don't mean we're lost."

"Marvin, I'm fine with wandering. But, no matter what, please do not leave me alone in this crazy city."

Before he could respond, shouts coming from a crowd on a canal bridge snapped Marvin's head around. Agreeable to any diversion from his unsettling thoughts, he said, "I've got ya'. Let's check out what's happenin' up there."

Once on the bridge, Marvin looked down in the canal at two

forty-five-foot-long rowboats vying for position as they sprinted toward the bridge. The boats had five rowers, women as well as men, on each side, and a coxswain directing the effort. Marvin looked up the canal and realized there were scores of the same class of boats heading their way.

As the boats were about to glide under the bridge to the roar of the approving crowd, the rowers, in a synchronized movement, pulled their oars out of the water and into their boats. Emerging on the other side of the bridge, the oars instantly plunged back in the water. Vying for the lead, the boats turned sharply left into another canal and under a different bridge. Again, the oars flew in harmonized fashion into the boats and then back into the canal. The crews were able to execute the oar maneuvers while constantly jostling for position with other boats.

The man to Marvin's right shouted encouragement in Dutch to one of the boats. Marvin asked him what was going on.

The man cheerfully responded, "It is a race through the city. There are over 150 boats here from all over Holland. Since we have little space for sports fields, we use what we have and we have much water!"

The deluge of racing boats mesmerized Marvin. They were painted every color of the rainbow. Marvin decided his favorite was a white boat with a blazing orange interior and matching orange oar blades. The crew's orange shirts and boater hats gave the boat a 3D look. He joined the crowd's supportive cheers and, as the crowd moved to another viewing spot, he moved with them.

On the third bridge he overheard two men say the race would end at the Amstel Hotel and it was time to run to the finish to see the leaders' final sprints. Without hesitation, Marvin ran with them.

Standing on the bridge spanning the Amstel River provided an excellent view of the finish line. As the boats raced to the finish line, the shouts of the coxswains and the groans of the rowers intensified. The energy of the cheering crowds was exhilarating and Marvin bent over the bridge's railing shouting, "Pull! Pull!" in unison with the crowd.

It was at that moment, bent over the railing and shouting encouragement, that a hollowing jolt of stomach acid froze him. He did a quick three-sixty; Constance was nowhere in sight. In fact, he had not seen her since the first bridge. *How long ago was that? An hour, two hours? I'm so stoned, I left Constance on the first bridge!*

He reached for his phone, only to realize he'd left it on his hotel bureau. Patting his back pocket, he was relieved to find his wallet. If push came to shove, he could get a cab. With no taxi in sight, he started jogging back in the direction of the first bridge. He was confident of the route back until he came to Warmoesstraat. He stopped, looked both ways, and turned right on a guess. As he hurried along, he looked up and down the street for familiar landmarks.

Passing an antique clock shop he thought he had seen before, he was convinced he was on the right path. Taking a left at the next alley, he found himself looking at City Hall—he knew he had never seen it before. Frustrated, he took a hard right into a crowded alley.

The alley was lined with bright display windows. Each window presented a barely clothed woman. He had wandered into the red-light district.

The crowd pushed Marvin along the narrow alley as if he was in a slow-running river. While Marvin strained to stop long enough to admire a beautiful Asian woman, a man wearing a Kelly-green driving cap collided with him and said in an Irish accent, "S'cuze der gov'na, just a wee bit distracted, if ya know what I mean!"

"No problem," Marvin responded while being pushed continuously down the narrow alleyway, unable to take his eyes off the display windows on either side. Some of the women were fantastically beautiful, others decidedly not.

The crowd dissipated at the end of the alley. In the last window, Marvin saw a meticulously dressed elderly man seated on a stool with both hands resting on top of his cane. His slender mustache was waxed to perfection. He appeared to be conducting a pleasant conversation with an unattractive woman in a too revealing negligee.

Marvin's head buzzed as if four different songs were playing at once. Finally exiting off Stoofsteeg, he power-walked down a crowded street until he came to Dam Square. Seeing a taxi line, he scurried across a busy street. Trying to squeeze through a bicycle rack to get to the cabs, his left hip caught a handlebar, creating a domino effect of a dozen falling bikes. He was far too focused on finding Constance to pick up his mess. As he opened a taxi door, a passing bicyclist hissed, "Asshole American." Closing the cab door, Marvin wondered, *How's he know I'm an American?*

When the taxi pulled up in front of the Pulitzer, Marvin reached for his wallet. His hands went into a patting fury as if his pants were on fire. His wallet was gone. All he had in his pockets was his hotel room key. The words he had heard in the alley echoed back to him: "S'cuze der gov'na, just a wee bit distracted."

Reality landed hard. He had been victimized by the oldest trick in the book, the "bump and lift." The humiliation deepened because it happened in a place he shouldn't have been, seeing what he shouldn't have seen.

The driver turned around and said in a Middle Eastern accent, "Sir, is everything all right?"

"My wallet was stolen; I have no money."

The driver coolly glared at Marvin. "May I suggest you ask the front desk for assistance?"

As Marvin stepped out of the taxi, he saw the doorman busily trying to wave down cabs for multiple guests. The street in front of the hotel was chaotic with taxi drivers jockeying for position while the narrow sidewalk was crowded with hotel guests. Then, he spotted Constance hurrying through the hotel's sliding glass doors and pulling her bag behind her. Juggling in his addled brain the stolen wallet, the spilled bike rack, the unpaid taxi, and now a departing Constance—he was paralyzed.

While Marvin stood frozen, Constance was in his face in a flash. "Where the hell were you? The last thing I said was please don't abandon me. Sure enough, you left me high and dry two hours ago!"

"I . . . just got caught up in the boat race. Constance, I'm so—"

"Save it for someone who cares." Constance's voice was growing louder with each word. "I told you—please don't abandon me!"

"Let's not make a scene," Marvin said plaintively as heads swiveled toward the couple. "Come back inside, we can talk this out."

"I am absolutely done with you!" Constance shouted. Elbowing Marvin aside, she threw her bag into the taxi's back seat, climbed in, and slammed the door shut. Marvin could see through the window that Constance and the driver were debating something while the driver repeatedly pointed at Marvin. Constance rolled down the window and yelled, "I'll even pay your fare, you sorry son of a bitch!"

With those words ringing in his ears and shouldering the weight of the crowd's contemptuous stare, Marvin watched Constance disappear.

33

Monday morning found Henry drawing to the end of his lecture at the University of Amsterdam School of Business. He could not help comparing his lecture on the 2008 US subprime mortgage crisis with Bernadette's lecture on Han van Meegeren. Was her subject more interesting or was she simply a better professor?

The students had started class in a typical Monday morning haze. Their disengaged faces looked like they were expecting a musical performance rather than a lecture. However, Henry thought his talk was beginning to spark a modicum of interest. The students had even turned away from internet surfing.

Addressing the American automobile manufacturers' 2008 campaign to secure a Congressional bailout, Henry flashed on the screen a photograph of the "Big Three" automobile manufacturers' chairmen sitting at a table fielding questions from their Congressional inquisitors.

"Here are the three chairmen of the American auto manufacturers making their pitch for a Congressional bailout," Henry said, turning to point at the screen behind him. "They blamed the sorry state of the US auto industry not on terrible labor contracts, not on unappealing product offerings, not on bloated, overpaid management ranks or misguided acquisitions. No, they testified that the US subprime mortgage crisis was to blame for their woes. That was bad enough. But, in an incredibly tone-deaf move, each man flew on his own corporate jet to Washington, DC, to plea for a bailout."

Henry was pleased to see many students shaking their heads in disbelief. "Here's what one congressman had to say about the chairmen of America's Big Three automobile makers." He flashed a quote on the screen.

"There's a delicious irony in seeing private luxury jets flying into Washington and the people coming off them with tin cups in their hands. It's like seeing a guy show up at a soup kitchen in high hat and tuxedo."

"Not surprisingly, Congress turned them down cold." As Henry mouthed the word "cold," he saw Marvin slip into the last row of the lecture hall. Marvin had never shown any interest in Henry's lectures, much less attended one. Intent on maintaining focus, he continued outlining the conditions for using funds from the Troubled Asset Relief Fund, known as TARP.

Ten minutes later, Henry said, "We'll stop there for today. For tomorrow's class, please be prepared to discuss whether it was legal to use TARP funds to bail out the car manufacturers, and if not, was it the right thing for the Bush administration to have done. I look forward to a lively discussion. Have a good day."

Henry gathered his notes while answering student questions. After the students exited, he started up the lecture hall's aisle toward Marvin. "Glad you could sit in for a few minutes. Everything okay?"

"Totally hunky-dory. You sounded like you knew what you were talkin' about up there. Pretty impressive, bro."

"Thanks, Marvin. Our apartment's right across the street. Come on up and see how the working class lives."

"Yeah, right. I'd love to see your apartment."

The brothers walked across Roetersstraat, past the massive bicycle racks next to the apartment building. Climbing the apartment house stairs, Marvin said, "Damn, Henry, these stairs will whip your butt into shape in no time."

"It's funny, but Marylou and I have gotten used to them. What's Constance up to?" Henry said as he unlocked the apartment door.

"Gone."

As the brothers stepped into the apartment, Henry asked, "Did you say *gone?*"

"Yeah, gone."

"Is everything alright?"

"Oh, I don't know," Marvin dissembled. "Maybe . . . maybe she concluded I wasn't a good long-term prospect."

"How insightful."

"Blow it out your ass, Henry."

"Sorry. Did you leave your sense of humor in Dallas? Is it over with her or just a time-out?"

"Don't know. If it's over, I'll sure miss her. She was the least fussy woman I ever met. But, tell ya what, I sure won't miss the pig hunts."

"Pig hunts?"

"Remember how I told you I was going on a pig hunt? She had me tearin' my sorry ass through East Texas bramble behind a couple of dogs chasin' down feral pigs to stab 'em to death. There was some weird psychological testin' stuff she had goin' that I can't understand, much less explain."

Henry knew he should stay silent but could not help himself. "Marvin, in my mind's eye, I see you half naked, war paint lining your face. I see you running with a pointed stick howling at the sky as you chase down a pig. It's a scene right out of *Lord of the Flies.*"

"Whatever," Marvin said, dismissing his brother's unwanted detour into the potentially intellectual. Looking around the apartment, he said, "I like this place. The plastered ceilings, or whatever they are, are pretty cool. Where's Marylou?"

"She's with Bernadette—you know, the author we went to hear. She lives upstairs with her daughter. The three of them are getting their nails done."

"That Bernadette's awful damn distracting."

"She's not your type."

"What's my type?"

"Good question. I've gotten to know Bernadette and she's not your type."

"Well, slap me silly! Am I smellin' a whiff of possessiveness comin' off you? Have you been behavin' yourself over here?"

"Don't be ridiculous!"

"Easy there. Henry, like I always say, you and me . . . we're like fingers in the same hand." Marvin theatrically wiggled his fingers at Henry. "We may be separate, but I can feel what you're up to. Don't you worry, just 'cause you've ordered don't mean you can't look at the menu."

"This is a ridiculous conversation . . . so what's the plan? You going home, sticking around, or what?"

"I'm not ready to go home. I reupped at the Pulitzer for three more nights. I lost my wallet, so I have to wait for VISA to deliver a new card. Thankfully my passport was in the safe."

"How'd you lose your wallet?"

"No idea . . . I may . . . have been pickpocketed."

"Where?"

"Not sure . . . ah, somewhere in center city."

"That sucks."

"Tell me about it. What are you up to the rest of the day?"

"I need to prepare for tomorrow's class, and we're having dinner tonight at a place called Five Flies." Henry hesitated. "We'd love for you to join us, but I've got to tell you one thing."

"What's that?"

"We'll be doing some research about a plan we have for Guy Wheeless."

"Jesus jumping Christ! Henry, let 'er lie."

"I knew you'd say something like that. But I've got an idea that will not only rock his world but will be great fun to execute."

Marvin gave out a world-weary sigh. "You're like some kinda hound returnin' to the same spot in the backyard time after time. I want no part in this. So it's just you and Marylou goin' to the Five Flies place?"

"No, Bernadette's coming and we're going to meet an art expert friend of hers."

"So Bernadette's coming," Marvin said with a tilt of his head. "Well, what the hell, I really don't have anythin' else for tonight. Tell me what kinda stunt you're cookin' up."

34

Edward O'Brian stood at the O'Brian Investment Partners' floor-to-ceiling glass doors. His life had never been in a better place. He had made some mistakes along the way, but he dismissed them as part of the passage to building a business.

Before tapping in the code to open the door to the secure space, he nodded to himself—the decision to set up the headquarters of O'Brian Investment Partners in the suburban office space was spot on. The inconspicuous space was far removed from the prying eyes of Wichita's downtown establishment in general and Guy Wheeless in particular. He looked over a single enormous room filled with side-by-side desks topped with throbbing double computer screens. The only private office was O'Brian's in the room's northeast corner.

When Wheeless was sentenced to prison, O'Brian's opportunity became blindingly obvious. The vast majority of the Wheeless Strategic Fund Investors called O'Brian to facilitate the withdrawal of their investments. Using his personal connections with the investors and assurances of robust future returns, more than seventy-five percent of the group had moved their money to O'Brian Investment Partners. After ten years of relentless ass-kissing and biting his tongue, O'Brian had found himself in the perfect position to rip Wheeless's empire out from under him.

At the start, it was just he and the Thompson brothers, men who understood success is not risk free. To manage the growing fund, he carefully chose former Wheeless Strategic Investment Fund employees with proven track records and no personal ties to Wheeless. He methodically negotiated with the chosen individuals, and eventually twenty-two of them moved to O'Brian Investment Partners.

Entering the offices through the heavy glass door, O'Brian moved like a politician working a crowd, nodding and waving to the young analysts as he strode across the open space to his office. Sitting at his desk, he reflected on his violent last moments in Wheeless's offices. Thinking about his humbling confrontation with Starsky, O'Brian reflexively bent over. Although a physical ordeal, the showdown had been a blessing. Expelled from Wheeless's office, he no longer had to live a double life—no more pretending he was working in Wheeless's interests while actually building his own fund at Wheeless's expense. No longer having to spend time in those offices was its own anodyne.

Although his life had never been better, two problems nagged him. He had failed to foresee that Wheeless was resourceful enough to get out of prison and immediately get to work on enhancing his public image. The *Wichita Eagle* and local magazines were awash with articles about Wheeless's newfound largess. But sooner or later, O'Brian knew Wheeless would turn his endless reservoir of vitriol on him. With Wheeless, Newton's third law was very real: for every action there is a reaction.

His second issue was the irksome Detective Ortiz and her endless questions about the passenger log. It was imperative that the original log never surface. However, O'Brian had run out of ideas as to where it might be so he could destroy it. And now complicating matters, Ortiz had somehow linked him to the camera left behind in her apartment. She had proved far more enterprising than anticipated.

O'Brian got up from his desk and entered the pulsating trading room. He surveyed the room for the first employees of O'Brian Investment Partners, the Thompson brothers. They were standing at the coffee station vigorously debating something. Walking over to them, he put his arm around the shoulder of the younger and better-looking brother.

"Let's talk in my office."

The raven-haired brothers, still debating, sauntered across the trading floor into the office. O'Brian wondered about the brothers' perpetual day-old beards. Did they go home and shave at night?

"How you doing?" asked O'Brian as he closed the office door and the three took seats at O'Brian's small round conference table.

"Everything's good," responded Brad, the older brother. "We're trying to figure out the most viable trade to take advantage of the new steel tariffs. The potential fluctuation of the Chinese renminbi is the wild card, tough to get a handle on it."

"Before you put that trade on, let's talk it through," said O'Brian.

"Absolutely," answered Rob, the younger brother.

"Let's review your Dallas trip one more time," O'Brian said, pinching the bridge of his nose with his thumb and forefinger. "The game plan was to get incriminating footage of Ortiz's aunt and use it to control Ortiz and keep her out of Wichita."

"Sorry about that," said Rob with a shoulder shrug. "That ditzy aunt wouldn't play ball."

"I remember you telling me you were irresistible to women," O'Brian said with a smirk.

"Well, this one was an outlier. But I did deliver the message from Wheeless to stay out of Wichita."

"Apparently Ortiz doesn't scare easily," O'Brian said. "You were supposed to use your so-called boyish charm to get incriminating video of the aunt. You not only failed to get any film but you lost my camera in the process."

"Sorry about that. I put on all my best moves. She asked me back to her place but that's as far as I got. And your camera, I must have left it at the hotel."

O'Brian weighed whether to tell the Thompson brothers that the camera had been left in Ortiz's apartment and Ortiz had traced it back to him. The brothers were brilliant on the quantitative front, but their practical street smarts were proving to be substandard. He concluded that the less they knew about Ortiz circling around him the better. He chose a different tack.

"Slapping the aunt wasn't smart," said O'Brian, frowning at Rob. "Violence against women is Wheeless's calling card, not ours."

"You're right. It went straight downhill from there. After I hit her, she screamed and that neighbor started banging on the wall. I'll admit it, I freaked out; I never should have hit her. But I still delivered the message."

"Look, this is all water under the bridge," said O'Brian. "Let's focus on what's important. We all know Wheeless not only committed the assaults here in Wichita but murdered his niece in Dallas. Right?"

"Right," the brothers responded, solemnly nodding their heads.

"The longer Wheeless is out of prison, the greater the chance he'll find a way to make trouble for us. Right?"

"Right," the brothers responded with greater conviction.

O'Brian waited a beat for emphasis. "You're sure that the aunt understood your message to stay the hell out of Wichita came from Wheeless?"

"Pretty sure," Rob answered tentatively. "But, the aunt is one major league space cadet. When we were in that dive bar and then in the car, she kept telling me I was emitting the brightest aura she'd ever seen, whatever the hell that means. When she invited me back to her place for a tarot card reading, I thought I had it made. But then she turned Miss Prim-and-Proper on me. I can't be sure she was capable of delivering any kind of message."

"Edward, should we take another shot at spooking Detective Ortiz?" Brad asked. "It was a kick playing mysterious foreign types."

"Are you kidding? No, way too dangerous. We need to back off. With all the evidence piling up against Wheeless, let's just hope Ortiz has the brass to make the case. Okay guys, let's talk later about that Chinese trade. Shut the door on your way out."

Alone in his office, O'Brian propped his legs on the desk. He robotically twirled his pen between his two fingers and thumb. His thoughts slowly came into focus. *Sending the Thompson brothers to Dallas to get an incriminating video was risky and, sure enough, they botched it. But maybe it would still pay off. Surely Ortiz's aunt told her the threat came from Wheeless. The attempt to intimidate her will undoubtedly sharpen her focus on Wheeless. The camera is an unfortunate new twist, but Ortiz seemed to accept my explanation about the burglary. Anyway, it proves nothing. Ortiz is a nuisance, that's all. Why spend time worrying about her—the passenger log has disappeared, and without it, she's got nothing on me—nada, zip.*

35

Marylou sat alone, but not by herself. It was happening for the first time since arriving in Amsterdam. As the black cat of depression curled up beside her, a lonely, sinking feeling enveloped her. She brooded over whether the cat's reappearance was triggered by her ambivalence about Henry's plan to foist a forgery on Guy Wheeless. Was it ridiculously risky and ultimately implausible? Even if successful and Wheeless was utterly humiliated, would that rid her of the black cat? Could she shed the cloud of depression without permanently eliminating Guy Wheeless?

A knock on the door broke into Marylou's reflections. She glanced at her watch; it was Bernadette, as usual right on time. She opened the door and put on a cheerful front.

"Bernadette, you look wonderful. Are those teardrop earrings new?"

"Yes they are, thank you for noticing. Lola helped me pick them out. I heard her talking on her phone, telling a friend how good her nails looked and that she would soon be wearing these earrings."

"That Lola's quite the planner."

"That is one way to describe her."

"Can we talk for a few minutes before heading over to the restaurant?"

"Of course," said Bernadette, taking off her coat. "First, tell me, how are your art classes going?"

"It's been a great experience. The classes are so hands-on and I really think I'm making some progress. One of the teachers named Yara does incredible work. She says copying classic works is a great training tool. To demonstrate, she painted a beautiful copy of a Caravaggio in less than a week. She's incredible. When I'm painting, I can't focus on my problems. It's real therapy."

As the two women sat down on the room's only couch, Marylou took a deep breath and said, "I so appreciate your willingness to use your connections to help us. But, I've been thinking—is it ridiculous to think that after all these years the *Perfect Strangers* painting could magically emerge from the shadows? After all, it's been out of sight since 1950."

"The answer is 'yes.' It happens more frequently than you think. Remember when we visited the Six Collection?"

"How could I forget?"

"Last week, Jan Six XI, the son of the family's current patriarch, made a startling announcement. He announced to the world that he discovered and purchased a new Rembrandt portrait. It is a delightful portrait of a young seventeenth-century man with bright red hair."

"How did he make the discovery?"

"First," Bernadette said, raising her index finger sending her silver bracelets tinkling up her forearm, "the young Mr. Six is a recognized Rembrandt expert employed by Sotheby's here in Amsterdam. It makes sense, since he was raised in a house with a Rembrandt portrait in the living room."

"Yes, I will never forget seeing that portrait of the first Jan Six. But how did he find the new portrait? How did it appear?"

"From what I read, he saw a photo of it in a Christie's catalogue. It was described as being from the 'Rembrandt School.' But the clever Mr. Six put together that the elaborate collar the young man is wearing was only in fashion for two years in the early 1630s. Rembrandt was only twenty-eight or twenty-nine at the time and had recently moved to Amsterdam from Leiden. He was a struggling artist and certainly had no school to support his efforts. Based on those facts and his own well-trained eye, Mr. Six concluded that Rembrandt himself must have painted the portrait. Since the purchase, Mr. Six has had the painting authenticated by over fifteen curators and art historians."

"Remarkable," said Marylou, shaking her head. "But where was the painting before it was handed over to Christie's to auction?"

"All I have read is that it was in a British family for several generations. Mr. Six paid only £137,000 for the painting. It is worth millions. But, my point is simply that genuine paintings reappear from time to time. If that were not true, how could forgeries exist?"

"I follow your logic. Is your friend we're having dinner with tonight an expert on forgeries?"

"Yes, I have known Bauke Dyksta for many years. He is a leading Dutch expert on art authentication. He is in Amsterdam for a conference. However, you need to be prepared. Bauke is a different kind of man and language is a problem for him."

"Does he speak English?"

"Not well and to tell you the truth, his Dutch is not much better."

"Why's that?"

"Bauke is from West Friesland, in the north of Holland. They have their own language called West Frisian. I do not speak it, so I am afraid we will need to communicate in English and his English is . . . challenging. It is good that he is a man of few words."

"Shall we walk to the restaurant?" asked Marylou.

"It is more than a mile away and the weather is not so nice. I suggest we walk up to the Hyatt Hotel and secure a taxi."

■■■

Exiting the taxi, Marylou looked down the narrow alley and spotted a black sign with silver outlines of five flies. Joining Bernadette she asked, "The canopy says 'd'VijffVlieghen.' Is that Dutch for Five Flies?"

"Yes indeed," responded Bernadette with a laugh. "Not exactly an appetizing name for a restaurant! It is a combination of five seventeenth-century houses. The restaurant is dark, mysterious, and delightful. The food is very traditional Dutch. I hope you will find it very nice."

Entering the restaurant, the women were greeted by an accommodating maître d' with a deep Italian accent and thick leather menus tucked under his arm. He guided them through a maze of narrow corridors past numerous dark dining rooms. Their table was in a low-ceilinged room with a black-and-white checkerboard floor. The walls were crammed with antique glasses, dusty wine bottles, blue Delft tile murals, and leather-bound guest books. Hanging in one corner was an ornate, four-foot-tall copper birdcage. The cage contained five six-inch copper flies. The room's faded gold wallpaper had a shine reflecting years of varnish. The maître d' pulled out a heavy wooden chair for each of the women.

"I've never been anywhere like this," said Marylou.

"It is unique even for Amsterdam. I have eaten here many times and in different dining rooms. In one room are two sketches by Rembrandt. Do you think it is nice?"

As Marylou was about to answer, she spotted Henry and Marvin bobbing through the low doorway.

"Talk about doin' the duck and jive! Those ceilings are lower than a cave," Marvin said as he bent over to kiss Marylou. "Your husband nearly decapitated himself in the first hallway."

Marylou could not help but smile. She had known the brothers her entire adult life; nothing ever changed. The needle could launch from either direction, but it was always there. Looking at them standing together, she mused that they looked like high school teachers—Marvin the enduringly fit gym instructor and Henry the revered history teacher.

Henry kissed Marylou and then kissed Bernadette in the Dutch fashion. Looking at Marvin, Marylou wondered why he was holding his hand against his chest and wiggling his fingers. She concluded it must be some kind of unknowable brother communiqué.

"I've been lookin' forward to properly meetin' you," Marvin said, wrapping Bernadette's hand in his. "Henry tells me you're one killer professor."

Marylou thought Bernadette looked a bit confused by Marvin's colloquial English. *With Bernadette's friend having challenges with English, is tonight going to be a train wreck of failed communications?*

As the men took their seats, Marylou said, "Tonight we're going to dine with a Dutch expert on forgery. He's joining us because of his friendship with Bernadette."

Marylou gave a little nod of confirmation to each brother to ensure they acknowledged their debt to Bernadette.

"His name is Bauke Dyksta. He's from the north of Holland, and I'm delighted he's taken the time from his conference to be with us tonight. Henry, would you like to order some wine? Some red and some white, please."

Twenty minutes later, a short, rumpled man in an ancient oatmeal-tweed sports coat entered the room. With his focus darting around the room and his fingers flexing up and down, he was a ball of nervous energy. His poorly cut mass of tight salt-and-pepper curls fell over his collar. The lenses of his Dutch-style ultra-narrow glasses were visibly smudged. Bernadette stood from the table and with a wave called out, "Bauke, here we are!"

One by one, Bauke took each person's hand in both of his and vigorously pumped it up and down as if pumping water from a well. After he had taken his seat, Bernadette asked, "What conference are you here for in Amsterdam?"

"It is very bearing stuff," Bauke said leaning over the table and making eye contact with each person. "Talk total the day about Atomic Absorption Spectrophotometry. It is way to tease the paints to see how hold they were. It is a modern virgin of authentication."

Marylou worked to avoid knitting her eyebrows. She was not sure she understood what Bauke had said. She asked, "Do you come to Amsterdam often?"

"I did went here before, yes," he responded as his head cheerfully tilted side to side like a bobblehead doll.

Marylou looked across the table at Marvin, the usual candidate to help direct a conversation. His poker face was set; he would only be a spectator. Glancing at Bernadette, she saw a fixed, supportive smile. Out of options, her left elbow tactfully poked her husband's ribs.

Henry gently cleared his throat. "Ah . . . Bauke . . . as Bernadette may have shared with you, my wife and I are interested in seventeenth- and eighteenth-century Dutch paintings. We're willing to pay a fair price, but we're concerned about forgeries."

"This is clearly not to do," Bauke said with a smile reflecting confidence he had said something clever. "I explain you."

Before Bauke could start his explanation, the waiter came to the table to take orders. For an appetizer, the women ordered the creamy soup of Dutch lettuce; Marvin and Henry chose the Dutch herring; and Bauke requested the terrine of smoked eel and duck liver. For the entrée, the table was split between the stewed spring lamb and the chicken casserole.

As the group waited for the food and talked about the places in Amsterdam to visit, Marylou felt blanketed by a sour, musky odor. She turned her head slightly, confirming Bauke as the source. She stole a glance at him. Inconsistent with the smell, his rosy skin glowed from a shave too close. She had an urge to move closer to Henry but held her ground.

Throughout dinner, Bauke chewed his food with an open mouth. When coffee was served, Bernadette asked, "Bauke, how big a problem is forgery?"

"This is something I have something to do with," he said, placing his cup in the saucer. "Some scholars say that forty percent of fine art is forgery. Bot, true, I not know."

"Excuse me," said Henry, "did you say forty percent?"

"Yes," replied Bauke. "Some say forty bot uders say forty-five."

"Is forgery a new problem?" asked Marylou.

"No new. Michelangelo was doing forgery. He buried a sculpture of Cupid to make it hold. Bot, today as prices high fly so do forgers."

"To detect a forgery, what should we look for?" asked Henry.

"I understand precise what you mean. I cannot give you an exhausted list. Shall I run it through?" Bauke responded with a broad smile and a head jiggle.

"Yes, please," Marylou answered, not entirely clear what Bauke had said.

"To meet an authentic painting, it is necessary to examine papers. So is it that certificates of authenticity, invoices, affidavits . . . is that the correct English? Well, uder paper from owners and record from auctions are important. Bot, don't understand me wrong, these uder documents can be forged."

"So, how can a buyer be sure a painting is real?" asked Marylou.

Bauke took off his badly smudged glasses and held them up to the ceiling light to determine if they needed cleaning. Apparently concluding cleaning was unnecessary, he put them back on. He looked at Marylou and said, "For paintings of old, the new science like we are discussing at conference is important. For paintings of new, the eye of expert is most important. It is one or the uder."

Marylou wished Bernadette would jump in and bring clarity to the discussion. However, it was clear that Bernadette would remain on the sideline in an effort to avoid undue entanglement in Marylou and Henry's forgery plan.

"Bauke, are you available to work as a consultant to evaluate authenticity of paintings?" asked Marylou.

"This is something I have something to do with. I hope to see you some uder time," he replied with another broad smile and another bobble of his head.

"That's good news, Bauke," said Henry. "We'll think over our strategy and get back to you."

Rising from the table, Bauke said, "Really, do come and search me up. Now I must meet uder colleagues from conference. We are ferry bussey, 'til soon." Before leaving he again gave everyone his two-handed water-pump handshake.

The group watched in silence as Bauke left the restaurant. Finally Marvin spoke, "Well, I'll be dipped if he wasn't a hoot—what a character! Gettin' involved with him would be like testin' deep water with both feet."

"Oh, he is a character," said Bernadette. "But what he said about forty percent of the fine art in museums and private collections are forgeries has support in the art community. As I tell my students, at the core, it is an existential problem. Should the attribution of a painting to a certain artist determine its worth or should the painting stand on its own merits?"

"I hear ya," said Marvin. "Given the realities of society these days, a big name will win 'er every time. That's probably why forgeries have exploded. And, that brings up a question that's been rattlin' my cage."

"What's that?" asked Henry.

"We hear from Dan Moore in Wichita that Wheeless is hell bent for leather to land some art work to pull his reputation out of the sewer. And your plan is to have that a-hole greatly overpay for a *Perfect Strangers* forgery."

"Correct," answered Marylou.

"Now, no offense intended, but before makin' this trip, I wasn't sure who Vermeer was and sure the hell didn't know diddly-squat about van Meegeren. I'm bettin' most Americans are in the same boat. So, why the hell would Wheeless overpay for a paintin' no one knows anything about by an artist they've never heard of? You got some sort of game plan?"

"Yes!" Marylou and Henry said simultaneously.

"Go ahead, Marylou," said Henry.

"The formula sits around this table. Here in Europe, Bernadette's book *Perfect Strangers* is already a big hit for good reasons—van Meegeren's story is fascinating and Bernadette is a great storyteller. We simply need to make the book a best seller in the States and everyone will be talking about van Meegeren. He's such a unique character, it'll be easy to catch the public's attention."

"You have a plan to ignite all this public interest?" asked Marvin.

"Indeed we do—my college roommate Penelope Smith! She's a nationally known literary publicist in Philly. I sent her the book; she loved it and has already started the promotional work. This week she got a commitment from *The New York Times* to review it."

"Okay," said Marvin. "You've set a match to the publicity fires. What's your idea about the paintin'? I know you're takin' a paintin' class, Marylou, but I assume you're not plannin' on paintin' it."

"No, definitely not. But, I've got an idea or two. Yara, one of the teachers at the art school, could definitely paint it. But I've got to figure out how to approach her."

"There's an incredible amount of work to do," said Henry. "However, for the sake of argument, let's assume we have the *Perfect Strangers* painting ready to go as well as the requisite public support for Bernadette's book. After the discussion with Bauke, I'm concerned about the last piece of the puzzle—creating the painting's provenance. I have no idea what would be believable about where the painting has been all these years. We're gonna need a whole lot more help than old Bauke."

"Don't be worryin' about the painting's provenance. Put that load on me," said Marvin. "I know just the man to drive that train!"

"So now you know something about art?" Henry asked, not masking his skepticism.

"Like I said, I got it. You handle the rest and lay the provenance and sellin' parts right on me, one hundred percent. None of you need to be involved one little iota."

"I will drink to that," said Bernadette, raising her glass.

"Back at ya," Marvin said, subtly jiggling his fingers in Henry's direction.

■ ■ ■

"What a night," Henry said as he unlocked their apartment door.

"One for the books."

"There's one thing bothering me."

"Just one?" Marylou responded as she hung her coat on a hook by the door.

"Do you think Marvin has a plan? Or is he winging it in hopes of coming up with one?"

"Past performance doesn't ensure future success, but it's a darn good indicator. Somehow, some way, despite all his clowning, Marvin always comes through," Marylou said while walking around the apartment turning out lights. "But—does he know anything about the art business?"

"If he does, he's done a great job hiding it."

"Do we have a choice?" Marylou said, unbuttoning her blouse.

"We have choice in all of this. Have you thought through what we're getting ready to do?"

"I assume," Marylou said, pulling her pajama top over her head, "I'm about to receive legal advice from my favorite attorney."

"Remember, I'm a reformed attorney."

"You love to say that. However, your so-called reformation hasn't stopped you from thinking like a lawyer. Can't this wait until the morning?"

"No, I want you to sleep on it. I've looked into the Dutch laws on forgery. As you can imagine, they don't take forgery lightly over here. At home we have so many potential federal and state criminal violations, I can't keep track of them. So far we haven't crossed any legal lines."

"Because our *Perfect Strangers* hasn't been painted?" Marylou said as she pulled back the comforter.

"When it's painted and even when van Meegeren's signature is forged on it, there's still no violation of law. It's not until we offer to sell it as an authentic van Meegeren that we step over the line."

"Terrific. We're still law-abiding citizens. Let's get some sleep."

"Hear me out. If this goes south on us, the Department of Justice will come after us under the Racketeer Influenced and Corrupt Organizations Act, you know, the thing called RICO. They've been real successful using the statute against forgers. How would you feel about being charged, in a very public way, with racketeering?"

"Okay, maybe the risk's too great. Have a better idea?" Marylou asked as she slid under the covers.

"Can't say I do."

"Then we better execute to perfection the one we have. Besides, as you just advised me, we haven't broken any laws yet, so tonight we sleep the sleep of the just. Good night, Henry, I love you."

36

Yara van Kilts was Marylou's favorite painting instructor. In the past, Marylou and Yara had talked in the airy, brightly lit Atelier Molenpad studio. But, given the increasingly sensitive nature of their conversation, Yara suggested her studio as a more appropriate spot. The studio was at the end of the hall in a three-story walk-up in Amsterdam's Oud-West neighborhood.

The studio was tiny, cluttered, and smelled of turpentine. Most of all, however, it was smoky. As Marylou sat down in one of the studio's chairs, Yara shook another filterless cigarette out of a light blue package, leaving the last one smoldering in an already crowded ashtray. Marylou had no choice but to endure the curtain of smoke stinging her eyes.

"Yara, when I saw how beautifully you painted that Caravaggio, I knew you would be the ideal person to paint *Perfect Strangers*."

"Thank you for that. I am willing to help you, but please understand it is only to pay my daughter's medical bills. This will be the one and only time I take on a project like this."

"I completely understand. This will be the one and only time for me as well. Yara, I know you are familiar with van Meegeren's work, but I brought some examples for us to look over. I thought it would be fun."

Marylou pulled her computer from her bag and opened it. "I've transferred them to a single folder that I'll email to you."

"Thank you, but please do not email me. There must be no dots to connect us."

Marylou nodded assent, and, as the two women bent over Marylou's MacBook Pro, Marylou began slowly clicking through her collection of van Meegeren paintings. The second photo was his famous painting of a skeleton dressed in a scarf, top hat, and monocle. A champagne glass and bottle were at the ready.

"This painting I am most familiar with,"Yara said, exhaling a cloud of smoke. "If I remember correctly, it is titled *Vanité*. It always makes me uneasy. It is like a death wish."

"Agreed," said Marylou, wondering if the perceived death wish had anything to do with the cigarette dangling from the skeletal mouth.

"Van Meegeren's dark soul is frequently on display in his paintings. This next one, although very different, is unquestionably dark as well."

On Marylou's screen appeared a painting of a naked, inebriated woman in a dance hall, slow-dancing with a fully dressed sailor.

"From what I've read about van Meegeren, he preferred life in the shadows," said Marylou. "This painting probably sprang from one of his hooker soirees. As you'll see from the next few examples, van Meegeren painted a fair number of café scenes. Maybe these will give you some ideas about what *Perfect Strangers* should look like."

Yara intently watched the screen as Marylou clicked through half a dozen café scenes. Yara held her cigarette at the side of her head, dangerously close to her wild mop of hair.

Keeping her eyes on the screen, Yara said, "I think the man's core talent was his ability to capture a specific moment in time. That will be my goal for *Perfect Strangers*."

"He was a unique talent. I'm amazed at how prolific he was. Where did he find the time to paint all his forgeries, pull the wool over the buyers' eyes, and still have time to paint under his own name?"

"He was a renaissance man of a peculiar type." Yara lit another Gauloises.

"I brought with me the description of his *Perfect Strangers* painting that was part of the documents from the 1950 tax auction of van Meegeren's property."

"Interesting," Yara said as she read and reread the auction details. "Although this is very detailed, I wish there was at least a photograph or even a sketch."

"The only other thing we have to go on is this book." Marylou took a copy of *Perfect Strangers* from her bag and handed it to Yara.

Looking at the front and then the back cover, Yara said, "I have heard of this book. It is a novel by an art professor at the University of Amsterdam, correct?"

"Correct."

"How would this book help to create the *Perfect Strangers* painting? I assume like everyone else, the author, this Bernadette Gordon, has never seen the painting."

"That's true. But, I . . . I went to one of her book events and the amount of research she has done on van Meegeren is impressive; she's impressive. Let me read you a passage she wrote in van Meegeren's voice. I love her description of the lovers' faces."

Marylou reached for the book, opened it, and read, "No other painter could have seized the instant that I captured for all time—the torrent of emotions shared by illicit lovers in their moment of profound disquietude."

"Yes, those words are impactful. I will read the book before I start to paint. Can you imagine what this Bernadette Gordon would think if she knew what we are preparing to do?"

"It's . . . ah, hard to imagine what she would think," dissembled Marylou. "Do you have enough background to execute the painting?"

"I can work with what we have."

"Great!"

"Marylou, we must do everything possible to minimize the risk involved in this project."

"Agreed."

Dropping her cigarette in the ashtray, Yara said, "When I finish the painting, you and only you must come here to pick it up. If you find the painting acceptable, you will pay me ten thousand American dollars in bills no greater than fifty dollars. After that, I deeply regret, it is best we do not see each other again for a very long time."

"I understand. How much time do you need?"

"No more than a month. First, I will need to find a suitable painting from the 1940s. I will scrap it and then paint over it. After the painting is complete, I will need to age it. Baking at a low temperature is best. It was one of van Meegeren's favorite tricks. Should I get started?"

"One more thing. I want the painting to incorporate an important detail."

"What do you have in mind?"

After Marylou explained what she wanted, Yara laughed the deep, guttural growl of a lifetime smoker.

■ ■ ■

Walking back down the long narrow hallway, Marylou reflected on what she had put into motion. In a month she would be the bag lady carrying an illegal payment into the building and leaving with a forgery. A year ago, the thought of promoting a forgery would have been preposterous. But, walking down the hallway, she felt buoyed by a new sense of purpose. She smiled from ear to ear—the detail she shared with Yara was the delicious final touch.

PART IV

THE UNVEILINGS

THREE MONTHS LATER

37

On a warm May afternoon, the psychiatrist's waiting room was the last place Detective Ortiz wanted to be. She unsympathetically surveyed her fellow patients, new faces but the same old mix of life's losers. She needed to convince Dr. Whitcome that her so-called anger management issues were resolved. Hopefully, this would be the last time she would have to sit with the waiting room rabble.

The six waiting patients assiduously avoided eye contact with Ortiz and appeared to be confused as to where they should be looking. A twenty-something woman hid behind a month-old copy of *Time* magazine. Consistent with the room's vibe, the magazine was held upside down.

The receptionist rescued Ortiz. "Ms. Ortiz, Dr. Whitcome will see you now." As Ortiz walked toward Constance's door, she secretly hoped Constance would notice her new, lighter hair color.

When Ortiz entered the office, Constance stood to greet her. She said, "Esmeralda, your hair looks great. The new color is so flattering."

"Thanks," Ortiz responded, unconsciously touching her hair.

As the women took their seats across from each other, Constance said, "My father used to say 'Any time a woman changes her hair color, something's up. Could be good, could be bad, but something's up.' Anything you want to tell me?"

Ortiz assumed her usual defensive posture for the session—crossed arms and legs. "Everything's alright . . . I just needed a change. I had a damn good week. I'm finally getting used to my new apartment. It's smaller than the one I shared with Sherrie, but it suits me."

"Is your aunt Sherrie still living with her mother?"

"Yeah, they've sequestered themselves down in San Antonio. After that jackass from the Grapevine Bar slapped her, she couldn't get comfortable in Dallas. Got to admit, I miss her more than I thought. With all her mumbo jumbo, she was a pain in the ass. But now that she's gone, I've got no one, not even the cat. Can you believe she took the damn cat?"

Constance wrote in her book, looked up, and asked, "When you go home, do you feel isolated?"

"Not sure isolated is the right word," Ortiz replied, moving her thin braid off her shoulder to her back. "It's more like I was abandoned."

"Feeling abandoned is a difficult emotion to navigate. Any new men in your life?"

"Hell no. Well . . . maybe. I met a cop in Wichita named Will Klepper. We talk the same language and he's awful handsome. But with my luck, nothing'll come of it."

"Maybe there is a little something up with your new hair color!" said Constance, giving Ortiz a playful smile.

"I'm not holding my breath."

"Are you trying to make new friendships?"

"Not really. I just spend more time at work."

"Okay, we'll come back to that in a moment." Constance turned the page in her notebook. "Speaking of work, how's work going?"

"Actually, it's about to be great."

"Tell me."

Unfolding her legs and arms, Ortiz leaned forward pressing her hands on her pant legs. "Remember my pathetic toad of a boss took me off every case other than the murder of that Southland University snowflake?"

"Yes."

"Remember how I thought for sure that the murderer was that pervert Wheeless in Wichita? You know, the victim's uncle, who somehow manipulated his release from Leavenworth for assaulting women?"

"Yes, I recall he was in prison and you were quite certain he murdered his niece."

"Constance . . . is this conversation privileged?"

"What you tell me in this room is absolutely privileged unless you reveal to me that you are about to commit a serious crime."

"Like back my car over my worthless boss?" Holding up her hands, Ortiz said, "Just kidding. Now, where was I? Oh yeah, a few months ago, I came across some new DNA evidence. I probably sat on it for too long and then it took forever for the DNA lab to process it. But, bottom line, I have a new major lead and it's one I haven't shared with my boss."

"So, new facts led to a new conclusion?"

"Isn't that what you're supposed to do? If facts change, you change your mind?"

"Indeed," Constance said with a laugh. "It's always been a mystery to me how changes in facts do not change minds. Do you feel good about the work you've done on the case?"

"Absolutely. Hell, work's all I got."

"Let's talk about that. Do you feel like work is all you have because that's how you choose to spend your time?"

Leaning back in her chair, Ortiz sighed. "Don't think so. Seems to me I spend all my time at work because I've got nothing else. Hell, maybe that's the same thing."

Constance closed her book, stretched her neck, and then looked Ortiz coolly in the eyes. "With your aunt Sherrie moving, it's understandable to feel abandoned. The fear of being alone is a powerful force. It has a number of clinical names, but the easiest to remember is isolophobia. Some people suffering from this phobia feel detached from their bodies when they're alone."

"Don't know about that. With this body," Ortiz said, pointing her fingers at her torso, "it's hard to feel anything but grounded. But I do stew about whether I'll be alone for the rest of my life."

"Are you disappointed that Sherrie moved to San Antonio?"

"Damn right. For years I paid her rent while she wasted her time with all that airy-fairy, spiritual bullshit. We have one little bump in the road and she leaves me high and dry."

"In fairness, Esmeralda, being assaulted in her own home is more than a 'little bump in the road.' Has your new living situation made you angry?"

There it is! She's finally probing about anger management. This is my chance to end these visits! "No, not angry. Sad, disappointed, but not angry," Ortiz replied with a slow shake of her head.

Constance tapped her lips with her forefinger. "That's progress. Understanding you can be sad without devolving into anger is an important step. That's all the time we have for today."

"Constance, are we done here? These sessions have been a real eye-opener for me. I feel I've resolved my issues. Can you recommend to the department that I've finished treatment?"

Constance hesitated. "I think we should put that decision on hold for another month. I'll see you same time next week."

■ ■ ■

Alone in her office, Constance stood at the window. Staring at the parking lot below, she concluded Detective Ortiz had not been forthcoming. The line that she was disappointed but not angry was too rehearsed. She needed more therapy.

More importantly, Constance was keenly aware of her own deceit. Her isolophobia diagnosis fit her, the doctor; not Ortiz, the patient. She had violated a prime tenet of the psychiatric world: she had resorted to psychological projection to make herself feel better. Projecting her problems onto a patient plumbed a new low.

It had been months since her spiral of descent was triggered in

Amsterdam. She reflected that, yet again, her troubles all came back to Uncle Charlie. His persistent efforts to take her father away had scarred her for life. Their relationship had been bad for decades but now it was growing worse. The week before, Uncle Charlie casually let drop, over dinner at the CW Ranch, that he and Marvin had become buddies. He even began referring to him by that annoying nickname, "Marvelous." Rubbing salt in the wound, he insinuated that he and Marvin were involved in an intriguing top-secret business transaction.

Constance pondered what Ortiz had said about the murder suspect named Wheeless in Wichita. She remembered driving to the CW Ranch with Marvin and how positive he was that Wheeless had murdered his niece, the Southerland University student. Wheeless seemed inordinately important to Marvin. Surely he would be interested in knowing there was evidence about a new suspect? Would this be an avenue to rekindle their relationship?

No. Screw Marvin. Despite her specific entreaties, he had abandoned her in the middle of Amsterdam. He was as bad as Uncle Charlie. Given Marvin's marital history, trying to mold him into an acceptable long-term companion was a fool's errand not worthy of her time.

But . . . maybe she should give Marvin one last try? He had sent numerous apologetic emails and even two letters; she had not responded. He was funny, handsome, and rich. And, he had passed the test; his performance during the pig hunt had been top-drawer. Based solely on that performance, maybe he deserved one more chance?

Constance stepped from behind her desk, locked her office door, and unlocked her secure drawer. It was filled with orange prescription bottles. She shook two bottles: they were empty. The third produced a rattle. She spilled out two round green pills.

She removed her mortar and pestle from another drawer and methodically ground the OxyContin pills into a fine powder. After carefully laying out two straight lines of powder on her desk, she rolled up a twenty-dollar bill and inhaled a line into each nostril. She gladly surrendered to the drug's pink cotton embrace.

An hour later, stirring from her dream state, she rose from her chair, carefully put away her equipment, and returned to her window. With arms folded across her chest, she thought through her plan to reconnect with Marvin. She would not only reconnect, but more importantly, she would disconnect Marvin from Uncle Charlie. The opportunity had finally presented itself; she would make Uncle Charlie feel the sting of abandonment.

Constance took comfort in knowing Marvin was not a complex man. Familiar with his instincts, she was confident in her plan.

38

The furniture had been pushed to the walls to accommodate the heavy Las Vegas–style poker table sitting in the middle of the Adolphus Hotel's Presidential Suite. When Marvin asked Charlie about the stakes for the Tuesday afternoon game, Charlie assured him it was the same as the stakes at the ranch—with a minor difference. Until Marvin sat down at the table, he didn't know that the minor difference was a single digit. Instead of a five-hundred-dollar buy-in, the Adolphus game was five thousand.

Marvin had agreed to play in part out of curiosity about the legends surrounding the hotel and poker. Built in 1912 by St. Louis's Adolphus Busch, the Adolphus Hotel had long been home to ultra-discreet poker games. Legend had it that for most of his years, H. L. Hunt rarely missed his Wednesday afternoon poker game at the Beaux Arts Adolphus.

Marvin's cards were bleak all afternoon as the group played hand after hand of Texas Hold 'em. By the time he had dropped twelve thousand dollars, he folded yet another hand. Marvin calculated that Charlie's stack of chips held his twelve thousand and a whole lot more. Charlie dressed the part of a card shark. He was wearing a heavily starched white shirt and a pinstriped vest adorned with a pocket watch with a gold fob stretching between the vest pockets. Other than in movies about riverboat gamblers, Marvin had never before seen a watch and fob.

When the player to Marvin's right relit his pungent green cigar, Marvin decided to call it a day. Pushing his remaining chips to Charlie, Marvin said, "I'm done, stick a fork in me. I assume it's okay to leave a check to cover the rest of this afternoon's thumpin'. This was like a pro-am tournament and I'm on the wrong side of the cut."

"Looking at the chips around the table, everyone enjoyed your company," replied Charlie with a laugh. "Boys, what do you say we take ten minutes? I need to talk over a couple of things with Marvin."

Marvin shook hands with the players and dropped his check next to the chip bank. The players moved to the bar and Charlie signaled Marvin to join him in the adjoining bedroom. Closing the door, Charlie said, "The cards were unkind to you today. We're happy to give you the opportunity to recover next week."

"Appreciate that, I'll let you know. Have you had time to consider my idea about the *Perfect Strangers* painting?"

"Marvin, in all the time I've spent in the art world, your idea is the most cockamamie thing I've ever heard."

"So, you're not gonna play?"

"Didn't say that. To the contrary, it's so bollixed up, it's got my juices flowing. I think it's worth a flyer."

"Hot damn."

"To avoid any misunderstanding down the road, if I pull the deal together, the proceeds from the sale come my way, right?"

"Right."

"So when's kick off?"

"I can get the painting to you whenever you're ready. I really appreciate you takin' this on, Charlie."

"Like you once told me, it's important to have something to do rather than have to do something. If we pull this off, we'll be able to dine out on these shenanigans for years to come." He pulled out his pocket watch and, looking like a train conductor, announced, "Time to get back to the cards."

...

Marvin walked down the hotel's hallway and squeezed into the narrow antique elevator already carrying three excited women. The elevator's mirrored panels made the space uncomfortably claustrophobic. From the women's conversation, Marvin deduced they were in Dallas for a real estate conference and fired up by the opportunity to shop in the original Neiman Marcus down the street. When the paneled elevator doors opened to the lobby, Marvin reached his long arm high to hold the doors open for three women, wishing them "happy huntin'."

As the women excited the elevator, Marvin glanced over their heads across the narrow lobby. He was startled. Constance was sitting on a low love seat under a huge round mirror in a carved oak frame. As he stepped into the lobby, she rose from the love seat and, after pulling a large black leather bag over her shoulder, walked to greet him.

Kissing him tenderly on one cheek with her fingertips lightly touching his other, she said, "Hello stranger. I've missed you."

"Constance, it's wonderful to see you . . . you look great . . . is . . . is everything okay?"

"No complaints. I hope you didn't lose too much money."

"How did you know I was here?"

"At dinner Saturday at the CW Ranch, Uncle Charlie made a big deal about you playing in his Tuesday poker game. I figured you'd be here and I'd offer you some sympathy for your losses."

"What makes you so sure I'm in the loser camp?"

"Uncle Charlie always wins."

"You're right about that. Constance, I feel so bad about what happened in Amsterdam—"

"Let's not talk about that now. How about I buy you a beer?"

"Hell yeah!"

Marvin followed Constance to the lobby bar where she bought drinks. Glasses in hand, she led the way to two plush green high-back chairs in the corner beside one of the lobby's oversized fireplaces. She set her bag on the floor. Marvin's head raced with all the things he wanted to say but the multitude of divergent thoughts rendered him silent. Finally, he lamely asked, "So, what have you been up to?"

"Things have been pretty quiet. Practicing medicine, enjoying the CW Ranch, catching up on my reading. Nothing exciting. I hear about you from time to time from Uncle Charlie."

"Really?"

"He likes to drop your name at dinner. He says you're working on some sort of project together." Constance stared at Marvin with unblinking eyes. "He's very secretive about it. Is there anything I should know?"

"Oh, it's no big deal. It's a business transaction with a fella in Wichita I've known forever. It's nothin' important, just kinda somethin' to do." *Do not get her involved with the* Perfect Strangers *plan, because girls talk. Change the conversation!*

"Constance, I'm sorry about Amsterdam."

"It's okay."

"No, I'm so sorry. Leaving you by yourself in the middle of that crazy-ass city was so wrong."

Constance looked down into her wine glass. After an awkward moment, she said, "During the past months, I've given that day in Amsterdam plenty of thought. There are so many 'ifs.' 'If' we hadn't smoked pot, 'if' we hadn't seen the boats racing down the canal, 'if' I'd held on to your arm, 'if' you'd had your cell phone with you. We got caught in a vortex of 'ifs.' I overreacted. I threw a tantrum. I'm the one who's sorry."

"Thanks for sayin' that, but I feel like you have nothin' to say sorry about. I let you down."

"As I tell my patients, don't let a misunderstanding devolve into a pity party. When you fall into a spiral of regret, make what happened a learning opportunity."

"Good by me," said a beaming Marvin. "How about we write that day off as 'Amsterdamage'?"

"Amsterdamage it is," Constance said with a laugh.

Forty minutes and two drinks later, Constance picked up her over-sized bag and put it on her lap. Marvin was disappointed she was getting ready to leave.

She unsnapped the bag and opened it. "I brought a little something you might enjoy."

Leaning over to look into the bag, Marvin was delighted to see a black negligee. Straightening up, he said hopefully, "Shall we . . . head back to your place?"

Constance gave him an enticing smile, reached into her bag, and pulled out an Adolphus room key.

39

Dan Moore had planned to arrive early for the meeting. His appointment was with a man he had known for less than a year, an invaluable source but also a perplexing one. When the man first approached Dan about a possible deal, Dan had his investigators produce a detailed background report. It reflected a lifetime of uninterrupted violence. However, the proposed deal was too good to reject.

Their meeting place was chosen to limit the possibility of being seen together—Penguin Cove in Wichita's Sedgwick County Zoo.

Dan's plan to arrive early was derailed by his terminal case of spatial dyslexia. Arriving at the zoo's entrance, he had only two directions to turn and, predictably, chose the wrong one. His decision was commensurate with a directionally challenged lifetime. The choice routed him the long way around, past Kookaburra Junction, Gorilla Forest, and Tiger Trek.

As he hurried along wearing his black backpack, he replayed his conversation the day before with Henry and Marylou. They were relieved to report that after weeks of negotiations, Wheeless had finalized the purchase of van Meegeren's *Perfect Strangers*. Marvin's art dealer friend had conducted the negotiation in a shroud of secrecy leading to the sale price of $2.5 million. The plan to sell the forged painting had gone extraordinarily well.

Finally coming to the exhibit of swimming and waddling penguins, Dan spotted the man sitting on a sunny bench calmly watching the birds. He held on his lap a package wrapped in brown paper. His black tee shirt read "Bend It Like Bikram."

Taking a seat on the bench, Dan asked, "Enjoying the exhibit?"

"Yeah, love to watch them walk. They remind me of shackled prisoners shuffling along," he replied in his hushed tone.

"Before we get into the rest of . . . all this stuff," said Dan, "what's Wheeless up to?"

"He's a mess. He may not be broken down on the side of the road but he's definitely out of gas. He deluded himself into thinking he would step out of prison into his former place in society. Although he and his PR lady have generated a barrage of good publicity, none of his investors have returned. By the way, I'm confident he's bonking that PR woman. Whatever. He's positive that skinny prick O'Brian has most of his ex-investors' money in O'Brien's new fund, but there's nothing he can do about it."

"It must be driving him nuts."

"Absolutely. He's also grown paranoid. As I told you, since he can no longer afford his chauffeur for protection, he's now packing a .38 everywhere he goes. I'd bet anything he's clueless about how to use it."

The two sat in silence watching the penguins. Two birds confronted each other. With beaks pointing at the sky, they pumped up their chests. Then with their vestigial wings stretched out, they swung harmlessly at each other. They looked like two inflatable clown punching bags knocking together to no effect.

"Those two remind me of Wheeless," Al Starsky said with a smirk. "He gets all pumped up for a fight but just flaps his wings. It's a miracle he survived inside."

"What's his financial situation?"

"Tapped out. I haven't been paid in two months."

"How did he pay for the painting?"

"Borrowed the money from the bank his father founded. The bank securitized it with every asset Wheeless has, probably including all those pimp suits he's so fond of."

"Sounds like he's all in on the painting."

"No doubt about it. He's convinced that the rumors about making the book into a movie are true. He thinks that the movie and all that goes with it will be his return ticket to the top."

"Is he worried about the retrial?"

"No, not really. Again, he's clueless in so many ways. He has no idea about all the work your guys have done to round up victims who didn't testify at the original trial. The #MeToo movement erupted while he was in Leavenworth. He's oblivious about women's new empowerment to go public with their grievances."

"How did you persuade Wheeless to buy the painting?"

"I really can't take credit for that," Starsky said, stretching out his legs. "After getting word from you to do everything possible to get Wheeless to buy the painting, I put together a whole dog and pony show about van Meegeren's story, the huge success of the *Perfect Strangers* book, and all the facts about the supposed purchase of the painting in Mexico. He, as usual, blew me off. Told me no one in the States gives a shit about what goes on in Holland. But when his PR woman told him some swanky Hollywood studio optioned the movie rights to the book, well, he got himself all worked up. Not a day went by that he wasn't asking where I was on the negotiation. And you know what?"

"What?"

"He's so out of it, he still hasn't seen the painting. He says he's waiting for the unveiling at the Wichita Art Museum. What a jackass. Enough about Wheeless. What about our deal?"

"Deal's the deal. You've done your part—letting me know exactly what Wheeless was up to. Your help selling the painting was above and beyond and I appreciate it."

"And, your part?"

"Here you go," Dan said, reaching into his backpack. "You're a new man.

You'll see in the envelope a Florida driver's license, social security card, two credit cards, and your passport. You're ready to launch life as John Brogan. As you'll see online, you've already had a full life on Facebook and LinkedIn."

Opening the passport, Starsky saw his photo over the name John Brogan. Leafing through the passport pages, he saw a dozen entry and exit stamps. To enhance authentication, John Brogan had already made a fair number of trips to Mexico and Europe. The documents were perfect.

"These are impressive," Starsky replied in his whisper voice. "I see the envelope of cash. Do I need to count it?"

"It's all there."

"Great. I can't stomach any more of Wheeless. I'll stick around for the painting's unveiling next week, then me and my new identity will get permanently lost in the Florida Keys. But, I have a going-away gift for you."

"What is this?" Dan said as he accepted a brown paper package from Starsky.

"It's the flight log from Wheeless's jet that O'Brian sold while Wheeless was in Leavenworth."

"Why are you giving it to me?"

"I thought it might be of some use in the investigation of the niece's murder."

"How so?"

Starsky raised his arms above his head signaling ignorance. "Damn good question. I've looked it over a dozen times and I don't get it. It shows the jet made one trip the entire week of the niece's murder, and that was to LA."

"Now you've completely lost me! Why are you giving it to me? What am I supposed to do with it?"

"That police detective investigating the murder, the Ortiz woman, asked everyone and their brother about the log and its whereabouts. I figure it must be important to her investigation in some way. Unless it somehow, some way, ties Wheeless to the murder, why would she be so interested?"

"So, you want me to get it to the detective?"

"That's up to you. I can't give it to her; I already told her I had no idea where it was. But here's the point: Why would she be so damn interested if the log doesn't somehow implicate Wheeless? Is there anybody that doesn't know Wheeless is the murderer?"

"I understand. I'll get it to her one way or another . . . I guess this is adios."

"Afraid so, but maybe I'll see you across the room at the unveiling. I understand half of Wichita will attend, and even the Dutch author is coming."

The men stood, shook hands, and walked away in opposite directions. Moore contemplated throwing the flight log in a dumpster but decided to hold on to it. If the log offered even the remotest chance to help convict Wheeless, he needed to get it into Detective Ortiz's hands.

40

On Charlie Whitcome's Ritz balcony overlooking downtown Dallas, the two men were in a celebratory mood. Raising his glass of scotch, Charlie asked, "Feeling good, Marvelous?"

"Damn good, and then some. As much fun as it's been stickin' Wheeless with that paintin', bringin' this chapter to a close feels mighty fine."

After clinking his glass with Marvin's bottle of Pabst Blue Ribbon, Charlie said, "That Guy Wheeless is one odd duck. I talked on the phone with him a number of times, but when I finally sat down with him to finalize the price, all he wanted to talk about was poker."

"What about poker?"

"He'd heard about the Tuesday game at the Adolphus, the one you played in. He was looking for an invite."

"Did you invite him to play?"

"Yeah, he struck me as a fish, and I'm not opposed to reeling in fish money. He met all expectations by dropping a bundle. He's supposed to make a return visit for the game the week after the great unveiling in Wichita. You want in on some of that fish cash?"

"I'm gonna pass. Given what we have in store for him at the unveilin' in Wichita, I'm pretty sure Wheeless won't be thrilled to see me."

"Suit yourself. Speaking of the unveiling, Wheeless still hasn't seen the painting. His lackey Starsky took a close look at it but not him."

"That's weird even for Wheeless. Didn't he want to see it?"

"He said he was too busy to come to Dallas to see it, and he wanted to wait for the full effect at the unveiling. He's got a few pages stuck together."

"He's got whole chapters stuck together," Marvin said, shaking his head. "But if you think about it, it makes sense. Wheeless doesn't give a crap about art, he's just lookin' for the spotlight. He'd buy a portrait of Minnie Pearl if he thought it would get him some good publicity."

"You're probably right about that."

"I'm headed to Wichita for the unveiling. You goin'?"

"God knows I love art events of every kind. But this one—this one I'll skip. Staying out of the limelight makes sense."

"Ah, come on. It'll be a once in a lifetime deal. To see the look on Wheeless's face will be worth the trip."

"It's best if I stay away. I've never met your brother or his wife, and it's best we keep it that way."

"You're probably right, Charlie. From what I've read, that van Meegeren was a world-class rascal. I bet he'd appreciate what we've put together."

"No doubt," Charlie said, putting his hand up for five. "This kind of tomfoolery would be right up ol' Han's alley."

"Can you give me the skinny on the paintin's provenance? How did you convince Wheeless's man Starsky that the paintin's authentic?"

"A trick of the trade." Charlie stopped to refill his glass. "In the business of selling paintings of questionable origin, you can never use the same trick twice."

"So, you've used this one up. Tell me."

"Some of the best stories are the ones left untold."

"Cut the bullshit Charlie, just tell me."

"Okay, okay. A lawyer I know down in Monterrey put it together. He drafted what they call a 'voluntad y testamento' for an old man named Paco Merino who supposedly passed away a year ago. The document outlines how Paco Merino bought the painting in the 1950s and left it to his nephew, Pedro Paderna. I, in turn, as duly reflected in another document, bought it from Señor Paderna. The lawyer in Monterrey, Mexico, had both sets of documents certified by his cousin, the probate judge. I had to pay both of them, but what the hell, it made for a clean trail and it's Mexico, so no one will ever be able to unravel the thing."

Marvin raised his beer bottle, toasting Charlie's cleverness. "Charlie, you done good and pocketed a nice bit of change for your trouble."

Charlie put both hands on the railing and stared out over the cityscape. "Marvelous, you're right. But I earned it. When you came to me, you had an awfully vague proposal. You wanted me to sell a painting that didn't exist to a very specific buyer I didn't know. You assured me your group would take care of creating the painting and generating enough publicity around a book by that Dutch woman that this very specific buyer would be convinced to buy the painting. Remember all that?"

"Yes, and I appreciate everythin' you've done . . . "

"You also made clear that neither you nor your little group could in any way be tied to the painting. As we stand here today, the one and only person connected with selling the painting to Wheeless is me. In other words, I'm the one shouldering all the risk. Where I come from, he who takes the risk gets the cash."

"Hard to argue with your logic."

"Good. For a minute I thought you were getting ready to try and recut the deal."

"Never crossed my mind," Marvin said. "Tell ya what has crossed my mind. Why did you agree to get involved in this circus in the first place?"

"Good question. It all goes back to the time we were in your office. You told me there's a big difference between having something to do and having to do something. Remember?"

"Can't say I remember, but I'm happy to take credit."

Turning from his view of the city to face Marvin, Charlie said, "When you came to me with your plan, I didn't have much going on. I wanted something to do, some fun, some mischief. I've always loved a bit of a scam—hell, it's one of the few things I get better at as I get older. I just figured what the hell, why not?"

"There ya go." Marvin raised his bottle. "Here's to 'what the hell, why not.'"

"Absolutely, what the hell, why not! When are you coming back down to the CW Ranch?"

"Constance and I have been talkin' about that. Just need to get a date on the calendar."

"So you two have patched things up?"

"I'm hopin' so. Never met a woman like her. She's about anythin' a man could want. But there's somethin' on the edges that Constance keeps to herself. There's a part of her she won't let me see. Has she said anythin' to you?"

"No. I haven't talked with her in weeks. Over the years, she's spent a fair amount of time pissed off at me for one reason or another. Long periods of silence aren't rare. Has she told you about her sabbatical?" Charlie gave Marvin a questioning look.

"I've been bidin' my time on that one, waitin' for the right moment. We're slow-walkin' things. In two weeks we're heading down to Cancún. We'll see how things go from there."

Charlie glanced at his watch. "Let's not fret about all that. Constance is a big girl, whatever's meant to be will be. It's time to hit the town— let's throw around some of Wheeless's money on an old-fashioned, down-and-dirty fandango!"

"What the hell, why not?" Marvin said with a broad grin.

41

It was Detective Esmeralda Ortiz's defining moment. The arrival earlier in the week of an anonymous package containing the Wheeless Strategic Fund passenger log was the puzzle's final piece. Sitting outside Captain Johannson's office, she felt more positive about herself than she had in years. She had finally solved the Southerland student's murder case.

As the office door opened, she watched Johannson warmly shake hands with one of her male colleagues exiting the office. Seeing Ortiz sitting in the corridor, her aluminum briefcase at her side, he simply said, "Next."

Seated in Johannson's office, she opened her briefcase and prepared to share her momentous news. Before she could start, Johannson launched in.

"I got a report last week from your lady shrink, that Dr. Whitcome. She says your anger management sessions need to continue for another month. This is costing the department. Are you paying attention or what?"

What a fat-ass dope. Here I am with a career breakthrough and he wants to waste time with anger management. Easy does it. "We continue to make progress and I deeply appreciate your willingness to invest in my career growth. Today I have some very important information to share with you."

"Yeah, what is it?"

"First, I have this," she said, handing the flight log across the desk.

"What am I looking at?"

"It's the flight log for the Wheeless Strategic Fund jet."

"How did you get your hands on it?"

"Someone mailed it from Wichita. Who, I don't know. I had it dusted for prints and there's nothing. Turn to page forty-two."

Flipping the log pages back and forth to find the correct page, he said, "This page lists a flight from Wichita to LA."

"Exactly."

"Look, Ortiz," he said shutting the book, "I'm not here to play twenty questions with you. Just spit it out."

"Page forty-two reflects the jet's activity the week Wheeless's niece, the Southerland University student, was killed. The so-called copy of the flight log Edward O'Brian gave me showed a flight to Dallas on the day of the murder, with Wheeless onboard. As you see, the actual flight log reflects only one flight that week and that was to Los Angeles. So, O'Brian must have forged the copy of the log to frame Wheeless."

"That's quite a leap of logic. Like I told you before, that copy you hauled back here from Wichita was useless without the original. Now you understand what I was talking about?"

Stay calm, deliver the coup de grace. "I appreciate your guidance. But now we have the original, which is very different from the page O'Brian gave me. As I said, O'Brian must have forged the copy he gave me to implicate Wheeless in his niece's murder."

"Or, this thing I'm holding," Johannson said waving the log, "that's mysteriously come into your possession, is itself a fraud. Why would O'Brian want to implicate Wheeless? I thought they worked together. Is this all you got?"

"No, in fact, I have the final link." Ortiz reached back into her briefcase. "Remember how at the murder crime scene there was one DNA hit we were unable to match? Also recall we were unable to locate any of Wheeless's DNA at the crime scene?"

"Yeah, yeah, and I told you to run down leads other than Wheeless. So, what do you got?"

"Well, when I was in Wichita interviewing O'Brian, he acted all squirrelly and made me suspicious. At the conclusion of the interview he left a pile of business docs on the conference room table . . . "

"Don't tell me you took possession of his documents without a subpoena!" Johannson slapped a hand loudly on his desk. "Have you somehow managed to screw up evidence again?"

Stay calm; deliver the knockout punch to this ignoramus. "No, in fact that's not what I did. O'Brian had a cold and blew his nose into some tissues and threw them in a wastepaper basket. As I learned in my criminal justice class, garbage is fair game. More importantly, any abandoned DNA in that garbage is a free-for-all. Anyone can use it for any purpose, any time, any place."

"So?"

"I snapped on my latex gloves, picked the tissue out of the garbage, put it in an evidence bag, and sent it off for DNA testing. All one-hundred-percent by the book."

"So?"

"Remember the unidentified DNA from the murder scene we've been wondering about? Well, that mucous-splattered tissue I picked up from O'Brian is a perfect match. So, to your question about why O'Brian would want to implicate Wheeless. Pretty simple: O'Brian, not Wheeless, is the murderer."

Take that, you swollen shit! Hold on—don't gloat.

"Okay, I see your point . . . Is there any other evidence implicating this O'Brian?"

Calm. He doesn't need to know about the camera. Telling him about it could ruin my career. I'll be the object of ridicule forever if I have to run through what happened that night at the Grapevine!

"What more do we need?" Ortiz responded.

"Then why're you sitting here? Get a warrant and arrest the son of a bitch. It's about time you got control of this mess."

42

It was past three AM and Guy Wheeless could not sleep. He appraised the scarlet hair cascading over the pillow next to him and gently pushed a wayward strand back into place. Janet Lancing had done an excellent job generating an endless stream of positive publicity. She also correctly foresaw that the resurfacing of the long-missing *Perfect Strangers* painting provided a unique public relations opportunity. And, she was wonderfully acrobatic in bed. But it wasn't enough. He deserved a little bit more.

In the coming afternoon, *Perfect Strangers* would be unveiled at the Wichita Art Museum gala. Art aficionados from around the country would attend, along with network film crews. Everyone who was anyone in Wichita would be there. The buzz about the painting, the book, and the movie was a cultural tsunami sweeping across the art world. With his financial tank running on empty, buying the painting was a risk that had to pay off.

The art groupies, whether they admitted it or not, yearned to be part of the unique story. The only path to the limelight they craved was to get close to Wheeless. And, the only way to get close to him was to be an investor in his fund. His path back to the top was clear.

Seeing Janet roll over in her sleep, he silently slipped out of bed. He walked to his closet, closed the door behind him, and reached for the box hidden away on the top shelf. He opened the box and deeply inhaled. It was a Doberman Pinscher costume hand-made out of human hair. When he was arrested on sexual assault charges, the police had confiscated his collection of dog costumes. The Doberman costume was brand new.

Wheeless closed the box, slid it back on the shelf, and returned to bed. After the euphoria of the unveiling, Janet would be unable to resist his entreaties to try on the costume. Once she slipped it on, the only thing in the world he craved more than money would finally begin, again. It was the little bit more he justly deserved.

43

Detective Ortiz paced nervously around Wichita's Dwight D. Eisenhower National Airport arrival room. Ortiz assured herself that some jitters were appropriate—she was about to make the biggest arrest of her career. Nerves just prove you're paying attention.

The full flight from Dallas had been abuzz with talk about a painting to be shown that afternoon at the Wichita Art Museum. She noticed that a number of passengers on the plane were reading a book titled *Perfect Strangers*. Somehow the exhibit at the museum and the book were connected. She made a mental note to ask Klepper about it.

Five minutes before the agreed-upon meeting time, Lieutenant Klepper appeared at the other end of the waiting room. Unlike their first meeting, Klepper had put some thought into his clothes. Ortiz thought he looked magnetic in his blazer and tie—she hoped he had dressed for her. He walked over to Ortiz and stuck out his hand. "Detective Ortiz, it's a pleasure to see you again. I like what you've done with your hair. I've got a car and Officer James waiting at the curb."

Elated that Klepper had noticed her hair, Ortiz slid into the front passenger seat. Klepper introduced Officer Ray James dressed in full police uniform and seated directly behind her. Klepper asked, "Got the arrest warrant with you?"

Patting her aluminum briefcase, Ortiz responded, "Right here, safe and sound."

"We're confident the target is in his office. Unless he's willing to waive an extradition hearing, it'll probably take forty-eight hours to have a judge hear it. I assume you'll stick around for the hearing?"

"Absolutely. I'm here for as long as it takes."

"Great. We'll be at his office in twenty minutes. Once we make the arrest, we'll get him back to headquarters for processing."

Looking out her window at the passing city sprawl, Ortiz said, "On the plane, a lot of people were talking about being in town for some art show. Do you know what that's all about?"

"For those of us who live here, it's impossible to miss. Our old 'friend' Wheeless purchased a painting by a Dutch artist who is famous for being a forger of some seventeenth-century artist. The painting has been missing since the 1950s. For whatever reason, the painting has received massive hype and today's the unveiling."

"Why is Wheeless doing this?"

"That prick," Klepper said, glancing sideways at Ortiz as he used his tongue to move his dip to the other side of his mouth, "is trying to buy back the city's respect."

"After what he did to those poor women, that shows unbelievable arrogance."

"You got that right."

"One more thing. Did you have the opportunity to check on whether O'Brian ever reported a burglary at his house?"

"Yeah, we checked it out. Never happened. O'Brian has never reported anything to the police."

"I figured as much. That line about his camera being stolen in a burglary was just another helping of O'Brian BS."

■ ■ ■

Klepper pulled his Crown Vic cruiser into a crowded parking lot in front of a blue-glass office building on Rock Road. Exiting the car, he said to Ortiz and Officer James, "Let's minimize the drama, okay? Like every police department these days, our every move is scrutinized to death. Let's serve the warrant, slap on the cuffs, Mirandize him, and get the hell out of Dodge."

The three police officers took the elevator to the building's fourth floor and walked down the corridor to the O'Brian Investment Partners offices. Through the huge glass doors they saw about twenty young analysts staring at their flashing computer screens. When Klepper rang the buzzer for entry, the analysts' heads swiveled in unison. One stood up and moved to the door. But, looking the group up and down, he put his finger in the air to signal he needed a moment. He headed toward the office in the corner of the large open workspace.

■■■

While the three police officers waited impatiently outside the glass doors, inside the O'Brian Investment Partners' only private office, Edward O'Brian was conducting a closed-door meeting with his chief lieutenants, the Thompson brothers.

"This afternoon is Wheeless's great unveiling at the art museum," O'Brian said with a smirk. "I guess our invites got lost in the mail."

"We should crash the sucker. We'd be the turds in the punch bowl," said Brad Thompson.

"As amusing as that might be, we're better off as far away as possible. For now, caution is key," concluded O'Brian.

Their conversation was interrupted by an urgent knock on the door. "Yeah!" O'Brian called out.

A senior analyst poked his head through the door. "There's three people at the glass doors. At least one of 'em's a cop. Should I let 'em in?"

"Thanks, Gordie, we'll handle this," O'Brian responded. "Brad, why don't you see what's up. It's probably another complaint about the allocation of parking spots."

Brad walked out of the office and closed the door behind him. Moments later, he burst back through the door. "We got to go! It's that Dallas cop, Ortiz. Rob, we need to get the hell out of here!"

Before O'Brian could say anything, the Thompson brothers were sprinting to the office's rear exit.

■■■

As the two men hustled to the rear exit, Detective Ortiz, still standing outside the glass doors, yelled, "God damn it!" as she pointed at the men. "Those pricks running for the exit are the brothers I met at the Grapevine Bar in Dallas. One of them beat up my aunt Sherrie."

"Detective Ortiz, what are you talking about?" Klepper responded.

"Arrest those two!" shouted Ortiz.

Klepper started banging on the glass, yelling, "We have a warrant for the arrest of Mr. Edward O'Brian! Open the door now!"

"They're getting away!" shouted Ortiz.

Klepper turned to Officer James, "Cover the rear exit. I'm calling in this mess!"

As Klepper called police headquarters for backup, he continued banging on the glass. During the chaos, the employees gathered in small groups, staring perplexedly at the police officers. Finally, Edward O'Brian stepped out of his office, smoothed his shirtfront, and calmly walked to the glass doors. Nodding to Ortiz, he buzzed the door open.

"Good morning, Detective Ortiz. What can I do for you?"

"Not a damn thing. You're under arrest for the murder of Nichole Kessler in Dallas, Texas."

After Klepper handcuffed and Mirandized O'Brian, O'Brian said, "You're making a big mistake here. I want to talk with my lawyer."

"You can make the call when we get downtown," replied Ortiz. "By the way, those two bozos that ran out the back door, I now know it was you who sent them to intimidate me. I also know one of them left your camera in my freaking apartment."

O'Brian stared at her silently and blankly.

Going nose to nose with O'Brian, Ortiz yelled, "Why the hell did they have to hit my aunt Sherrie?"

■■■

With O'Brian securely behind county bars, Klepper and Ortiz sat down in his cramped office to debrief. "That was pretty chaotic in O'Brian's office," said Klepper. "Remember we agreed no drama? I think you have some 'splaining to do, don't ya think?"

"Yeah, believe me, I had no idea we'd run into those brothers."

"Start at the top," he said, folding his hands on the desk.

"All of this mess started with Wheeless," Ortiz said with a sigh. "Given his assault conviction here in Wichita and the poisonous relationship he had with his niece, I was positive he murdered her in Dallas. But, looking back, some of the pieces never fit."

"Like what?"

"We talked about this before. Not only were we unable to find any of Wheeless's DNA at the crime scene, but we did find a DNA sample we were never able to ID. Then, out of nowhere, two men who said they were brothers from Georgia—as in, near Russia—doing some import business in Dallas when I met them—"

"Whoa, slow 'er down a notch. You're losing me. How did you meet brothers from Georgia?"

"I . . . we, my aunt Sherrie and I, met them in a bar." Ortiz gave him a sheepish look.

"Okay . . ."

Swinging her braid down her back, she continued. "The brothers supposedly from Eastern Europe were, in fact, those two turkeys who ran for the exit. Obviously they recognized me. When they were in Dallas, one of them slapped around my aunt Sherrie and told her to give me a message. He said their message, to stay the hell out of Wichita, came from Guy Wheeless."

"This O'Brian is one devious SOB."

"He's that and a whole lot more. When I came back to Wichita for some interviews, one was with O'Brian. He had a cold and kept blowing his nose. He discarded the tissues in the wastepaper basket. I picked one up and had it tested. Sure enough, it was the same DNA as that at the crime scene."

"Nice work, detective. Was that the evidence you used to get the arrest warrant?"

"Yes, but the story gets juicier. The first time I came to Wichita, O'Brian gave me a copy of a page supposedly from the passenger log of the old Wheeless Strategic Fund jet. The page he gave me showed Wheeless had taken the jet to Dallas the day of the murder. That was a major piece of evidence pointing to Wheeless as the murderer."

"I'm smelling a rat."

"Correct again. Last week someone mailed me the original passenger log. It was mailed from Wichita, from who, I have no idea. We dusted it for prints but got zero. Someone put in a lot of time and effort to wipe it clean. The original log showed there was no trip to Dallas the week Wheeless's niece was murdered. Obviously, O'Brian forged the copy he gave me to show that Wheeless had been in Dallas at the time of the murder. He did it to frame Wheeless."

"So, this was all about O'Brian trying to frame Wheeless?" Klepper said, shaking his head. "Doing something that devious involves love or money every time."

"From what I've seen of those jokers, it's hard to imagine a lot of love in their hearts. Must have been about money."

"No doubt. Hold a minute, Officer James is calling in."

Ortiz listened to Klepper's end of the conversation. He said "got it," "fine," and "nice job, Ray" a number of times. Ortiz liked everything about Klepper. He was a tough guy with a caring edge. But, he was a cop. Her proscription against dating cops was firm; he was a prospect she would have to let slide.

Klepper clicked off his phone. "James says he picked up those geniuses at one of their apartments. They were packing their bags. Their names are Rob and Brad Thompson and they'll be here in short order. I assume you'll want them extradited to Dallas as well?"

"Absolutely."

"This has been quite a day for you. And I guess for Wheeless too. In an hour he'll be basking in the glow of his unveiling. Any chance you might want to go down to the event?"

"Nope, I'm not real interested in art. I'll hang here and have a chat with the Thompson brothers."

Klepper looked down at his shoes and then into Ortiz's eyes. "Since you'll have to stay over for the extradition hearing, any chance . . . any chance we might break bread tonight? My buddy manages the best steak house in town."

Ortiz felt a flutter in her chest, a flutter not felt in years. She quickly calculated. Why should her prohibition against dating policemen have extraterritorial effect? Surely it should apply only within Dallas's boundaries. And, maybe Aunt Sherrie's tarot card reading about the Eight of Wands signaling love arrows in the air was finally coming true. Maybe, just maybe the arrows were headed her way at this very moment?

"Yeah, steak would be great," Ortiz responded, trying out her most winsome smile.

44

Wheeless sat at the conference table reviewing Janet Lancing's draft speech for the *Perfect Strangers* unveiling. He was annoyed that, as usual, she was more interested in her phone than in him.

"So, how confident are you that this will be the best attended event in the museum's history?"

"There is no question it will be," replied Lancing, continuing to text. "Let's be real, the bar's not that high."

"And you're sure crews from all the networks will be there?"

"Yes, it's all in hand. Do you want to make changes to your remarks?"

Wheeless stood to look at his reflection in the glass of a lithograph. He slicked back the sides of his hair with both hands, enjoying his reflection. "Is the stage positioned like we talked about?"

"Yes, just like we planned. Do you want to make changes in the remarks?"

"I think I'll just wing it," Wheeless said, insolently tossing the pages on the table. "You know, get the feel of the crowd and whatever's in my gut, let it fly."

Looking at her phone, Lancing said back over her shoulder, "Be back in a minute, have to take this call."

As she pushed open the conference room door, Starsky caught the door from the other side and, with a mock bow and scrape, beckoned for Lancing to exit before he entered.

"Well, I'll be damned," said Wheeless. "Look at you all dressed up like an adult. I didn't know you owned a suit and tie."

"I don't," Starsky said in his whisper voice. "I rented the entire outfit. Ready for the big event?"

"Yeah, this is going to be the start of a new era for all of us. When we look back, this will be the day that the Wheeless name was resurrected."

Ten minutes later, when Lancing reentered the room, Wheeless asked, "What's wrong with you? You sick or something?"

"You're not going to believe this."

"Believe what?"

"On the phone was my connection at the Wichita Police Department."

"And?"

"She says there's been an arrest in the murder of your niece, Nichole Kessler."

"And?"

"It's Edward. Edward O'Brian was arrested."

Wheeless and Starsky stared incredulously at each other.

Finally, Wheeless with clenched fists at his sides said, "I told you that son of a bitch was up to no good!"

"Guy, don't get all exercised," Starsky said softly. "Can you imagine better news? Doesn't this mean the money that went to O'Brian's fund will be flowing back your way? With this news and the unveiling in less than an hour, isn't today stacking up to be like the best day of your life?"

Wheeless stared into space. Finally, Lancing asked, "Guy, are you alright? We need to get to the museum."

"Damn right I'm okay. Never felt better."

45

Marylou walked down the corridor of the Ambassador Hotel in downtown Wichita. From the rugs, to the prints of trees on the walls, to the room doors, everything was a shade of purple. When she was growing up in Wichita, the boutique hotel had been the Union National Bank building. During the years the city turned its back on the downtown, the building had been vacant. She was delighted to see evidence of her hometown's successful revitalization efforts.

On her way to the suite occupied by Bernadette and Lola, she reflected warmly on her days in Amsterdam when the mother and daughter lived upstairs. It had been a time of personal discovery and renewal.

Marylou gently knocked on the deep purple door, and Bernadette greeted her with the warmth of an old friend. When Marylou stepped into the suite, Lola called out, "Hello, Marylou" from her cross-legged position on the bed. Surrounding her were a dozen tourist pamphlets she had collected during her mother's North American book tour. She was busy striking different selfie poses with her brochures.

"You are just in time," said Lola. "Mother and I are discussing which American city is our favorite."

"One guess which was Lola's favorite," said Bernadette, rolling her eyes.

"I'm betting Las Vegas," said Marylou.

"Exactly," said Lola, jumping off the bed. "When I get out of school, I will move to Las Vegas. The lights, the music, the excitement, it is my destiny. I will be a dancer with the feather headpiece."

"Not exactly what I have in mind," Bernadette said *sotto voce* to Marylou.

While Lola busied herself packing the tour guides into her gold lamé backpack, Marylou asked Bernadette, "How're you holding up? A ten-city book tour is no easy task."

"This has been a dream come true. The chance to tour the United States and meet so many people who have read my book has been life changing. Marylou, you made it all possible."

"That's not true. I introduced you to a few folks, but it was you and *Perfect Strangers* that made it all happen. And, now a movie!"

"And now a movie," Bernadette repeated, shaking her head in disbelief. "This month has flown by. But, I must admit, I am ready to fly home tomorrow."

"Not me!" interrupted Lola.

"Lola, we need to leave for the museum in a few minutes. Please, get dressed."

"I am dressed," Lola said, pointing at her torn jeans and neon-pink tee shirt.

"Oh no you are not. Please get to it."

When Lola had closed the bedroom door behind her, Bernadette fell into one of the suite's three lavender settees. Marylou followed her.

"Marylou," she said in a low voice. "Are you scared about this afternoon?"

"I guess a little. We've come so far with this crazy idea. What's the worst that can happen? The painting is exposed as a forgery? That might be a good thing, since it would enhance the excitement around your book. You know, a forger's forgery. Does Lola know what's going on?"

"Heavens no. She would crash the Dutch internet in minutes. Where's Henry?"

"He and Marvin are at an old friend's office, Dan Moore. He runs a private investigation firm here in Wichita. You'll probably meet him at the museum."

"Was their friend, this Dan Moore, involved in . . . in all of this?"

"Oh, yes."

"I do not want to know details."

"I understand. Before you go, I've got good news and bad."

"Please, give me the good."

"We're going back to Amsterdam. Henry signed on for another semester at the University of Amsterdam."

Both women jumped up into an exuberant hug. "Oh, what wonderful news!" said Bernadette. "We have so much to explore together in Amsterdam."

Then, holding Marylou at arm's length, she asked, "And the bad news?"

"Henry and I have talked endlessly about this. We decided that I shouldn't attend today's unveiling. If I'm seen there, it could ruin what we have in store for Wheeless. I hope you understand. I'll drop you and Lola at the museum."

"I think you have made a wise choice. Will I see you later?"

"I'm afraid not. Henry and I are leaving this evening for San Francisco. It's our granddaughter's fourth birthday."

"Oh, that is so nice. Then the next time we will see each other will be in Amsterdam. I am so excited!" Bernadette looked at her watch and called out toward the bedroom door, "Lola, please, you will make us late."

46

Walking up the steps of the Wichita Art Museum, Marvin and Dan Moore debated the prospects of the Southerland University basketball team. Henry tried to turn off the noise. He wanted to focus on the events about to unfold. He stopped and said, "Gentlemen, lock in your poker faces."

"Aye-aye, captain," Marvin saluted. "Into the fire, boys!"

Once inside, the group stopped at the desk for name tags. The ceiling above the desk was the glass-enclosed Chihuly "Bridge" sculpture. Sandwiched between glass panels were biomorphic glass shapes of blue, yellow, and orange. Looking up at the sculpture, Henry could see patrons walking across it. The first floor's ceiling was a walkway on the second.

They climbed the stairs to the grand ballroom where the unveiling would take place. The three-story ballroom was packed with a festive crowd. Seemingly everyone had a champagne flute in hand. The news cameras and their sloppily dressed cameramen were relegated to a corner of the ballroom, removed from the elegant buffet tables and bars.

The room's main feature was the tumultuous Chihuly "Confetti" chandelier, hanging from the center of the ballroom's ceiling. The sculpture was a detonation of crayon-colored glass in shapes both elongated and squat—a balloon blower's shapes.

Henry spotted Bernadette and Lola standing toward the front of the ballroom. Joining them, he surveyed the newly constructed stage. The low platform was set in front of the sixty-foot windows overlooking a wide, majestic turn in the Arkansas River. The stage blocked the museum's premier view. Looking around the room, Henry wondered why the stage had been set blocking the river view.

Across the ballroom, Henry saw a beaming Wheeless triumphantly making his way through the crowd. He wore a blood-red tie and his perfect hair gleamed. Trailing behind him was an attractive woman with bright scarlet hair. Wheeless shook every extended hand and seemed to have a word or two for everyone in the room.

Marvin leaned into Henry's ear and whispered, "Look at that giant rooster. He could strut sittin' down."

After Henry reminded Marvin about his commitment to maintain a poker face, Marvin retreated across the room to join a group of friends.

Henry watched Wheeless move around the room heading toward the group where Marvin was standing. As always, Marvin's head stood conspicuously above the crowd. Wheeless and Marvin locked eyes. Marvin gave him a goofy smile that momentarily extinguished the grin on Wheeless's face. Instantly, his smile switched back on as he changed direction to avoid Marvin.

As Wheeless climbed the stairs to the podium, Marvin and Dan joined Henry, Bernadette, and Lola. Dan whispered to Henry, "I love it. Just seeing us probably ruined his day. I know, I know, poker face."

Looking at Wheeless on the stage, Henry realized why the platform had been positioned in a way that blocked the river view. From across the room, it looked like Wheeless was walking on water. "What a jackass," he mumbled too loudly.

"Excuse me?" said an elderly man standing next to him.

"I said, 'What class,'" feigned Henry.

"This is a great day for the city of Wichita," Wheeless shouted from the podium. "It's wonderful, very wonderful, to see so many friends here today, so many good friends, to support the fantastic Wichita Art Museum. This city and its citizens deserve the best, only the very best. Today, the unveiling of Han van Meegeren's long missing masterpiece *Perfect Strangers* is one of many steps I have taken, and will continue to take in the future, to support this city and its citizens. I love this city! I have never felt better about Wichita than I do today!

"There are so many of Wichita's civic leaders and important people from all over the country here today. Everyone wanted to be here, everyone. I'd love to give a shout out to each and every one of you. But, I know what you're here for—you're here to see this beautiful painting. So, for the sake of time, I'll shout out to only one person. In fact, she came all the way from Amsterdam just to be with us today. She's the author of the terrific book with the same name as this painting. Read her book. It will soon be a blockbuster movie, a real blockbuster, really big. It's going to be really big! Where are you, Bernadette Gordon?"

A surprised Bernadette sheepishly half-raised her hand, making her bracelets sing as they fell down her arm. While the room politely applauded Bernadette, Henry looked over in her direction. Just past her was Marvin—his hand on his ribcage, gently wiggling his fingers at Henry.

"Good to see you, Bernadette, and thanks for coming all the way from Holland just to be with us today. I bet there's no one more excited about seeing this magnificent painting than you. So, what you've all been waiting for, here is Han van Meegeren's masterpiece, *Perfect Strangers*."

Two museum employees carefully lifted the dark blanket covering the painting. With "oohhs" and "aahhs," the crowd burst into appreciative applause.

Henry was pleased with the work—the painting captured the couple's flash of angst, what Bernadette's book described as their moment of "profound disquietude."

Henry closely watched Wheeless. He was so absorbed in the audience adulation, he had not yet examined the painting. Finally turning to the painting, he was able to sustain his triumphant smile—but his eyebrows knitted and his eyes narrowed suspiciously.

Lola, standing next to her mother, put both hands over her mouth as she bubbled over with giggles. Pointing at the painting, she said, "Look, Mother, the woman in the painting looks like . . . no . . . is it . . . it *is* . . . it is Marylou!"

Tightly gripping Lola's arm and bending close into her face, Bernadette issued a stern warning in Dutch.

■ ■ ■

After basking in the room's adoration for a minute too long, Wheeless invited the attendees to form a line to get a closer look at the painting.

"One riot, one ranger," Henry said to Marvin and Dan. "I'll handle this; let's talk later."

As Henry got in line, he saw Marvin, Dan, and Bernadette heading for the exit. Lola was trailing behind her mother with her head down like a scolded dog. Predictably, Marvin had his arm around Dan's shoulder as the two tittered like teenage boys sharing a dirty joke. Henry fought a grin.

Henry watched Wheeless shake hands with each patron after their brief time in front of the canvas. Twenty minutes later it was his turn. He stopped in front of the painting admiring his wife's wonderful likeness. Marylou's art teacher had captured her soft beauty and intelligent eyes. The sweep of her hair was perfect. Stepping toward Wheeless, Henry stuck out his hand. When Wheeless hesitantly took it, Henry leaned in close to his ear and whispered:

"No one needs to know. No one will know unless I so much as smell you on the wind. Then the whole world will know you're a sucker. Nice chatting with you, asshole."

47

Wheeless burned as he watched Henry exit the museum. He had known Henry since high school and never lost his feral distaste for him. Two inconvenient truths were undeniable: Henry's wife, Marylou, was in the painting, and the painting was, therefore, a worthless fake. His only hope was that no one recognized the woman as Marylou. His focus turned to pointing the finger of blame. Art Starsky had the most contact with the art dealer, Charles Whitcome. He looked around the room and saw Starsky standing by himself in a corner.

Crossing the room to confront Starsky, Wheeless strained to maintain a fixed smile. Along the way he was repeatedly stopped by well-wishers extending congratulations. By the time he'd crossed the room, Janet Lancing had joined Starsky. Wheeless's mood had grown so dark, even the mental vision of Lancing in his new Doberman costume failed to spark any interest.

"Art," Wheeless said standing uncomfortably close to Starsky, "how well do you know Charles Whitcome, the art dealer you negotiated with to purchase *Perfect Strangers*?"

"I met with him a couple of times and got to examine the painting. It's beautiful, don't you think? I did a Google search and everything came up clean. He's an experienced art dealer with a solid reputation. He took me through the painting's provenance through Mexico, and everything checked out. You've played poker with him, so you probably know him better than me. Why are you asking?"

Wheeless stared silently at Starsky. Like many ex-cons, Starsky was impenetrable. Wheeless realized a museum filled with admiring guests was not the right place for a confrontation.

"Nothing about today is making any sense. Do you believe that son-of-a-bitch O'Brian? There were an awful lot of people who thought I killed Nichole. Killed my own niece?"

"Guy, Guy, relax. There's nothing bad here, it's all good. The unveiling was a great success, and O'Brian's arrest gives you a perfect opportunity to rebuild your fund. How can you possibly be upset?"

Wheeless could not read Starsky. He decided to get him back to the office where he could interrogate him without onlookers. "You're right. It's an opportunity. Today's the day we start setting things right. Let's head to the office and get started."

"No can do," Starsky said softly. "I'm on my way to Seattle to take a new job, get a new start. This is au revoir, Guy."

"Why leave now, just as things are looking up?"

"What better time will there be? You're back on your feet, so my work here is done. Next week I'll email you my new details."

Wheeless watched Starsky leave the museum. He was confidant Starsky was not heading to Seattle and quite sure he would never receive the promised email.

48

Henry, in his pajamas, tiptoed barefoot down the creaky stairs of his daughter's narrow townhouse in San Francisco's Russian Hill neighborhood. The day after landing in San Francisco, they received a detailed text from Dan Moore reporting the arrest of Edward O'Brian for the murder of Wheeless's niece. They were dumbfounded. Marylou predicted with certainty that, when the facts came out, in some way Wheeless would be implicated. Henry committed to himself to withhold judgment until the details were known.

He had promised his granddaughter pancakes to start off her birthday celebration. He walked to the kitchen, quietly made coffee, and arranged the pancake ingredients on the counter. He pondered whether all the risk of creating and selling the *Perfect Strangers* forgery had been worth it. Sure, Wheeless had been humiliated; but were he and Marylou truly back to normal? He dismissed his ambivalence, concluding that his forgery plan had worked flawlessly and Wheeless would not dare reenter their lives.

Preoccupied with his thoughts, he turned his phone on. There was a series of texts from Marvin. With each one, Marvin's request for Henry to call him grew shriller. Henry thought that Marvin was calling with details about O'Brian's arrest.

"It's about time," Marvin answered.

"What's the emergency? Do you have news about O'Brian's arrest?" Henry whispered.

"Why are you whispering?"

"Because everyone else is asleep. It's two hours earlier here. So, what's up?"

"This is not about O'Brian. Constance was at my place last night. We were about to hit the sack when I got a call from her Uncle Charlie. He had some really bizarre news."

"What news?"

"Like every Tuesday, Charlie was playin' poker at the Adolphus. It was the regulars and a couple of new guys sittin' in. The new players came in hot and pretty-faced. They started losin' big and talkin' loud. Charlie was dealin' Texas Hold 'em when he turned over the river card . . . "

"Sorry, what's the river card?"

"It really don't matter, let's just say it's a card that all the players can use in their hands. Charlie turned over the card and it was the one-eyed jack, the jack of diamonds. One of the new players bolts out of his chair like he's been shot out of a cannon. He stares daggers at Charlie and then slams his hold cards on the table. One of his hold cards is another jack of diamonds!"

"Holy shit!"

"You got that right. He then pulls out a .38 and shouts, 'Not twice, you son-of-a bitch.' Well, from what I hear, Charlie dove on the floor like he's goin' after a loose ball on the hardwood. The gun goes off and the bullet hits the wall. A couple of Charlie's friends wrestle the gun away and subdue the shooter until hotel security arrived."

"Is Charlie alright?"

"As you can imagine, he's pretty shook up. He broke a wrist when he hit the floor, but otherwise he's okay. But Henry, there's more to this."

"Okay." A twinge of foreboding hit Henry. Uncharacteristically, Marvin was dragging out his news.

"Henry, you know the shooter."

"What?" Henry said, sitting down at the kitchen table.

"Henry . . . the shooter was Guy Wheeless."

"Holy shit!" Henry's hand went to his cowlick.

"They're holdin' him at the Dallas County Detention Center. But Charlie's refusin' to press charges—he told the police it was just a big, fat misunderstandin'. I bet he thinks pressin' charges will open up the whole can of worms about the *Perfect Strangers* paintin'."

After a few moments of silence, Marvin said, "Henry, you still with me?"

"Yeah, yeah I'm here. Dan told me a while back that Wheeless had taken to carrying a gun."

"Why the hell didn't you tell me he was packin'! I would have made sure Charlie barred him from the game, and then this mess wouldn't have happened."

"You're looking at this all wrong. I'm sorry Charlie got hurt, but if you think about it for a second, this whole incident is terrific news."

"How the hell is that?"

"Because a condition of Wheeless's bond was he could not leave Kansas. Carrying an unlicensed firearm across a state line and then firing it is a one-way ticket back to prison."

"Are you sure?"

"Positive. Marvin, I got to go."

Henry immediately hit his "favorites" button for Dan Moore in Wichita. Dan answered on the second ring.

"Dan, have you heard about the shooting in Dallas?"

"Yeah, I spoke with Marvin last night. The Wichita police told me this morning that Wheeless is being extradited straight back to Leavenworth. He's toast."

"How are you feeling about his retrial on the assault charges?"

"Henry, I could not be more confident. We interviewed three new victims, and these women are credible, ready to testify, and adamant about making the charges stick."

"This is a ton to digest. Got to go."

Henry heard a toilet flush upstairs. Five minutes later, Marylou buoyantly entered the kitchen. Already dressed in a red-and-black running outfit topped with a University of Amsterdam baseball cap, she sparked with positive energy. Handing her a glass of orange juice, Henry gently kissed her and thought to himself, *We're finally on the road to recovery.*

"This will be a wonderful day," Marylou declared. "Who was on the phone?"

"Just Marvin."

"Anything new?"

Henry instantly decided he was on the right path and would not allow Wheeless to scar this day.

"Ah . . . not really, just same old, same old. It can wait. Want to help with the pancakes?"

"Always happy to be your sous-chef. Henry, I abandoned that black cat back in Wichita. With all our problems in the rearview mirror, I feel wonderful!"

They shared a warm, long hug of relief.

49

Sitting in her University of Amsterdam office, Bernadette looked warily at the pile of term papers in front of her. Grading term papers was like getting a new puppy—the joy of newness quickly dissipated as the reality of the hard work set in. She was about a third of the way through the papers and, as always, gratified by those whose hard work paid off in cogent and well-organized arguments. Slackers were exposed in their initial paragraphs.

Setting her red pen down on the pile of term papers, she got up from her desk to pour her fifth cup of coffee, when her office phone rang.

"Hello, this is Professor Gordon," she said, sitting back down.

"Is this Bernadette Gordon, the author of *Perfect Strangers?*"

"Yes."

"Your book is fantastic. I have read it twice."

"Thank you so much. With whom am I speaking?"

"My name is Stijn Kok. I am calling from Utrecht."

The combination of the name Kok and Utrecht triggered a wave of apprehension in Bernadette.

"I am glad you enjoyed the book, Mr. Kok."

"I so enjoyed it. I understand it will be a movie. Very exciting for you."

"Yes, it is exciting."

"You and your book are all over the internet. I read about your book tour of the United States. That must have been wonderful fun."

"Yes, it was very nice." Bernadette wondered about the conversation's direction.

"I also read you attended the unveiling of the painting at a big event in Wichita. What did you think of it? Was it what you hoped?"

Bernadette stood up and began nervously pacing behind her desk. "Mr. Kok, I appreciate your interest in my book. However, I am in the middle of grading term papers. I need to get back to that work."

"I am calling to retain you for an art project."

"Oh, what do you have in mind?"

"I believe you have heard of my grandfather. His name was H. A. J. Kok."

A bolt of anxiety rattled Bernadette. "Was your grandfather the purchaser of the *Perfect Strangers* painting at the 1950 tax auction of van Meegeren's assets?"

"Yes. I have lived my entire life in my grandfather's house."

Bernadette's tension swelled. "That is very nice, Mr. Kok. What is the project you have in mind?"

"I was hoping you would help me with an authentication. Did you authenticate as a van Meegeren the *Perfect Strangers* painting you saw in Wichita?"

"No, I was never asked to authenticate it."

"I understand. As an expert on van Meegeren, what are your thoughts on the painting?"

Bernadette felt apprehensive goose bumps. "It was extremely well-executed and consistent with known van Meegeren paintings. Why do you ask?"

"When my grandfather bought *Perfect Strangers*, he immediately placed it above the living room fireplace, where it has remained ever since. In fact, at this moment, I am looking at it."

Trying to lubricate her dry mouth, Bernadette asked, "Mr. Kok, this is all very interesting, but what is it you want from me?"

"It is simple. The painting in Wichita is, without doubt, a forgery. I would like to retain you to authenticate the painting in front of me. I have two other experts who have already agreed to help with the project. As the author of *Perfect Strangers,* you are the most logical person to lead the team. I am happy to pay your fee."

"I am totally focused on grading term papers at the moment. May I call you back in a few days?"

Bernadette carefully returned the phone to its cradle. She stood up and bent over her desk, placing both palms flat on the desktop. She hung her head for a moment but raised it with a smile on her face. Why should she be anxious? What did she have to worry about? Her connection to the painting hanging in the Wichita Art Museum was, at best, tangential. Nothing tied her to the forgery. In fact, the news was all good. She would not only fulfill her dream of seeing the *Perfect Strangers* painting but would lead the authentication team. And, the publicity around the resurfacing of the painting would turbo-charge her book and the coming movie. Her longing for a higher perch in the art world was about to become a reality.

She would need to call her friend Marylou to alert her to the remarkable turn of events. But for now, she had a job to do. She reached for the pile of term papers.

BIBLIOGRAPHY

Bailey, Anthony. *A View of Delft*. New York, 2001.

Dolnick, Edward. *The Forger's Spell: A True Story of Vermeer, Nazis, and the Greatest Art Hoax of the Twentieth Century*. New York, 2008.

Enquist, Anna. *Where the Lord Washes His Hands*. Delft, 2016.

Lammertse, Frisco; Garthoff, Nadja; vande Laar, Michel; Wallert, Arie. *Van Meegeren's Vermeers: The Connoisseur's Eye and the Forger's Art*. Rotterdam, 2001.

Lopez, Jonathan. *The Man Who Made Vermeers: Unvarnishing the Legend of Master Forger Han van Meegeren*. New York: Mariner, 2008.

Mak, Geert. *Amsterdam: A Brief Life of the City*. London, 1995.

Rijkens, Maarten. *I Always Get My Sin*. Amsterdam, 2005.

Schjeldahl, Peter. "The Sphinx," *The New Yorker*, April 16, 2001.

Schneider, Norbert. *Vermeer: The Complete Paintings*. New York, 2001.

Shapiro, Greg. *How to Be Dutch*. The Hague, 2016.

Shorto, Russell. "Rembrandt in the Blood: An Obsessive Aristocrat, Rediscovered Paintings and an Art-World Feud," *The New York Times Magazine*, February 27, 2019.

Shorto, Russell. *Amsterdam: A History of the World's Most Liberal City*. New York, 2013.

Six, Jan. *The House of Six*. Amsterdam: Six Art Promotion, 2001.

Wheelock, Arthur. *Vermeer & the Art of Painting*. New Haven: Yale, 1995.

Wheelock, Arthur. *Vermeer, the Complete Works*. New York: Abrams, 1997.

READING GROUP GUIDE

1. Talented authors take readers on journeys that they might never take in their real lives. If you could visit a scene from *The Forger's Forgery*, would you head to Amsterdam for dinner at the restaurant d'Vijff Vlieghen, pack your outdoor clothes for a hunting trip in East Texas, or gear up for some weekend shopping and spa treatments in Dallas? Or would you pick some other place from the book that caught your attention?

2. This novel is based on an historical event, the forgeries of Han van Meegeren in the 1930s and '40s. Discuss why you think the author chose to base his mystery on a real-life character, rather than creating a fictional tale and if it made the story more interesting.

3. Who was your favorite character? Discuss the reasons you liked this character and what questions you might ask them if you had the chance to meet.

4. When Henry first learns van Meegeren's story, he's surprised that the forger wasn't reviled for being a con man. Rather, Bernadette describes van Meegeren's rise to notoriety as the swindler of Nazi Hermann Göring. When van Meegeren chose to admit to forgery rather than admit to selling a Dutch treasure to a Nazi, did this surprise you? Discuss why.

5. Many of the characters underwent transformations. Discuss which character you think changed the most or the least in the novel and why. Discuss whether it's important if a character does change in the course of a story.

6. The evil deeds of Guy Wheeless would be hard to forgive. Discuss whether the judge's actions surprised you and why you think he acted as he did.

7. Many readers will likely do an internet search for the van Meegeren forgery, *Perfect Strangers*, described in this book. If you did that, discuss what you discovered.

8. What emotions did you have at the reveal at the Wichita Art Museum?

9. If you imagine this book as a movie, which actors would you cast: for Henry? Bernadette? Marylou? Starsky? Wheeless? Detective Esmeralda Ortiz? Others?

10. If you could have a drink or cup of tea with the author, Clay Small, what questions would you like to ask him?

AUTHOR Q & A

Q: After writing *The Forger's Forgery*, would you share a new favorite place or places where you like to spend time in Amsterdam?

A: *The Rijksmuseum is my favorite museum in the world. Not only does it house fantastic seventeenth-century paintings like Rembrandt's* The Night Watch *and Vermeer's* The Milkmaid, *but the building and surrounding grounds are fabulous. At the end of the day, I'm frequently at the Brouwerij 't IJ. My favorite restaurant is a tiny place run by two Italian brothers called Cucina Casalinga. Don't go if you're in a hurry!*

Q: Your fictional story is based on the true story of master forger Han van Meegeren, who made quite a name for himself by forging the works of some Dutch masters in the 1930s and '40s. What drew you to van Meegeren's story?

A: *It was Vermeer who drew me to van Meegeren. I became interested in Vermeer when I started travelling to Amsterdam on business in the 1990s. I made it a goal to see as many Vermeers as possible. (I have seen 30 of the 36.) I saw an advertisement in an Amsterdam newspaper for an exhibit in Rotterdam of all known van Meegeren forgeries of Vermeer. After seeing the exhibit, I was hooked on van Meegeren's sheer criminal genius.*

Q: Do you have a favorite scene in *The Forger's Forgery*? Would you tell us about it and why it holds special meaning?

A: *That's like asking who's your favorite child! Since we have three children, I'll highlight three scenes. First, Bernadette's lecture at the University of Amsterdam. This scene forced me to distill all I have learned about van Meegeren into a few pages. Second, I enjoyed the scene of Marvin and Constance chasing wild pigs in East Texas. That scene required a fair amount of research* *since I've never been on a pig hunt. Third, I enjoyed writing about the boat race in Amsterdam. I saw such a race in 2017 as a memorial to Eberhard van der Laan, the very popular mayor of Amsterdam.*

Q: You seem to know a lot about art and artists from all ages and backgrounds. Would you talk about whether you have a background in art, or is it a newfound love inspired by a particular experience?

A: *In college, I was an English literature major. To graduate, students had to take either art or music appreciation. I chose art. That course launched me on a lifetime interest in paintings.*

Q: Would you like to tell us about your inspiration in creating a character as vile as Guy Wheeless?

A: *I don't want to go there! As Marvin says in the book, some people are just no damn good.*

Q: Do you have a favorite character in *The Forger's Forgery*? Would you discuss why this character was your favorite?

A: *Bernadette is my favorite. Her calm and logical personality is so Dutch. She is an accomplished woman, very comfortable in her own skin. She is loosely based on my landlady and friend in Amsterdam.*

Q: Did you find that some characters took over your writing process and did things that surprised you? Or were you in control of them the whole time?

A: *I like to think I was in control of all the characters except Marvin. He is a wildcard, but I try to be vigilant about not allowing him to run off the page.*

Q: Who are some of your favorite writers or writers whose works have influenced you?

A: *My favorite writers are: Tom Wolfe, David Foster Wallace, Ian McEwan, and Don DeLillo. I was most influenced by Tom Wolfe and his ability to blend fiction into real life situations.*

Q: If you could do a book reading in Amsterdam, do you have a favorite bookstore you would pick to host it?

A: *That one is easy. For my first book,* Heels Over Head, *I did a reading at the American Book Center on Spui. That experience led me to have Bernadette do her book reading there in* The Forger's Forgery. *I look forward to returning there.*

Q: How did writing *The Forger's Forgery* change you? What did you learn about yourself or any other particular topic?

A: *One of the most fun things about writing* The Forger's Forgery *was researching the history of forgery. I was stunned to learn that many experts believe 40% of art in the world's museums and private collections are forgeries!*

ABOUT THE AUTHOR

CLAY G. SMALL is the former Senior Vice President and Managing Attorney for PepsiCo, Inc. In that position, he was responsible for all of PepsiCo's global legal issues and personnel. He is currently an Adjunct Professor at the Cox School of Business, where he teaches a variety of courses including *The Legal and Ethical Environment of Business* and *Perspectives on American Business through the Lens of General Motors*. Mr. Small is also an annual Visiting Professor at ESADE in Barcelona and Vrije University in Amsterdam where he is a member of the law school advisory board.

Mr. Small is a graduate of Ohio Wesleyan University, where he was a two-time All-American soccer player. He was drafted by the Dallas Tornado of the North American Soccer league. He received his J.D. degree from Southern Methodist Law School and is an inductee of the school's Distinguished Alumni Society. He serves on the board of the Baylor Health Care System Foundation and the Executive Committee of the Dedman School of Law. He is also a founder of Inverdale Investments, a hedge fund in Dallas, Texas.

Mr. Small's first book, *Heels Over Head,* received the Texas Association of Authors' award for the best book in 2017 in its category.